PRAISE FOR THE WRITING OF MARGERY SHARP

"A highly gifted woman . . . a wonderful entertainer."
—*The New Yorker*

"One of the most gifted writers of comedy in the civilized world today." —*Chicago Daily News*

"[Sharp's] dialogue is brilliant, uncannily true. Her taste is excellent; she is an excellent storyteller." —Elizabeth Bowen

Britannia Mews
"As an artistic achievement . . . first-class, as entertainment . . . tops."
—*The Boston Globe*

The Eye of Love
"A double-plotted . . . masterpiece." —John Bayley,
Guardian Books of the Year

Martha, Eric, and George
"Amusing, enjoyable, Miss Sharp is a born storyteller."
—*The Times* (London)

The Gypsy in the Parlour
"Unforgettable . . . There is humor, mystery, good narrative."
—*Library Journal*

The Nutmeg Tree
"A sheer delight." —*New York Herald Tribune*

Something Light
"Margery Sharp has done it again! Witty, clever, delightful, entertaining." —*The Denver Post*

The
Flowering
Thorn

The Flowering Thorn

a novel

MARGERY SHARP

OPEN ROAD

INTEGRATED MEDIA

NEW YORK

Cover design by Mimi Bark

ISBN: 978-1-5040-5085-2

This edition published in 2018 by Open Road Integrated Media, Inc.
180 Maiden Lane
New York, NY 10038
www.openroadmedia.com

The
Flowering
Thorn

PART I

Chapter One

I

There is good evidence for believing that an American gentleman staying at Beverley Court once so far forgot himself as to clean his shoes: what is probably not true is that the head boot-boy subsequently borrowed the chef's carvers and committed *hara-kiri*. A chef's carvers are very difficult to come at, and it is also most unlikely that any member of the pantry-staff could have penetrated unchecked as far as the kitchens; but the story is useful as illustrating the almost fanatically high standard of Beverley service.

The management, indeed, worked, and worked successfully, on the basic assumption that their tenants as a class were not intended by nature to boil eggs, wash socks, sew on buttons, walk up or down stairs, have children, keep dogs, or put up friends on the sofa. They were stunted creatures; but like animals in captivity, astonishingly contented. The waiting list for the smaller apartments was as long as Deuteronomy.

In this heaven of the civilised, Lesley Frewen's mansion was inevitably small, for at the Beverley Court letting office the parable of the needle's eye had long been reversed. Entertaining, however, only on the most intimate scale, and rarely at home except to change and sleep, the lack of floor-space hardly struck her. Almost it was an advantage, for with the nomad instinct of the hyper-civilised she dreaded nothing so much as the accumulation of possessions; and as this creed was as widely subscribed, if not as widely practised, among her friends, all their gifts for many years had either gone up in smoke, or shrivelled on the stem, or melted in the mouth. Miss Frewen's personal belongings, indeed, would have gone into a hat-box; and for clothes there was the big fitted cupboard whose doors, when open, practically bisected the bedroom. They were lined with two long mirrors, between which, at about a few minutes past six on the 20th of March, 1929, Lesley Frewen stood adjusting the angle of a small black hat. Beneath the tilted brim a face immaculately plucked, rouged and powdered met her final glance with a well-grounded confidence: she was looking just as every other woman wanted to look, and could continue to do so for at least four hours.

From the telephone by the bed came a low repeated burr: the taxi was waiting. A rapid glance into her handbag assured her of lip-stick, powder, cigarettes: complete in every material detail, and with mind serenely attuned to social intercourse, Lesley Frewen went to the party.

II

Arriving at Pont Street, however, the sum of her perfection was slightly diminished. Facially, all was still well. But in her feelings she was ruffled, though only a little: partly because a shoe-string needed tightening, and partly because she had just observed on the door-step a young man who was threatening to commit suicide unless she accompanied him to Warsaw. He was completely uninteresting, and had never, even in the wildest flights of passion, suggested their travelling anything but third, so that the triumph of Lesley's virtue had been little more than a walkover; but her refusals, though frequent and frank, had as yet made no impression, and with equal persistence the youthful Bryan continued to press his suit.

'Damn the child!' thought Lesley, 'why the hell does Elissa let him in?' And with a frown under her eye-veil she paid off the taxi, knocked at a high blue door, and a moment later was absorbed into the party.

"Darling!"

"Darling!" countered Lesley swiftly, and looking round to see who had addressed her. But it was impossible to tell, for the mob in Elissa's drawing-room shifted so quickly that the only jointed conversations were carried on toe-to-toe like an old-fashioned boxing-match. At the other end of the room a piano was being played, though not professionally: the glasses rattled on its lid and people far over by the windows talked at the tops of their voices. The heat, noise, and congestion were alike considerable, and with every farther step Lesley's spirits rose. An agreeable press, a stimulating babel: the complicated atmosphere—of electric heating, scent, and good furs—at once so familiar and so exhilarating in the nostrils: and gathering her wits, she abandoned the futile search for Elissa to lay instead a course for the buffet. It was slow going. Those who had achieved their drinks continued to linger at the fount, those still unslaked pressed thirstily on; and her progress was further impeded by the early departure of Mrs. Carnegie.

"Darling!" cried Lesley, this time getting in first.

Mrs. Carnegie purred absently back: a round little woman, French by birth, American by marriage, plumply-breasted as a robin, and with not the slightest objection to making herself conspicuous by an almost Edwardian display of pearls. She wore them even in bed, she told people, in order to preserve their colour: and from all Lesley had heard about her, the statement would never lack corroboration.

"You are looking for Elissa, hein?" said Mrs. Carnegie. "She 'as gone to see why there is no more gin. When she comes, will you say I am very sorry, I 'ave to go?" She glanced expertly round, and from the mob at the piano singled out a tall and beautiful young man. "Paul! Paul, we are going!"

But the beautiful young man did not want to leave. He was enjoying himself. He said so loudly, first in Polish and then in translation.

"But I do not want to go! I am enjoying myself!"

"You will enjoy yourself where we are going!" promised Mrs. Carnegie. "You will enjoy yourself more!"

With the trustfulness of a child Paul stopped playing the piano and made his adieux. They included, at the sight of Miss Frewen, a heel-clicking pause and a long pressure of her hand—not exactly kissed, but bowed over to the extreme limit. He knew she had no money; she was aware of his knowledge; and the disinterestedness of the tribute afforded both a certain pleasure.

"Paul!" cried Mrs. Carnegie.

"I wish you were coming too," said Paul simply; and with a last melting glance moved elegantly away.

Slightly but agreeably flattered, mocking at herself for being so, Lesley resumed her course. She was by this time thirstier than ever, and in definite search of a man to do her pushing for her: but for all that it was with a faint sinking of the heart that she perceived young Bryan Collingwood standing squarely in her path.

"Lesley!"

The crowd was thick, but there was no time to hide. Miss Frewen sighed.

"Come out on the balcony, Lesley. I've got to speak to you."

"My dear, don't be so absurd! I haven't seen Elissa!"

"Please come. I implore you to come."

She observed, with no emotion beyond a faint impatience, the extreme pallor of his lips: he had probably been one of those horrid little boys who can hypnotise themselves into nausea at the sight of a milk-pudding. But since he was quite capable of making a scene in the middle of Elissa's drawing-room, she gave in and followed him through the French window.

"Well?"

"If you don't come to Poland with me I shall kill myself."

He stood with his back to the railings, pressed hard against the iron and devouring her with his eyes; and as Lesley watched him there rose deep in her sophisticated soul a sudden fierce pride, a sudden anger at the insolence of such misery. How dared he follow her with that starving look, run at her heels and scratch at her door! And now this blackmail, this suicide—he was impossible! And she heard her own voice, very cold and distinct, saying:

"This is intolerable. I refuse to be blackmailed by a peevish child."

The white lips moved in answer, but without a sound. She shrugged her shoulders and stepped back into the room.

"*There* you are!" exclaimed the gentleman behind her.

It took Lesley no more than a mere second of concentration to remember everything about him except his name. Retired stockbroker, lots of money, hands-off-capital-and-shoot-the-unemployed. . . . And he was carrying things.

"Dry Martini and caviare. Have I remembered?" asked the stockbroker coquettishly.

With real gratitude she held out a hand.

"Perfectly. Is that your secret of success?"

He beamed at her; and Lesley, sipping, smiled admiringly back. The delicious coldness—for Elissa always had plenty of ice—made her lips tingle, and with a cavalier thus ready to hand she had no hesitation in emptying the glass.

"Now let me get you another," said the stockbroker; and Lesley let him. The crowd, however, was by now even thicker than before, and his progress being correspondingly slow she took up a good central position under the lights and had there been five times addressed as darling before he ever reached the buffet. There was also an invitation to dine, an invitation to lunch, and the offer of a desirable town residence for the next fortnight. The first two Lesley accepted, the last put regretfully aside: for though the Yellow House was charming indeed—a delightful modernised cottage in a mews behind Green Street—she could not quite make out whether the owner himself would or would not be also in residence. From his insistence on the second bathroom, decided Lesley, it seemed at least probable; and she had never liked the owner quite so well as that. Besides, two weeks . . . if her suspicions were correct, surely a month would have been more flattering? So sweetly but firmly Lesley shook her head.

"It's a very beautiful idea," she said, "only I happen to have a home already. You've seen it."

"Well, lend it to someone else," suggested Mr. Ashton, with the easy resource of a man who never has to think about money. He wrote songs, both words and music, at the rate of two dozen a year, employing in the process a vocabulary of about thirty-five words—the figures were Elissa's—and six musical phrases. One heard them on every gramophone, the latest, called '*Love-hut for Two*,' having sold no less than a quarter of a million records; and it was only by a severe mental effort (Lesley felt) that the composer affected to despise them.

"Well, if you change your mind in the next two days, give me a ring," said Toby Ashton. "I hope you will. . . ." He looked earnestly into her eyes and moved on with the stream, thus making room for an invitation to tea, which Lesley refused, and another to dance, which she accepted. By the heat and bustle, now at their extreme, she was no more oppressed than is a swimming fish by the weight of water; a Magyar count lit her cigarette, and her complexion continued perfect.

III

In a little room off the hall Elissa was doing her Yogi. Tall, pale and slender, dressed in grey, white and black-and-white check, intricately coiled upon a sofa of black, red and silver tapestry, she looked as much like the cover of a fashion paper as was humanly compatible with the usual organs. Between her long hands lay a rosary of amber, loosely strung on a silk cord: with every bead she drew a deep breath and thought of infinity. And if that wasn't everyone's idea of Yogi, at least it was Elissa's.

'Infinity-click,' thought Elissa, 'Infinity-click . . .' for it was almost impossible, as she had early discovered, to think the infinity without thinking the click. There were all those people upstairs, soon she would have to go and give them more drinks; but it was always on occasions like this, with the house crammed and the gin flowing, that she felt the strongest impulse to meditation. On a table at her side stood a bowl of lilies and a telephone with the receiver off: they reminded her respectively of the negation of being and a message from the hairdresser—Madame's regular assistant having gone down with 'flu, would Madame trust somebody else, or change the appointment? That would have to be seen to, and a fresh supply of Martinis.

Meanwhile . . . the Way, the Life, the Threefold Gate. Nothingness eternal. The end of doing, the end of wanting, the end of being! Well, either Monsieur Lecoq himself should do her hair, or no one. It wasn't worth the risk. Had Toby Ashton come yet, and if so, would he be able to stay on? Toby and Lesley, and possibly Hugo Dove— they could all make a scratch supper off the remains and then go somewhere amusing. Or if that stockbroker person had the Rolls with him? In any case, something or someone was sure to turn up. The end of planning. . . .

'Infinity-click,' thought Elissa.

IV

"But why not to-morrow?" pleaded the Count, who had come rapidly to the boil.

"Because I'm going out already," said Lesley.

"To-night, and to-morrow, and the night after that! Can it really be so?"

"Easily," said Lesley.

"I do not wonder," explained the Count. "I grieve." It was quite true: he really did grieve, for Lesley with her dark slim elegance conformed almost exactly to his favourite type. He grieved for ten seconds. Then he remembered a girl he had seen on arriving, equally dark and with very beautiful ankles. She was still somewhere about, but there was no time to lose. As swiftly as was compatible with a broken heart, the Count bowed, sighed, and turned sadly away into the arms of the stockbroker.

"Dry Martini and gentleman's relish. The caviare's all gone," said the stockbroker.

Lesley received him gratefully, professing an extreme solicitude for the welfare of his person. The crowd round the drinks, was it really as bad as people were saying?

"Worse. Far, far worse," replied the stockbroker heroically. "But no matter. Every time someone hacked me on the shins I saw your lovely lips and struggled on." He paused. "This time to-morrow I expect I'll be asking someone to hack me again."

Lesley smiled like a woman who is flattered; and then all at once, in the drawing of a breath, her mood changed, and a sudden cold detachment ran chilling through her veins. She thought, 'Why am I exerting myself to attract this rather stupid, middle-aged stockbroker? He is wealthy, and pretends to admire me; but if ever he asked me to become his mistress, I should certainly refuse, and there is notoriously no other means of getting at his money. Physically he is far below the average policeman, and for intellectual companionship I should prefer the lift-boy. Then why?'

Her gaze, which had been mechanically fixed on his small pale eyes—bright, clear and colourless as the windows of an empty house—shifted to a group by the balcony door; and again, without warning, her thought twisted aside. For no possible reason, but sudden as an arrow from the sky, anxiety pierced her. She glanced quickly round the room, hoping to see young Collingwood, but he was not there. Gone home, then?—or perhaps still out on the balcony?—and if so, what was he doing there? The questions raced through her head, too swift for any rational and reassuring answer. It became imperative that she should go and see what Bryan was doing on the balcony.

With an incoherent murmur she turned on her heel and walked straight across the room. The long windows were pulled-to, but the latch being on the inside had prevented his fastening them, and Lesley stepped out with five seconds to spare.

"Put that thing down at once," she said crossly.

For a moment young Collingwood tried to out-stare her, the revolver still wavering at his temple. Then eyes and hand dropped together and the gun dangled ridiculously by his side.

"Now give it to me," said Lesley.

This time he obeyed at once. She opened her bag—fortunately a very large one, in the latest mode—and stuffed the thing inside.

"But—but . . . Lesley!"

"Well?"

"I l-love you!"

"Nonsense," said Lesley coldly. "You don't love me in the least. You simply like to have an emotion."

And without even waiting to see whether he threw himself over the railings she stepped back through the window and almost on to Elissa's toes.

"Darling! I didn't think you'd got here! Have you had anything to drink?" From under the preposterously long but still genuine eyelashes Elissa's bright intelligent glance flickered over the hat, gown, complexion and accessories of her dearest friend. "Come and have one of my new sandwiches and tell me if they're all right."

"But darling, I'm just going home!"

Again that bright intelligence flickered out, this time over the assembled guests.

"They are rather a mess, aren't they? But just hold on another ten minutes and we'll throw out the riff-raff and go on somewhere amusing. You and me and Toby and Hugo. . . ."

Lesley shook her head. Not that Elissa wasn't right. It was a mess, a mess of people and a mess of emotions, a purposeless mingling of fret and pleasure and fifty perfect strangers. A silly mess, that nothing but gin could ever hold together . . . Aloud she said,

"I can't really, darling. I'm dining out."

"Who with?"

"Douglas Ford."

And a sudden spring of happiness warmed her heart.

V

All the way home in the taxi Lesley's mind raced ahead, planning in ridiculous detail the employments of the next hour. To turn on the bath: to lay out shoes, frock, undergarments, stockings: to rub on the first and swiftly-to-be-removed layer of face-cream—all these would take at least a quarter of an hour. Then the bath itself, and after the bath another quarter of an hour, this time of complete relaxation, before beginning to dress; then the face, the hair: five minutes for the hands. There was time, but no time to lose; and with an odd feeling of crisis Lesley left her fare to be settled by the porter and stepped straight into the lift.

On her outer door-mat, however, she had to pause and look for her latchkey. That ridiculous revolver was still stuffing up her bag, making everything very difficult to find; and with a final spurt of dislike for all men under thirty she reflected that she would probably now be liable to a heavy fine for being in unlicensed possession of firearms. Unless of course one got up very early in the morning and went and threw it into the Round Pond. . . .

And pushing open the door, Lesley smiled. No doubt Douglas would know what to do with it; and in any case the story—very delicately hinted, no suspicion of giving a man away—ought at least to convey, to that rather preoccupied intelligence, certain . . . well, certain implications. 'An absolute child, my dear, and being very silly about me. . . .'

But the thing was spoiling her bag nevertheless, and weapon in hand, as though to face a burglar, Lesley went into her sitting-room and switched on the lights. But there was nothing stirring, not even a mouse; since from Beverley Court both mice and burglars were equally excluded by the board of management.

Chapter Two

I

About five hours later, between midnight and the quarter, Douglas Ford stood up to go. The smoke of many cigarettes faintly blued the air, for they had returned, at Lesley's suggestion, a little early.

"I'll come and show you the lift," she said. "The doors are so ornamental that no one recognises it."

Douglas Ford laughed.

"I know them of old. An Aunt of mine lives on the top floor. She says it's just as good as a nursing-home, and much more convenient for the shops." He laughed again, and for once, as he stood loosening his shoulders, Lesley took notice that her room was small. The bulk and solidity of men! A thought struck her, and she said,

"In your Arctic kit—didn't you look enormous?"

"So the other fellows used to tell me. But out there there's room."

He lifted his hand, as though suddenly interested in the size of it; then changing the gesture to one of farewell, took Lesley's ungloved fingers and bade her good-night.

"Don't lose your way!" she said.

When he was quite gone, and when the lights of his car had vanished from below the window, Lesley went slowly to her bedroom and looked in the glass.

The image she sought there—so curiously, eagerly, as though for the first time—was tall, poised and precisely as slender as fashion required. Gown, gloves and single orchid were impeccably chosen, while the dark, smooth shingle, close as a silken scalp, set off a certain neat elegance of head and shoulders. A lady, one would say, of at least sufficient income, enjoying considerable taste, and not more than twenty-eight years old.

Without the slightest warning, Lesley Frewen burst into tears.

For a moment, while the sobs were still beyond control, her only desire was to fling herself down on the bed and bury her face in a pillow. But she was standing, as has been said, before a mirror, and the sight of the havoc therein—the disintegration, as it were, of so much elegance—acted at least as well as sal volatile. Swiftly as it had come, the storm passed over: Lesley dried her eyes, powdered her nose, and returning to the sitting-room sat down to consider the extraordinary phenomenon of her own tears.

II

Extraordinary indeed; for purely on her own social merits, and with an income which to many of her friends would have seemed microscopic, Lesley Frewen was universally admitted to lead an exceptionally full, varied and interesting life. She had as many dinner engagements, someone once said, as a young man about Town, and could be relied upon as neighbour for either ambassadors or poets. Music, art, the theatre (all modern) were absorbing interests. She was a foundation member of the Ballet Circle. Hostesses liked her, and occasionally asked her advice. A more fortunately situated young woman, in fact, it would have been hard to conceive: and to crown all, she had just been dining alone with Douglas Ford.

A good many women would envy her that. Elissa, for example, who had first introduced them, and then a little regretted it; and for the length of a cigarette Lesley sat by the fire and thought of Douglas.

He was exactly—she admitted it without disguise—the sort of man she liked and admired. Although little over thirty, he had already made a name for himself in scientific exploration: was universally expected to go on to even greater triumphs of pure research: and had in addition a sophisticated and delightful sense of humour that exactly matched her own. Nor was it the only quality they shared. Golf and the French cinema, skating, bridge and D. H. Lawrence— the list of their common tastes was endless. And he admired her looks, thought her extremely intelligent; would ask her opinion on current affairs. . . .

"Then what was it?" cried Lesley aloud; and so at last admitted what still seemed almost impossible, that the evening had been a failure.

They had dined, they had laughed and talked, in every mir- ror she had watched herself looking her best: and yet, for want of some tiny, ultimate pinch of happiness, the whole evening had been flawed.

Thus, step by step, she approached the heart of her black mood, the reason for those unreasonable tears; and presently, for the bitter reward of her courage, the last turn straightened to the centre and there was no more looking aside.

She had wanted Douglas Ford to make love to her, and he had not been sufficiently attracted.

There had been a moment, perhaps ten minutes ago, when lean- ing forward for a last cigarette she had deliberately displayed, with an exaggerated turn, the smooth contour of her delicately-rouged cheek. If he had kissed it, she would have said—what?—'My dear Douglas!'—very lightly, more amused than rebuking; and she would not have drawn back.

An angry shame burned at her centre. To have so offered herself, to have been so refused! That the offer had passed unnoticed, that the refusal had been unwitting, she could and did believe; but the bitterness was not thereby lessened. Beside it nothing else mattered: in all her life at that moment, nothing else even existed. And having thus stumbled on the ultimate truth, Lesley remembered her generation and lit a cigarette.

It was true. Away from Douglas, nothing was real. That afternoon a man had tried to kill himself for love of her, and it had been no more than an incident at a party. Nothing was real, not even death. And this had been so, moreover, as she now suddenly and strangely realised, for far longer in time than their brief acquaintance. Before ever they met, the truth had been there. She had glimpsed it, now and then, in a wakeful dawn, a solitary midnight. But always in the morning the waiting had begun again: the waiting that was her purpose and occupation, her present and her future.

'So that's what I have been doing all these years,' thought Lesley. 'Waiting. . . .'

There was now, however, nothing more to wait for. There was nothing to want, because nothing had substance.

"Substance!" said Lesley aloud.

And so with the spoken word an old phrase came to her—so old, indeed, that her wondering eyes had first deciphered it under the frontispiece of a child's reader: *Thus by grasping at a shadow, the foolish dog has lost the substance too.* A foolish dog indeed! Fat and curly, Lesley remembered, and of the same curious breed that produced Good Dog Tray. A rather humiliating comparison.

Suddenly, on a table at her side, the telephone was ringing. In an idiotic flutter—'*Lesley, have you gone to bed yet? No, Douglas, why?— Then can I come and fetch you? I've just met some people who are going on to Claridges*—' She reached out and silenced it.

"Lesley darling—"

It was Bryan. He had evidently not thrown himself from the balcony.

"Yes, what is it?"

There was a slight pause, and Lesley hoped that he was not about to pull the trigger of a revolver in order to let her hear the shot.

"Listen, Lesley—"

"Well?"

"Would it be an awful nuisance if I came round and used your gramophone for an hour or two?"

"It would," said Lesley. "It's a quarter past one, and I'm just going to bed."

Again the pause, this time enlivened by a faint murmur of voices at the other end of the line. He seemed to be consulting somebody: when he spoke again it was in a tone of exquisite reason.

"But listen, darling, it really is rather important. I've a man here who's just come back from Bulgaria with some amazing records of folk-music, and I've broken my sound-box. They've never been heard in England before, and—"

"Well, I don't suppose anyone else will hear them before morning," said Lesley tartly. She did not really wish him dead, but a slight resentment at his being still alive inevitably coloured her feelings.

"Darling, don't be so beastly! If you like we'll come and get your sound-box—Lesley! I say, don't ring off! Lesley—!"

But the receiver was already clicked down on his yammering: clicked down too on the sound of Lesley's voice. A rather odd sound, like an ejaculation. . . .

"Love!" said Lesley, contemptuously.

And in that instant, as though resentful Love had heard and come to wound her, there slipped into her mind, already bodied in words, a strange and dreadful notion. She thought,

'Perhaps I am not a woman that men do love.'

She thought,

'There are women like that. Attractive women. . . . And if that is so, and if . . . that is what I have been waiting for, what am I to do now?'

The intricate, daily patchwork was still there to work at, the innumerable dovetailing fragments still lay ready to hand: but it now seemed to her, and for the first time, that her work had no pattern.

"I want something new," said Lesley aloud.

On the table at her side lay a tiny pocket-book, bound in black silk and stuffed a month ahead with every variety of familiar engagement. Automatically she picked it up and began fluttering the leaves. To-morrow—to-morrow promised the rather rare event of tea out at Cheam with her aunt Mrs. Bassington.

Chapter Three

I

"It really *is* a problem," said Lady Chrome, thoughtfully helping herself to a piece of chocolate cake.

"My dear, I dream about it at nights!" wailed Mrs. Bassington; and all three—Mrs. Bassington, Lady Chrome, and Lesley by the fireplace—turned with one accord to take a look at the problem himself, who was seated very comfortably on a wolverine rug and playing with a box of bricks. The game was a simple one, consisting merely in building the eight blocks into a tower and then knocking them down again; but the problem played it for all he was worth. He fell upon the tower, destroyed it, razed it to the ground: the blocks rolled far and wide, farther than the cake-stand: one would never have guessed, to look at him, what a problem he was.

"It will have to be an orphanage, of course," murmured Mrs. Bassington, "but I suppose even that involves *some* financial consideration. I mean one can hardly leave him outside Dr. Barnardo's. . . ."

She looked genuinely worried, poor woman: and indeed had every right to. Exactly a month earlier, and after reading a very moving article on the plight of the unmarried mother, she had engaged as companion a young Scotswoman with a four-year-old boy. (That Nora Craigie afterwards turned out to be a genuine widow, with her marriage lines in her trunk, is neither here nor there: it was the intention which counted, and which, in Mrs. Bassington's eyes, deserved a better reward.) The Scotswoman proved charming, capable, and as grateful as could be wished: unfortunately she also suffered from heart trouble. This disability she managed to conceal, however, until about fifteen minutes before dying of it; and it was the deception, the slyness of it, which Mrs. Bassington now professed herself unable to forgive. Or at any rate, it was something one could decently complain of, and what with all the trouble of the funeral and the worry of the future, she felt she must either complain or burst.

"When I'd treated her really like—like my own daughter!" cried Mrs. Bassington.

From the other side of the cake-stand Lesley heard her unmoved. She was feeling, for these two flabby and bleating old women, an almost homicidal dislike. The mood of the previous evening was still upon her; she wanted to hurt, to shock, to take her revenge.

"But are there *no* relatives at all?" marvelled Lady Chrome. "Not even a grandmother?"

"My dear!" Mrs. Bassington threw up her hands in despair. "We've advertised in things like '*John Bull.*' I even made them put 'something to their advantage,' because after all there are the effects as well. And not a single debt—I will say that much for her. But both she and her husband I know were orphans, because she told me so herself, and in these cases it's always the grandparents who come forward." She broke off, breathless with so much emotion. It was all even worse than she had thought.

"If only," mused Lady Chrome hopelessly, "you could get someone to adopt him! After all, dear, he—he's quite a *nice* child."

"Or why not advertise him too?" suggested Lesley. '*Boy, four years: healthy, ginger hair, no incumbrances: nominal to good home.*' It sounds rather attractive."

And turning again in the direction of the rug, she suddenly saw that she had spoken no more than the truth. There really *was* something rather attractive about him, something to do, perhaps, with his complete imperviousness to all but the matter in hand. Far overhead, remote as the Fates, three irrelevant women babbled or were silent: they had no bearing on his game, so he took no notice of them. Bang! went his fist, crash! went the tower; and all was ready to start again. Once he sat down heavily on an unexpected brick: frequently on the bare parquet floor: but even as he rubbed, the other hand was always busy at rebuilding. With a growing fascination, Lesley watched.

"A place in Essex," murmured Lady Chrome vaguely, "run in connection with some church or other. . . ."

Orphanages again! From all one heard, the food was now quite decent; but it would be rather wasteful if all that crowing, relishing energy, that bundle of clean and vigorous life, were simply to be forced, along with a hundred other inferior bundles, into the one most convenient mould! For comparing him with the other children (admittedly few) of her acquaintance, Lesley had little doubt that the Problem, as raw material, was of exceptional quality. His game, for example, was an equal mixture of joyful pugnacity and careful construction. At the constant bumps to his behind he displayed a natural concern, but no resentment. And it was probably an optical illusion, but he seemed to be growing as one looked at him.

'Maternal pride—it really *is* understandable,' thought Lesley curiously. And yet, and yet—a child of that age was a woman's full-time job. He had to be washed, fed, exercised and instructed from about eight in the morning till about seven at night. After that, she supposed, one could go out to dinner in the usual way: but what about getting the hair waved? There was a place in Bond Street where they took charge of dogs, even Alsatians, but nothing was said about small boys. . . . And then there would be *his* hair to get cut, and a thousand other things as well. Yes, a full-time job if there ever was one, though probably not quite such a martyrdom as women were apt to make out: for was there really any reason why from seven o'clock onwards life should not go on precisely as before?

Any full-time job, on such terms, would lose half its terrors: then why not this one in particular? Moreover, there was something—what was it?—something so extremely real about it. It was worth doing; and suddenly, idly, chiefly from a desire to upset someone, Lesley heard herself say,

"Don't bother about that advertisement, Aunt. I think I'll adopt him myself."

II

Almost before the words were out of her mouth, in a split second of perfect lucidity, Lesley Frewen had realised two things. The first was that she had not the least desire to adopt a child; the second, that the child had heard her.

Though without comprehending. Comprehension—of those two swift phrases—how could she even for an instant have imagined it possible? It was only that, like a dog at a familiar voice, he had suddenly raised his head and fixed her with a long expectant gaze. . . . And all at once there flickered through her brain something she had heard from Douglas Ford: that a dog takes his orders less from the actual words than from the compulsive thought behind them.

"But, my dear!" It was Lady Chrome who first found her tongue, leaning purple with emotion above her own stately bust. "But my dear, you must be *crazy!*"

"Rather foolish, dear child, and not really very amusing," corroborated Aunt Alice.

Both these opinions coinciding exactly with her own, the only rational course was obviously to submit and pass the cake: and in the company of any two persons less purple and authoritative, Lesley would no doubt have done so. But the pop-eyed stupidity of Lady Chrome, the complacent imperviousness of Mrs. Bassington, had already produced their usual unfortunate effect; and raising her beautiful eyebrows, Lesley said provocatively,

"It would be such a new experience. . . ."

Lady Chrome released a long breath.

"But—but you don't even *like* children!'

"Not in the least," agreed Lesley. "That's why it would be new."

"In any case, the idea is impossible," cut in Mrs. Bassington decisively.

Her niece, however, was not so easily to be intimidated.

"Why, Aunt Alice?"

"Because you're far too young, in the first place. You don't know what you're doing. People would say—would think—"

"But they do already, Aunt," pointed out Lesley blandly. "When I went to Salzburg last year everyone thought I'd gone with Toby Ashton."

"Lesley!"

"But unfortunately Toby is almost as dark as I am, so as long as he stays ginger it won't look quite so bad."

From Lady Chrome's *bergère* came a sound like a suffocating Pekingese. Mrs. Bassington, with greater self-command, merely pursed her lips and continued to pour out tea. And all at once, from being slightly amused, Lesley was irritated beyond endurance. She said coldly,

"I'm perfectly serious, Aunt Alice."

"Nonsense, my dear."

With a considerable effort Lesley controlled her temper. The impertinence of old women! A tie of blood, however thin, and how complacently they advanced to the limits of rudeness! Her resolve hardening, she said,

"There's really no need for any more discussion. I quite understand your feelings, Aunt Alice, but unfortunately you don't understand mine. It probably comes of—"

For the first time Mrs. Bassington raised her voice.

"My dear, there's no need to tell *me* what it comes of. I know. It comes of letting you have your own money at eighteen. Eighteen!" She took a fierce little sip of tea: over the rim of her cup her eyes popped angrily. "I said at the time it was ridiculous, but no one listened to me, and now this is the result. You think you can behave exactly as you please. You think you can fly in the face of convention and get applauded for doing it. Well, I shan't waste any more breath trying to stop you. You're ruining your life, my dear, but as you are no doubt preparing to tell me, it's your own life to ruin."

She broke off, breathless and slightly mottled. Lesley smiled.

"How well you know me, darling!"

"And don't call me darling," added Mrs. Bassington in parentheses. "It's ridiculous, a meaningless trick and I won't have it. You go your own headstrong way and then try to placate me by foolish endearments. You won't think yourself, and you won't let others think for you. I know exactly what your income is, my dear: a bare five hundred and fifty, and you spend every penny of it. What's going to happen, may I ask, when the child goes to school?"

Lesley thought rapidly. Then:

"Uncle Graham, darling," she said; and with a secret enjoyment watched her aunt's face. For old Graham Whittal was both wealthy and distinguished; and he had publicly referred to his sister-in-law as a pompous old busybody. "He's a governor or something of Christ's Hospital," Lesley elaborated, "with two nominations. It's one of the best schools in the country."

The riposte being unanswerable, Mrs. Bassington ignored it. Instead, she drew herself together and played her trump card.

"Very well, my dear, since you're so determined. But there's one thing I warn you: you'll have to take him tomorrow."

Whatever she felt, Lesley betrayed no emotion.

"I'll come down with a car."

"You've realised, of course, that you'll have to leave your flat? And that no respectable place is going to take you in?"

At last Lesley paused. The second threat worried her not at all: times had changed since Aunt Alice read *East Lynne*. But to leave Beverley Court! And leave she must: they didn't take children. Tomorrow, moreover: a bare twenty-four hours' notice after nearly seven years! Her personal possessions, fortunately, would all be eminently portable, and with a waiting list like the Beverley's, there would be no difficulty in letting; but all the same, to leave Beverley Court. . . .

'It is rather perfect,' thought Lesley reluctantly; and with her mind's eye she suddenly saw the big wicker basket, rather like a laundry-basket, which arrived every Tuesday morning to collect her mending. And the following Thursday the basket reappeared and the mending was done. In case of any real crisis—a laddered stocking or a ripped hem—emergency assistance could be summoned by the ringing of a bell. . . . And that was only one of the amenities. On the first of April in each year a man came round with a dozen pink geraniums and filled the two window-boxes, which from then until the first of October became the responsibility of the under lift-boy. In the early hours of the morning he watered, groomed and when necessary replenished; and on the appointed day the man came back and put in privet instead. . . .

"Oh well," said Lesley, emerging from her brief homage to the past, "there are other places in town besides the Beverley. If I'm down by three o'clock, Aunt Alice, will you see that his things are ready?"

"They'll be ready on the door-step," said Mrs. Bassington grimly.

With an agreeable sensation of victory, Lesley gathered up her gloves, made a formal adieu, and walked towards the door. Half-way across the room, by the scattered heap of bricks, she paused and looked down.

"To-morrow you're going to come and live with me, Patrick."

He nodded off-handedly and got on with his tower.

Chapter Four

I

Among the many epitaphs which Mr. Ashton constantly composed for himself there was one so exquisitely apt that he sometimes felt tempted to scrap all the rest and compose no more. It ran, very simply—though with perhaps a reminiscence of Stendhal—to no more than six words: 'He made songs, and understood women'; and such being the case, he experienced not the least surprise when Lesley Frewen rang up to say she had changed her mind.

"My dear, of course I meant it," he assured her. "Come in to-day—now—whenever you like." Under the flowered dressing-gown, for it was no more than ten in the morning, his heart, without actually beating faster, felt all the pleasurable emotion of prophecy fulfilled.

"But what about you, Toby?" asked the voice of Miss Frewen. "When do you want to get out?"

The moment had come. He would have liked to move to a more comfortable chair, for the conversation promised to be lengthy: but a pause at that point, however slight, would almost inevitably suggest that . . . well, that necessity was needing time to become a mother. With no pause at all, therefore, Mr. Ashton said rapidly,

"Oh, really, my dear, it's all rather odd. I've just had a wire from Paris, and they don't want me till the week *after* next. So you see how it is. I mean, would you mind awfully if I stayed? There *are* two bathrooms." And he waited with real interest for the answer. For Lesley Frewen—after all, what did one know about her? As hard-boiled a virgin as any in town, he shouldn't wonder . . . and yet if so, with an almost uncanny gift for stopping a lover's mouth. Or was she even now—for the pause continued—working up a flow of righteous vituperation?

But Lesley's voice, when at last it broke the silence, came cool and untroubled.

"But of *course* I don't mind, my dear. I think it's terribly nice of you to let us come!"

And now, at the other end of the line, Lesley waited with at least equal interest. The first result, however, was disappointment, for as soon as he got his breath again Mr. Ashton merely cursed the exchange.

"Darling, this 'phone's so rotten I can't hear you. What did you say?"

"I said we wouldn't mind a bit, Toby, and it was terribly nice of you. Because—did Elissa or anyone tell you?—I've just adopted a baby boy."

This time the pause was so long that she began seriously to wonder whether the shock, at so early an hour, had not been altogether too great. But Mr. Ashton had not actually fainted: to be astonished to the point of swooning implies at least a standard of morality: and this, except in art, the composer of 'Loving for Two,' was admittedly without. He was surprised, but not bowled over; in proof of which, and with an undeniable gallantry, he broke the silence on a note of congratulation.

"But darling, how original of you! Most people always farm them out. Shall you be bringing a bassinette!"

"Not even a pram, my dear. He's four-and-a-half. How nice you are, Toby!"

"Yes, aren't I?" said Mr. Ashton. "I'll tell Mrs. Lee. She runs the place, you know—very trustworthy, only mustn't be hurried. When shall you be along, darling?"

"About four o'clock, then," said Lesley unhesitatingly. "Will that be all right?"

"Perfect, my dear. Oh, and by the way—"

"Yes?"

"There is just a chance I may have to go to Madrid," said Mr. Ashton.

II

The other man to whom Lesley telephoned that morning was her uncle-by-marriage Graham Whittal. Their relations being normally confined to the annual exchange of a ninepenny Christmas card, her summons to a five o'clock rendezvous in St. James's Park caused him extreme surprise. He continued to feel surprised, moreover, all through the afternoon: for though his niece was obviously wanting something out of him, he could not for his life imagine what. There were always debts, of course, and in these days the young women were probably as bad as the men: but he had the curiously defi-nite impression that she was not the sort that gets into a mess over money. But what then? What else drove the young into the company of their elders? Love? Not in these days! As puzzled as when he sat down there, Mr. Whittal rose from his club window, retrieved his hat; and taking a taxi as far as the Horse Guards, walked slowly to meet his niece in the neighbourhood of the pelicans.

'And why the pelicans?' he thought suddenly. Hideous plucked-looking creatures! Ungainly even in flight! But made very good mothers, one heard—or didn't one, nowadays? So many theories being exploded, it was probably only a matter of years before the earth was flat again! In any case—good mothers or no—hardly a reason why that young woman should wish to contemplate them.

And just then he thought he saw her, only she was accompanied by a child.

"Hello, Uncle Graham," said Lesley. "Aren't these creatures hideous?"

Mr. Whittal removed his hat.

"Good afternoon, my dear. I was just thinking the same thing. Also that your escorts are usually a good deal older."

"Four-and-a-half exactly, Uncle. I'd tell him to say good afternoon, only I'm afraid he might not."

"Shyness, or vice?" inquired Mr. Whittal sympathetically.

"Oh, vice, I hope. It's so much more natural."

He had the distinct impression that she was carrying something off.

"Ah, that means you're judging by your own generation. This young man may be at the other end of the swing. But in any case, it's hardly your responsibility."

Under that really ridiculous hat his niece looked at him oddly.

"Oh yes it is, Uncle Graham," said she.

The retort had been irresistible: but it left too much to the imagination. With genuine interest Mr. Whittal looked from Pat's flaming head to her own dark shingle.

"His name," said Lesley explicitly, "is Patrick Craigie, and he is the son of Aunt Alice's companion, who died a month ago, by a father unknown, also dead, but legally married. I've adopted him."

"Dear me," said Uncle Graham.

On the other side of the railings a pelican suddenly shook out its wings, spread-eagling with gawky pride before a couple of indifferent companions.

"And where do I come in?" asked Mr. Whittal.

Lesley looked at him intelligently.

"Well, I was going to lead up to it," she said, "but aren't you something to do with the Bluecoat School?"

So that was it! Of all things on earth she was out after school fees! And deep in his heart there was something that sighed. Axes to grind—there was no getting away from them! Well, it was very natural: the old had, and the young wanted.

"I am," said Mr. Whittal, quite unaware how long he had been silent. "I happen to be a Governor."

"And you can get small boys into it?"

"I can nominate them, if that's what you mean. The small boy has also his share. He has to be able to read and write, for example—"

One hand on his arm, Lesley smiled delightfully.

"Come back to my Club, darling, and tell me there. You won't believe it, but the sherry's marvellous."

Graham Whittal looked at her. Whatever she wanted she was obviously going to get: but it was long indeed since a young woman had made eyes at him. With a perfectly clear view of his own motives, therefore, he followed her into a taxi and prepared himself for the shearing.

Chapter Five

I

The old, noted Lesley, are always wrong.

The reflection, in all its gnomic simplicity, occurred to her at the breakfast-table, having been crystallised, as it were, from a hundred scattered musings, by the simultaneous arrival of three invitations to dinner and a card for an At Home. In circles unknown to Mrs. Bassington her niece's adoption of a baby boy was being hailed as something so amusing and original that Lesley had not yet lunched or dined off the Yellow House china.

The Yellow House was charming, and they had it to themselves. Exactly a week earlier their host had welcomed them with his foot on the doorstep and a passport in his hand: the man in Paris, he said, would be there after all. Lesley expressed her regret, honoured such devotion to duty; and with a single interested glance at the colour of Pat's hair, Mr. Ashton flung himself into a taxi and was seen no more.

'Dear Toby!' thought Lesley. She felt quite a genuine affection for him; she even toyed, over the last of her coffee, with the idea of a second and unchaperoned visit at some future date. For the Yellow House, out of which he had so gallantly ejected himself, was exactly her idea of a small Town residence: compact, picturesque, and with one really large room over the next-door garage. One could give some very amusing parties there, in—other circumstances; it was definitely something to bear in mind. In the meantime, however, on the other side of Mr. Ashton's breakfast-table, Patrick Craigie sat finishing a rusk.

Lesley looked across at him, over the black-and-yellow china, and wondered what, if anything, to say. The news, the weather, the invitations?—all obviously impossible: and she had already seen he had enough to eat. Conscientiously but in vain Lesley sought for a suitable topic: in a year or two's time, no doubt, one could take him the *Daily Mirror* or something: until then it looked as though they would breakfast in silence.

Glancing again, she decided that Patrick at any rate was feeling no social embarrassment. He was a silent child, almost stolid. He never prattled, but his articulation was good. Whenever he addressed her, which was rarely, he did so as Frewen, which was also amusing and original, and made a good point at dinner parties; but what really went on in his mind Lesley had so far no idea. The sudden change in his circumstances had caused, so far as she could gather, neither surprise nor emotion: he accepted them silently, stolidly and with apparent content. Whether he ever thought about his mother she could not guess: that he should want her in the night sometimes never entered Lesley's head; for Patrick at the Yellow House slept next to Mrs. Lee, and it was she who rose secretly in the middle of the night.

Gathering up her letters, Lesley rose from the table and lit a cigarette. The morning—a hairwave and lunch in town: Pat could go shopping with Mrs. Lee. Afternoon—rather miscellaneous; an exhibition of Negro sculpture, and possibly a new hat. And then back and rest and change for bridge at Elissa's, followed by a midnight matinée. . . .

The door opened and Mrs. Lee came in. She was stout, cooklike, and with Lesley at least completely impassive; but for once a slight animation seemed to be working within her. She had no need to ask, she had merely to remind, and the flow of her pleasure was therefore unchecked.

"You do remember, Madam, that I'm going for the night to my sister's?"

Lesley remembered perfectly. Hadn't there been a note from Mr. Ashton about it.

"That's right, Madam. I shall leave the table ready, and the chicken in the refrigerator. Master Pat's supper I can do before I go."

With equal good humour Miss Frewen confirmed the arrangements, omitting, however, to mention that the chicken would not be required. Mrs. Lee was invaluable, but her prejudices dated from the flood, and Lesley had no intention of either staying at home herself or of wrecking the long-laid private arrangements of a first-class cook. She was going to begin, in fact, as she meant to go on.

Through the smoke of her cigarette Lesley smiled securely. The evening, besides being amusing, was also going to be important: a test case so to speak, in which should be proved with what perfect confidence one could leave a four-year-old child until three in the morning. For one night at least, or at any rate for a considerable part of it, Patrick should sleep by himself in the Yellow House.

II

In pursuance of this resolution, therefore, Lesley went up about seven o'clock, saw Pat peacefully dreaming, and bathed and dressed as quietly as possible. It was an occasion for full fig, in this case a new dead-white moiré of extreme backlessness: the smooth, heavy silk clung snugly about her thighs, the narrow crossed shoulder-straps settled immaculately into place, and never in her life had Lesley felt more successful.

"How maternity agrees with you, darling!" said Elissa in Pont Street. "One of these days I shall go to Battersea myself. Cut for partners, someone, and let's play rather high. . . ."

With no more than a pleasant sense of its being her due, Lesley picked up a safe Three No Trumps. She did not know it, but she had about another two hours. She had, in fact, until exactly ten o'clock; when having just raised her partner to Three Spades, her inner eye was suddenly distracted by a lively cinematograph impression of young Patrick Craigie setting the house on fire.

He was doing it with matches. . . .

"*Darling*, your lead!" said Elissa sharply.

Rapidly concealing her agitation, Lesley laid a card on the table, discovered too late that it was the Ace, and apologised all round. His sleeping-suit was made of flannel.

'*Flannel!*' thought Lesley impatiently. 'His mother ought to have had more sense.' If flannel caught alight it simply went up like celluloid; and now she came to think about it, there was celluloid there too—that absurd floating swan brought in by Mrs. Lee! It lived by Pat's bed, looking very much out of place, Lesley remembered, on a steel book-table. . . . Flannel and celluloid!

"Having no hearts, partner?"

She looked: she had. The game progressed while Pat charred to a cinder. She tried violently to concentrate, but it was no good; and with a growing disgust, Lesley felt herself to be experiencing the traditional emotions of the absent hen. Her nest was bare, her chick unguarded: for in such nauseating similes did her predicament naturally express itself. Intellectually, she could conceive no possible cause for alarm: and it was therefore all the more unfortunate that what she had now to deal with was a matter not of intellectual conviction but of female physiology. She was discovering, in fact, that it is almost a physical impossibility for any normal woman to leave a small child alone from seven at night till three in the morning; and her bridge suffered accordingly.

"Game and rub," said Elissa, reaching for the score-card. "What is it, darling, drink or the digestion?"

"One on top of the other, darling," replied Lesley, with a suitable languour. "So much so, in fact, that I think I'm going to cut the matinée."

"But my *dear*"—Elissa's hair-thick eyebrows went up and up—
"you aren't as bad as all that, are you?" She looked really quite
anxious—it was so unlike Lesley to break up a bridge party, and a
nuisance into the bargain. A damnable nuisance, for what the hell
were they to do until it was time to go? Aloud she said,

"Have a brandy, darling, and don't give way. There's nothing like
bridge for taking the mind off it."

For the first time within memory, however, that perfect social
conscience was no longer in command. Apologetically, indeed, but
with no sign of relenting, Lesley rose to her feet: she was sorry for
Elissa, but she was in an agony for Pat; and steadily refusing both
cars and cordials, Miss Frewen slipped into her cloak and almost
ran downstairs.

III

From the windows of the Yellow House not a flame issued. Lesley let
herself in, ran quickly upstairs, and there found Patrick peacefully
asleep and no matches in the room.

For a moment she stood gazing, though without æsthetic appreciation, at his pink cheek on the white pillow; then turned back on
to the landing and swore from the heart.

Her return to form being as sudden as complete, she could not
now for the life of her conceive what had happened. There had been
something—God knew what—that drove her from Elissa's bridge-
table; that caused her to lie, feign sickness, and let down her hostess;
and which now, having done its worst, had abruptly departed. It was
all utterly inexplicable.

'Of course he was all right!' thought Lesley, looking back over
her shoulder. Through the open doorway she could just see Pat's
bed, low and pale and with a mound in the middle. The mound
was Patrick, and it never stirred. Probably it had never stirred in all
the time she was away; would doubtless continue unstirring should

she go away again. The thought was tempting: the night was young: and as though to add its persuasion, a clock downstairs chose that moment to chime.

'My God!' thought Lesley. 'It's only half-past ten!'

She stood and listened: the whole house urged her out. It was charming, intimate, a pleasure to the eye: but it did not expect to be inhabited at half-past ten at night. By a whole crowd of people, yes: by two people, perhaps: but not by just one person. . . .

With sudden resolution Lesley picked up her white moiré fishtail and went softly downstairs. The telephone was in the hall, where Patrick could not hear it; and there would be ample time, if she rang up at once, to waylay the party before they left for the Adelphi.

She stretched out her hand, she touched the receiver: and in that instant her bluff was called.

'Burglars!' said a voice within her mind.

'Nonsense!' snapped Lesley.

But it was no use. Even as her lips formed Elissa's number her mind switched back to the smell of burning.

'I tell you there aren't any matches!' argued Lesley with herself.

As quick as thought her mind immediately substituted a masked face at the window, a sudden beam of light—Patrick sitting up shrieking, and a hand over his mouth! Like the original fire-piece, the scene flashed before her with an extraordinary perfection of detail: she could see the hairs on the man's hand, the stitching on Pat's collar. . . .

Her hand dropped back. Even her hand was in the conspiracy. Lesley regathered the folds of her dress and turned again to the stairs. For her hand was perfectly right. The momentary panic had become a permanent frame of mind; and Lesley had little heart to go out in the certain knowledge that half an hour later she would once more be driven back. Her fears had been disproved, and by the mere sight of Patrick's slumber: at the bare thought of leaving him, they were again raising their heads.

With a sudden fierce resentment, a feeling more like hatred than any she had yet experienced, Lesley moved softly into Pat's room and stood looking down at him. Sweet, deep, untroubled: only a child could sleep like that, a child secure in its tyranny; and for the first time, sick with prevision, she saw that she had given herself into bondage.

Which would seem to show that the old are sometimes right.

Chapter Six

— ❋ —

I

The following morning Lesley woke to a mood of cold and bitter lucidity: the mood that should have descended, a week or more earlier, in Mrs. Bassington's drawing-room. For half an hour, in Toby Ashton's bed, she lay marshalling the facts, co-ordinating them into a whole, and considering the result with a complete lack of enthusiasm. For the first and dominant fact was this: that her new and permanent home, which incidentally should be found as soon as possible, would have to contain, in addition to Patrick and herself, a maid who slept in. It would mean extra food, extra wages, above all an extra room; it would mean a fifty per cent increase in expenditure, and with nothing to show but the same liberty of movement to which she had always been accustomed.

Lesley turned over in bed and reached for a cigarette: then suddenly altered her mind and took the dressing-gown instead. A certain natural efficiency, almost atrophied by disuse, was urging her to be up: she felt an impulse towards paper and pen, towards rows of figures and division by fifty-two. Bathing, dressing, powdering, the impulse persisted; till at breakfast she took a pencil and did arithmetic on *The Times*.

The result was so depressing, and many of the items so inevitably provisional, that she scored all through and turned instead to look for a flat. At the enormous number to be let her confidence returned a little; and having noted down the addresses of the dozen most attractive, Lesley put on her hat and went out for the morning.

II

The first of the flats was in Hyde Park Terrace, the last in Campden Hill: at each of which addresses, as at the ten intervening, there successively took place either one or other of the following dialogues.

"Good morning," said Lesley.

"Good morning," replied the housekeeper. (She was twice a landlady, and once a reception-clerk: but the term will serve.)

"I want," continued Lesley, "four rooms, furnished, kitchen and bath."

The housekeeper, smiling affably, would then lead the way. All housekeepers smiled to begin with, for there was something in Lesley's appearance—a businesslike elegance, an air of solvency—that went straight to their hearts. After a swift examination of premises, however—

"I shall have with me," added Lesley, "a small boy."

It was a phrase she had pitched on after considerable thought, but the effect on the housekeepers was not always happy.

"A small boy, Madam?"

"Yes, four-and-a-half."

"I'm sorry, Madam, but we don't take children...."

That was the first version. The second, proceeding smoothly past Patrick to the question of rent, lasted about five minutes longer, was terminated by Lesley instead of the housekeeper, and always on the same note.

"It's charming, of course," agreed Lesley, "but far too expensive." The words were on her lips, in the course of that morning, at least five times. During the next few days they practically lived there.

She was at last experiencing, in fact, the disadvantages of so small a town; for the residential districts as Lesley visualised them amounted to no more than a dozen square miles or so between Chelsea and the Regent's Park. Within this desirable area lived all the people one knew, so that it was naturally rather crowded; but Lesley would no more have thought of looking over the fence, so to speak, than of booking a seat in the upper circle.

In a moment of disquiet, however, she did wire to Paris to beg Tony's hospitality for a further week: and with ten days' grace instead of three returned once more to her round of house-agents.

They all said the same thing.

For the accommodation Madam required, and at the rent Madam was prepared to pay, Madam would probably do better to try the suburbs.

Lesley listened incredulously: it was as though they advised her to try Australia. There *were* the suburbs, of course, through which one occasionally passed in a car, and where people out of *Punch* borrowed each other's mowers: but as for *living* there—

'Impossible!' thought Lesley; and so reached the disturbing conclusion that in the whole of London there was nowhere to live. All was impossible, Town outside the ring-fence, the suburbs outside Town; and so step by step, fighting every inch of the way, she was driven into the country.

III

"But *darling!*" exclaimed Elissa, with her first breath after the bomb-shell. "You surely don't expect you'll like it?"

"On the contrary," replied Lesley, "I expect to loathe it. But it's only till he goes to school."

"Four years, my dear!"

Lesley shrugged.

"Unfortunately, there's no alternative."

For perhaps two minutes they smoked in silence. Then Elissa drove the stub from her holder, and said abruptly:

"Darling—we all think you're splendid, of course, but aren't you being rather a fool? Surely you don't intend giving up your whole life to the child? It's—it's unreasonable."

"It's hardly a question of 'intending,'" said Lesley wearily. "I've taken the thing on and I've got to see it through. I can't afford to see it through in Town, so I've got to see it through in the country. As I said before, there's no alternative."

From Elissa's second cigarette rose an immaculate smoke-ring.

"But darling—I may have got it wrong—but from what you first told me—you haven't done anything actually *legal*, have you?"

"No, it didn't seem necessary. There was no other claim, and I simply . . . undertook him."

"Well, then," Elissa looked up, her long black eyes full of a bright lucidity. "Quite honestly, darling, wouldn't it be better to face the facts and push him into a home?"

At the other end of the couch her friend was perfectly still. 'To get rid of him!' Lesley was thinking. 'To get rid of him and be free!' It was what she longed for with her whole soul. . . .

"Seriously, why not, darling?" asked Elissa again.

Lesley looked up, for the question started a curious train of thought. If with her whole and sovereign soul, then why not, indeed? What was it that could prevent her? And examining her soul more closely, Lesley at last became aware that the general state of its opinions was by no means what she had been assuming. There was a very definite feeling, it appeared, in favour of holding on: a feeling so powerful and unexpected that she could liken it only to a minor revolution. She thought, 'If I don't see this thing out I shall have something rotten inside me for the rest of my life.' Rotten like an apple—the brown decaying core under the firm red skin. . . .

And aloud she said,

"No good, my dear. The boats are burned. I shall take an attractive little cottage somewhere, not too far from Town, and have people at the week-ends. It might really turn out rather amusing."

Elissa regarded her with a contained astonishment. Unlike some other of Lesley's friends, she had never hesitated to express an absolute belief in the story of Pat's parentage; but the strain on her faith was growing momentarily heavier. She reached for her bag and took out a powder-box.

"You're amazing, my dear," she said sincerely. "*I* couldn't do it, not even with Yogi. When shall you go?"

"As soon as I can. Poor Toby's still in Paris, waiting to come home. And . . . Elissa. . . ."

"What, darling?"

"Don't cut me off with a shilling."

For the first time in an intimate friendship of six years' standing emotion touched them. With genuine self-forgetfulness Elissa left her nose unfinished and put out a long, narrow hand.

"Darling! Of course not! We'll all come down and see you in shoals. I adore the country really, if there's anything to go for. And I know what I *will* do, darling—I'll give you all my old records to take away with you."

As well as she could Lesley disguised the bitterness of her answering smile. She had been without her gramophone for the last five years—ever since going to the Beverley, in fact, where the latest electric models were built into soundproof walls; but Elissa's memory was notoriously bad. And feeling already a little like a charitable institution, Lesley kissed her friend on either cheek and walked uneasily home to Toby's Yellow House.

IV

The news that Lesley Frewen was looking for a cottage automatically enriched her acquaintance with more writers and painters than she had ever known before. They brought one another to the Yellow

House, they gave studio parties from Hampstead to the King's Road, they hovered, in short, like bees round a honeysuckle: and in the pocket of each was the five-year lease of a cottage on the Welsh border. Or such at any rate was the impression left on Lesley: who also formed the opinion that painters as a class (even more than writers) were extraordinarily reckless about signing agreements.

To this point she herself attached the utmost importance; and on a lease of that length would have turned down the Trianon. Accessibility from Town, furniture with the cottage, a monthly tenancy—such were her essential requirements. Next in order ranked indoor sanitation, bathroom and electric light: a telephone she was prepared to put in herself. Only long before the telephone made its appearance, the writer or artist of the moment had always drifted disconsolately back to the bar, leaving Lesley (except for an increasing familiarity with modern art) exactly where she started. After agreeably wasting about three days, therefore, she again sought the counsel of age. Not from Mrs. Bassington, of course, whose counsel had arrived unsolicited, and remained largely unread, in a letter of five pages; but from old Graham Whittal.

"If I were an estate agent in heaven," said Mr. Whittal thoughtfully, when she had finished detailing her requirements, "I might be able to help you. As things are, I can only suggest Harrod's. Have you tried them?"

"This morning," said Lesley. "They're all too big and beautiful. No, why I came to you, Uncle Graham, was because I thought you'd know land-owners."

"In these days, my dear? The ones who could have sold, and the others have gone bankrupt."

"All the better, darling, they'll be quite pleased to let me a cottage. Try and think who you were with at Eton: lots of little boys must have been landed in those days."

Obediently, Mr. Whittal thought. Back and back to an age when money was never mentioned and a young man of fashion had bought his first opera hat. . . .

"There's old Kerr. He's got a place in Bucks."

Lesley's face cleared.

"Bucks! That's just right. An easy run."

"But I don't know whether he's got any cottages. You see, most of them, my dear, are being lived in already."

"But you can find out," prompted Lesley.

"I'll write to him, if you like."

"Why not 'phone?"

"He hasn't got one."

"How ridiculous!" said Lesley. "Then I suppose the cottage won't have one either?"

"You may be practically certain of it, my dear," said Mr. Whittal gravely.

With equal irony she met his glance.

"Yes, I'm used to my luxuries, aren't I, darling? I shall have one put in."

'What's she carrying off now?' thought old Graham. An uncomfortable young woman, with her bitter-sweet voice and the underlying harshness! And yet—and yet—what did he or anyone else know about the young? Was it the underlying harshness, or the underlying hurt? What had been happening to her all these years?

And aloud, very gently, he said to her,

"My dear, have you ever considered the future?"

Lesley took out and employed a lipstick. When she had finished, and with mouth renewed in a hard scarlet line, she said,

"Don't worry, Uncle Graham. I know what I'm doing."

"I know a good deal of what you're feeling—"

For a moment she looked at him, startled.

"— And whatever happens in the immediate future, I can promise to get him into Horsham. That takes care of his education. But as for your going and burying yourself in the country, giving up everything you enjoy to play the incompetent nursemaid—it—it's fantastic. After all, my dear—he's got along quite successfully for the last four years."

In the pause that followed he saw that his niece was trying not to laugh because she still wanted something out of him.

"Darling—"

He made an odd gesture of irritation.

"Don't bother, my dear. You can have it without."

"All right, Uncle Graham. It's only a trick of speech." As quick as thought she was back to that odd underlying bitterness. "But you will talk as though he were my adored bastard. It's terribly funny."

For a moment, under their thin, very wrinkled lids, the old eyes held her in steady scrutiny. At last he said,

"In that case—what in heaven's name are you doing it for?"

('Rotten apples!' thought Lesley.)

"A new experience, Uncle Graham. You will write to the land-owner, won't you?"

"Certainly, if you wish it. I shall write and say my niece has gone suddenly demented and needs complete seclusion."

"Thank you, darling. That will be perfect," said Lesley cordially. "I suppose I can't put you up for the Ballet Circle in return?"

With his very natural refusal the interview came to an end. Leaving the room, a feeling that she had been definitely less than gracious made Lesley turn and look back. He was standing in the traditional attitude of ruffled authority—back to the fire, feet a little apart, brows bent upon the pattern of the hearth-rug.

Lesley shrugged her shoulders. It was no good. He didn't believe her. His mind ought to be in a museum.

V

Returning about an hour later to the Yellow House, Lesley found standing in the hall a large leather trunk. It had an old-fashioned dome lid, two stout straps, a garnish of brass nails, and by contrast with Toby's wallpapers might just have been unloaded from the Ark. Lesley pulled off her hat and summoned the housekeeper.

"Does this belong to Mr. Ashton?"

Mrs. Lee looked slightly offended.

"Oh, no, Madam, it's for you. Carter Paterson brought it about half-an-hour ago. And it won't go upstairs, Madam, it's too big."

Advancing a step nearer, Lesley looked at the lid. There were two sets of initials; in the middle, a small N. McB. executed in brass nails: a little below, amateurishly painted, N.E.C. in white.

"It was paid in advance," added Mrs. Lee fairly. "Otherwise, of course, I shouldn't have took it in."

In a flash of understanding Lesley remembered her Aunt's letter. That unread third page! And sitting down on the edge of a steel chair she pulled out the crumpled sheets and spread them in the light.

'*Poor Mrs. Craigie*'—that was it—'*Poor Mrs. Craigie's trunk still here, so I got Denman to pack it and have sent it to you at Yellow House. There were also a few things of Pat's which she says she has put in the tray.*'

Lesley folded the letter back into its envelope and looked again at the heavy domed lid and mighty straps. No one strapped a trunk like that unless the locks were broken, so that she felt fairly confident of being able to get in; but the business was distasteful nevertheless, and she was still debating whether or not to let Patrick's belongings go when Mrs. Lee returned for further instructions.

"Yes, undo the straps, please," said Lesley, suddenly making up her mind. "And then get on to Whiteley's and ask them to come and collect it. Say it's for storage." With the loosening of the buckles curiosity had at last stirred; but a vague disrelish, as at a breach of taste, still kept her motionless. When Mrs. Lee had gone to the telephone, however, Lesley knelt down on the grey carpet and slipped back the locks. As she had suspected, they were both completely useless, and without further resistance the lid gave way.

At the very top, on a sheet of tissue paper, were several very small undergarments, half-a-dozen red bone chessmen, and a much-thumbed copy of *The Tailor of Gloucester*. Lesley lifted them all out on to the carpet. The vests looked much too small and would probably have to be thrown away: the *Tailor* and the chessmen Pat could have at once, to take down to the country if he still wanted them. But she hoped that he would not, for they represented, to her eyes, the unmistakable beginnings of Junk. Junk! The trunk was full of it. As though drawn by a morbid attraction, her hand reached out and twitched aside the blue paper.

In one corner, a bundle of letters tied up with a white ribbon. Two hymn-books. An old chocolate box, also tied up with ribbon. Two white silk blouses, quite clean and neatly folded. A man's glove. And in a sort of nest of paper, pinned to the stuff of the tray, a buttonhole of waxen orange-blossom.

It was junk of the worst description.

With an instinctive and fastidious gesture Lesley thrust down the lid. A wiser Pandora, she had no mind to release a swarm of sentimental microbes. Sentiment and junk. The two things she had all her life most sedulously avoided—only to receive them at last delivered to her door! It was almost amusing. Wholly amusing, in fact, when one remembered the hackneyed, theatrical-property contents of the tray: but for all that she was taking no risks. The trunk should go at once to Whiteley's, there to be stored, amid all the safeguards of modern invention, until such time as Patrick was old enough to be given the receipt. About eighteen, perhaps. Though what a depressing birthday present! Meanwhile—

"Pat!' she called suddenly. "Where are you? Come here a minute."

From the room on the right came a soft thump. He had evidently been sitting on the window-sill. A moment passed, filled, for Patrick at least, with interesting endeavour. Then the door was pulled open and he stood victorious on the threshold.

"Look, do you want these?" asked Lesley, holding up a red knight.

"Chessmen," said Pat.

"Yes. Do you want them?"

In that same instant she saw that he had recognised the trunk. Step by step, one eye still on the chessmen, he moved towards it: and with a first faint stirring of scientific interest Lesley watched for his reactions.

They were few. He recognised; but did he associate? It was difficult to tell, for when still about three paces away his attention was completely diverted by *The Tailor of Gloucester*. This he fell upon literally and figuratively, with his whole heart, turning and tearing the shabby pages until he came to the picture of Simpkin the cat putting mice under tea-cups.

"Simkin," said Pat; and drew a long breath of satisfaction.

'My God!' Lesley thought in horror. 'He's used to being read to! . . .'

Chapter Seven

I

Four days later they went down to the country.

Like an unenamoured but determined bride, Lesley was hurrying upon her fate. She would have taken the White Cottage without seeing it, if Sir Philip's solicitor had not insisted on a meeting: and finding it small, ugly and inconvenient, she took it all the same. It was thatched, but not picturesque: there were four tiny rooms and a smallish barn, the whole standing alone in a very old orchard at the end of a pig-infested lane. This comparative seclusion, and the electric light (put in by Sir Philip in an isolated moment of enthusiasm) were its best, and only, points: but they would at least relieve the tenant of the smell of oil and of the horror of living in a row. The first of the village buildings was a small farm, also opening on to the lane, whose yard ran parallel with the bottom of the orchard: it was owned by people called Walpole, said the solicitors' young man, whom Lesley would find very respectable and trustworthy neighbours.

"So long as they keep their pigs on their own land," Lesley told him coldly, "I don't mind if they're criminal nudists."

"Oh—I don't think you'll find them that," said the solicitors' young man doubtfully; and without pursuing the subject further led her gingerly across the orchard to where a primitive combination of bucket, chain and crank enabled water to be drawn from a thirty-foot well.

"I see," said Lesley, with her eyes on the apple-trees. They looked incredibly senile, many leaning on crutches, and all as though twisted and gnarled by a vegetable gout. A company of greybeards, she thought, gathered round a well. . . .

"You won't get much fruit, I'm afraid," said the young man apologetically. "They're too old."

"Fruit! I should hope not," cried Lesley. The idea was positively indecent, reminding one of those dreadful Victorian old men who got children at seventy by a second or third wife. But she did not develop the simile aloud: quite a lot of clever conversation, in fact, passed wastefully through her head as she listened to the young man's confidences. The thing in the barn, it appeared, was a copper; the thing in the kitchen, a Primus cooking-stove. The hole in the wall was really a serving-hatch, the place like a tool-shed—well, that was an outside lavatory. There was also a hip-bath to bathe in, a meat-safe for the meat, and an unusually large quantity of first-rate clothes-line.

"Now that," said the young man proudly, "is what I call completely furnished."

Lesley looked at him in silence. He was thick, red, raw and bounding; but the mere fact of his being there—of his being actually in conversation with her—lent him a transitory interest. 'So this is what it's going to be like,' she thought: 'talking to people like this about outdoor sanitation.' And aloud, as though to practise, she said severely,

"As I should probably be here so long, do you think Sir Philip would add on a bathroom?"

"Long?" said the young man, startled. "They told me about four or five years. Isn't that what you were thinking of?"

"Even one year," explained Lesley patiently, "is long to go without a bath. Ask him about it, please, and let me know."

With a face of extreme doubt the young man took out his pocket-book and made a note in it. He wrote like a policeman, every faculty in play: and while he laboured Lesley walked back to the barn. By clearing it of lumber—and it at present seemed to contain almost as much furniture as the cottage itself—one would treble the floor-space and have somewhere to give parties. That was important. The rest of the place, of course, would hardly bear thinking of: it was hideously ugly and hopelessly inconvenient. With a shrug of her shoulders Lesley stepped outside again and took it on the spot.

II

By an unfortunate coincidence, the day Lesley went down to the cottage was also the day of Mrs. Carnegie's luncheon, the Magyar Count's cocktail-party, and a reception for a Czech pianist, to each of which entertainments Elissa had accepted an invitation. She had accepted, she would go: but she had also, with characteristic generosity, promised Lesley the use of Hugo Dove's car, and without making the trip in person it would be almost impossible to preserve the distinction between Hugo's lending his Minerva and Elissa lending Hugo's car.

"So you see, darling," she told Lesley over the 'phone, "we won't be able to pick you up till about six. But Hugo says we can do it in three-quarters of an hour, and my dinner isn't till eight-thirty. You will be ready, won't you?"

Lesley frowned. It was then nearly half-past twelve, and she had been ready packed since ten.

"Couldn't Hugo run us down this afternoon? Leaving here at six means getting there practically in the dark," she said.

"Darling, I'm sure he would, only I've got a hairwave at three-thirty, and then there's the cocktail-party. . . ."

"Darling, if it's the least bit inconvenient to you, why not let us go down by ourselves?" suggested Lesley. "You're being most terribly sweet about it, but I'm sure we're upsetting your day."

All down the line emotion quivered.

"Let you go alone to a desolate cottage!" cried Elissa indignantly. "I wouldn't think of it! We'll be there at six sharp, darling, and mind you're ready."

Lesley hung up the receiver and made no attempt to feel grateful. Her trunks were strapped. She had tipped Mrs. Lee; a basket of provisions stood ready to hand. Her only special preparations—the opening of an account with Fortnum and Mason, and of a double subscription with Mudies—had occupied exactly half-an-hour on the previous afternoon. And the most trying part of all, the final and bitterest drop, was that at both the luncheon and the cocktail-party she herself might also have been present. Both Mrs. Carnegie and the Count had pressingly invited her: and she had refused, rather spectacularly, with an amusing reference to love in a cottage. . . .

"Damn," said Lesley; and ringing for Mrs. Lee (she had been very well tipped indeed) ordered lunch at home.

The period of waiting, however, was unexpectedly diversified, if not exactly shortened, by the arrival of a visitor. Shortly before three there was a knock at the door, a step in the hall: it was Mrs. Bassington in person, come all the way from Cheam to advance her crucial argument.

"But, my dear Lesley, supposing you ever want to marry? You can't have considered the extreme awkwardness—the impossibility—of such a situation. *No* man would stand for it."

Lesley raised her eyebrows.

"My dear Aunt! I thought we'd gone into that once and for all about seven years ago?"

It was quite true. Like many another wise virgin of her generation, she had early advertised a disinclination for marriage. The dangers of such a line, however, being only too obvious, she had chosen her attitude with particular care: there was nothing aggressive, nothing embittered about it: far from liking no one man well enough, it was the commonly accepted interpretation that Lesley Frewen liked too many men too well. But the root principle was there nevertheless, and properly understood should have saved Mrs. Bassington a good deal of anxiety. . . .

Not unpricked by annoyance, Lesley got up and looked out of the window: Aunt Alice's remarks were probably everything that a young girl should have heard in 1860, but their application to herself showed a certain lack of faith.

"I'm expecting a car," she explained untruthfully, "to run us down to the cottage. Do stay and see it, Aunt Alice, it's the second longest in London."

Mrs. Bassington rose. She did it rather effectively, ruffling out her feathers like a turkey in a story-book: and her voice too was like a turkey's—not quite so dignified as the rest of the picture.

"If it wasn't for your poor dead mother," she said, "I should never speak to you again. But I'm your only living relative, my dear, and I know my duty if you don't."

"I'm sure you do," agreed Lesley politely. "You'd like me to continue to come to you, I suppose, whenever I'm in trouble?"

The feathers quivered.

"I *was* going to say, my dear, that as soon as you come to your senses again I shall be perfectly willing to see you at Cheam. But that," said Aunt Alice finishing bitingly, "is perhaps looking too far ahead."

When she had gone Lesley went upstairs, turned on a hot bath, and lay there for an hour. The perfection of the appointments, however, started a series of unfortunate comparisons, and the treatment soothed her less than usually. She then had her tea, and immediately afterwards assembled Pat, the luggage and the basket of provisions, and placed them all in readiness in a room off the hall. The result was a modern *genre* picture—The Last Day in the New Home—of considerable authenticity: only two boxes, and only one child. Lesley looked at him curiously: on being told that he was now to live in the country he had displayed no more emotion than on being told that he was now to go for a walk: on the actual point of departure, he was displaying even less. Well, it was a comfort in a way; and settling herself in the window Lesley took up and opened the first of her Mudie's books.

It was fortunately quite interesting, for the car was a good deal late.

It arrived, in fact, at exactly twenty-five past seven, when Pat had just been given his supper; but as Elissa was naturally in haste to be off, Lesley sent it away again and bundled him into his coat. The injustice, however, scarcely saved time, for he at once went into the lavatory and remained there interminably. Mrs. Lee had given him a banana, and he was eating it to make sure.

"Darling, if you call that house-trained, I don't," said Elissa crossly. She was worried about her hair, which had not set as well as usual, and also about the Czech pianist, whom she had met in New York and who she feared might have forgotten her. Once on the road, however, her humour improved; she made no objection to stopping for a drink; and all the way down, with her head screwed down and her chin on Hugo's shoulder, she gave Lesley advice.

"The one thing that's really important, darling, is not to know *any* one. Then you can do just as you like and shock the whole village. We'll all come down and help. And be specially careful about the Vicar, darling, and that new kind of rat—the one that was imported and then began to burrow. Don't you feel excited, darling, starting on your new life?"

"Terrifically," said Lesley.

As well as she could in her rather coquettish position, Elissa suddenly looked intense.

"It's like a new incarnation," she pointed out. "A new incarnation, going—" The car swerved violently, and also gave her an instant to think. The country and hard labour—was that up and up, or down and down? She compromised. "— Round and round. You'll probably change enormously, one way or the other. Only do be careful of your figure, because that's always where the country tells first. Exercises, darling—do *lots* of exercises on a wooden floor. . . ."

In the back of the car, however, her friend repaid her with little attention. Lesley disliked inefficiency, and she disliked being made to wait: they had stopped twice already for a drink, and the daylight was steadily waning. She said,

"What time is your party, Elissa?"

The word, as always, produced an instant reaction: from Wendover onwards the hedges began to flash. The cars they overtook stood still, the cars they met exceeded the speed limit. Every few minutes Pat bumped over sideways and hit himself on the basket. He was three parts asleep and so fairly well armoured; but with every fresh collision Lesley half expected tears. He did not habitually weep, but nor for that matter did she; and it was from her own sensations, as they at last turned up the lane, that she gathered the clue to his.

"Here you are, darling! How delicious it looks!" cried Elissa gaily. Out went the suitcases, out went Pat, out went the basket of food. "And now for God's sake get a move on, Hugo, or I shan't have time to dress."

III

For a minute or two longer Lesley stood just as they had left her, motionless among the packages, young Patrick pressed close to the folds of her coat. The air felt fresh, and colder than the air of London: it was so quiet that she could quite easily follow the first mile or two of the Minerva's progress.

When the last throb had died away, leaving all still again, she took out the big key and pushed it into the lock.

"I don't like this place," said Patrick suddenly.

From the sound of his voice she knew the tears to be near: but no impulse to console awoke in her, only a faint shiver of revulsion. A crying child, a dark house. . . .

"I don't like it either," said Lesley.

The door gave under her hand, they were over the threshold. From a blackness deeper than the night's, and far colder, the dim proportions of walls and furniture gradually emerged. (Where was the electric light switch? To the left or to the right?) What with fatigue, darkness and excitement, Pat's tears, the only sound in that unnatural silence, were rapidly overwhelming him.

"Be quiet, Pat," said Lesley coldly. A deep and secret antagonism hardened her voice and her heart. To the pressure of his body against her side she deliberately denied response.

And now the light leapt out under her fingers, so that they were suddenly standing in a strange room. It was hideous, neat and dusty, and the clock did not go.

PART II

Chapter One

—— ✻ ——

I

About four centuries before the invention of cottage architecture, someone built the White Cottage. That there were ever any ground-plans is extremely doubtful: rather is it to be supposed that one day in the late sixteen hundreds a man and a boy went with spades, paced their distances, and began to dig without further deliberation. They dug well: like oak-trees the outer walls took surface-level at scarcely less than their middles. But it also seems probable that the boy paced the south side and the man the north, for the rectangle they drew was not a true one; all the floors ran together a little, and no corner was absolutely square. By the great brick chimney, of course, they cannot be judged: it bears unmistakable signs of rebuilding, and indeed could scarcely have smoked so badly for three centuries without someone laying a hand to it. The barn, too, dated from a good deal later, wood-built throughout and beamed with quartered tree-trunks: men had worked on the place from generation to generation, until when Lesley Frewen took it the amenities included an outside lavatory and a substantial tool-house. But none of the builders, one felt, had been professionals; they were all just men who could build a bit, and with an amateur's self-distrust they had each of them made sure and built solid. From without at least the effect was not unpleasing: the cottage squatted down like a hare in its forme, close-pressed against the earth and friendly to the apple-trees.

Once over the threshold, one might have been in Brixton.

"*Brixton*, darling?" echoed Elissa, making her first call over the new telephone.

"But *exactly*, darling," Lesley assured her. "The wallpapers have chrysanthemums on them." With a conscious effort she flicked her voice to irony. "And there's a lot of stuff I think must be rep—it's got bobbles all round the edge."

"Darling! How terribly funny! Is there an aspidistra?" asked Elissa greedily.

Lesley glanced over her shoulder.

"No, but there's a coloured picture of two cats sitting under an umbrella. And a china mug—this is perfectly true, darling—with 'A Present from Margate' on it."

"My dear, you mustn't alter a *thing*," said Elissa, audibly impressed.

"I'm not going to. It's only temporary, thank God. When are you coming down to the house-party?"

"Darling, but the minute you invite me! Only not perhaps this week or next, because I've rather a lot on. . . . And then of course it's June, which is always hopeless. But I'll see you soon, darling. . . ."

Lesley hung up the receiver and went to the window. Outside in the orchard a couple of Walpole pigs were grunting round the apple-trees, but the technique of chasing them away was utterly beyond her. Patrick was out there too, thumping up and down with a bean-pole between his knees: she looked at him with an intensity of dislike so nearly bordering on hatred that her own features, could she have seen them at that moment, would have seemed completely strange to her. And even without seeing, it was as though she guessed: for in all their enforced companionship she never once spoke to him without consciously masking her face. It was a hatred to be ashamed of, ignoble and unjust: but she did not love him the more for making her ashamed.

Nor was there anything endearing—for so variously does hatred feed—in the fact that half-an-hour later it would be time for his bath: which meant that water would have to be drawn from the well, poured into the copper, bailed out again, and finally thrown away. With a deep and passionate conviction she reflected that it wasn't worth it.

'In any case, it's only his face and hands,' thought Lesley. 'There's enough for that in the kettle. . . .'

As once before, her spirit wavered. To give in, to let things slide, to be ruled, if only for an hour, by the weary body instead of the exacting mind! . . . And then as once before, from some deep and unexpected reserve, she found either courage or obstinacy to set her teeth and hold on. On the table with the telephone lay her heavy gloves. Lesley picked them up and went out to the well.

II

The first week was a pure nightmare of laying fires, drawing water, driving out pigs, making beds, washing-up and wrestling with the Primus: a squalid domestic turmoil, during which Lesley gathered only the vaguest notions of her general surroundings. At the bottom of Pig Lane, she was aware, lay the main thoroughfare of High Westover: half street, half square, with the Three Pigeons on one side and the Post Office on the other. The Post Office was simply a cottage with a notice-board, the Three Pigeons a late Victorian edifice of bright yellow brick; and neither of them lent the least picturesqueness to an essentially uninteresting view. From the other end of the square a road ran slanting to the church and Vicarage, which could also be approached across country from Pig Lane: but this Lesley did not expect to do. There was always, of course, the possibility of a Parochial visit, those impertinent descents which loomed so large in the conversation of Aunt Alice; but Lesley felt confident that by a little judicious atheism, or at any rate by a little judicious incivility, she would be perfectly able to nip them in the bud. In the meantime, however, the days went by and the only callers were a remarkably saturnine postman, and Arnold Hasty the constable, who appeared very early one morning to ask if she had lost a small white-and-tan terrier.

"No, I haven't," snapped Lesley, with her wrists in the washing-up water. "I don't keep a dog."

"Ah," said Arnold reflectively, "then it *wouldn't* be yours, then. I just thought it might." He smiled at her bashfully; he was as young as a duckling. Lesley pulled out a meat-dish and began to swab it vigorously.

"Well, if you *should* be wanting eggs," said Arnold suddenly, "my mother'd be very pleased to let you have them."

"Thank you," said Lesley, "but I'm getting everything from Town . . . good morning." And that was the end of Arnold.

Apart from that one visit she spoke to no one at all except Patrick and Florrie Walpole, a handsome red-haired slattern, who supplied the cottage milk. Patrick, she believed, talked occasionally to the pigs. For bread Lesley telephoned to Aylesbury, where a baker named Twitchen offered to deliver twice a week, and punctually on the Wednesday morning a van arrived from Fortnum and Mason and decanted her first order: an attractive selection of ready-cooked foods, rusks for Patrick, and a small piece of bacon for angels on horseback. That same afternoon, the state of the kitchen becoming at least noticeable, she realised with a shock of dismay that in addition to the duties already enumerated it would also be necessary to scrub, sweep, dust and polish. For three days she did so; and at the end of the first week, with roughened hands and aching shoulders, came to the reluctant conclusion that she would have to get help.

'Some local woman' she thought, 'who can come in in the mornings, do the heavy stuff, and then clear out again. She can draw water, lay the copper, keep the Primus clean, wash up—all that sort of thing.' The picture grew attractive. 'And really if she can cook,' thought Lesley, 'it's going to be quite possible.'

From this hopeful conclusion, however, the next step was not so simple as might have been imagined. The village of High Westover supported no registry office, and Lesley had a shrewd idea that most business of that kind was probably transacted through either the Post Office or the Vicarage. The dilemma thus presented—between Church, so to speak, and Home Office—was sharp indeed: to apply to the former, without at least some show of civility, was obviously impossible: but the ice once broken, what might not result? Invitations to tea, quite possibly, followed by questions and advice and conversation about Girl Guides. . . . The Post Office, on the other hand, was a Government Department, impersonal and aloof: so after getting her own breakfast for the eighth time in succession Lesley put on her hat, confined Patrick to the orchard, and walked down Pig Lane to Rose Cottage. There was a notice-board in the porch with a good deal of varied information about wireless licences, foot-and-mouth disease, how to join the Army; over the door itself, in clear official lettering, the words 'High Westover Post Office' stood boldly forth. Her mind now almost completely at ease, Lesley pushed open the door and walked in.

It was not nearly so impersonal as she had wished.

Of the two little girls presumably in charge, one was nursing a baby, the other peeling potatoes. They did not stop to parley, however, and at the sudden (and apparently unexpected) sight of a customer at once jumped up and disappeared through an inner door. Thus abandoned—though presumably not for long, for she could hear their cry of "Father" all down the garden—Lesley turned her attention to the Post Office itself. There was a counter, a yard or two of grill—all the paraphernalia, in fact, that the public demands; but there was also a red plush overmantel, a down-at-heel rocking-chair, and half the stock of a small general store: from a brief inspection of whose leading lines Lesley gathered that the village in general wore strong cotton underwear and suffered from constipation. Before there was time to go further, however, the inner door opened again, and she had a confused impression of several newcomers all trying to see through at the same time. But only the Postmaster came in.

"Good morning, Ma'am," said the Postmaster, so huskily that Lesley wondered how on earth he managed the telephone.

"Good morning," said Lesley: "I'm Miss Frewen, from the White Cottage. Do you know of any reliable woman who could come and work for me?"

"Mrs. Sprigg," replied the Postmaster, without the least hesitation. "She'd suit you nicely." He masticated.

A trifle taken aback by such readiness, Lesley elaborated.

"I want someone who can manage all the rough work of the cottage, and possibly cook a little. If you think Mrs. Sprigg can do it, you'd better tell her to come up and see me."

The Postmaster nodded: and suddenly, as though he had at last succeeded in disposing of some impediment, his voice rang like trumpets.

"Agnes! Agnes, when could Mrs. Sprigg go up'n see Miss Frewen?"

With the extreme promptness that apparently characterised the whole establishment, the door flew open and Agnes joined them.

"Eleven o'clock before dinner or one-thirty after, whichever Miss Frewen says."

"Eleven o'clock, then," snapped Lesley, not to be outdone: and returning to the cottage sat down to await the interview. The unwarranted repose was extremely grateful to her; and though feeling determined to sift, with the extreme of domestic perspicuity, all Mrs. Sprigg's qualifications, it is nevertheless worthy of notice that she made no attempt to wash up.

III

At eleven o'clock precisely (and thus earning a good mark for punctuality) Mrs. Sprigg arrived. She was considerably older than Lesley had expected, with brown, bright eyes, very thin wrists and ankles, very large hands and feet: and in short resembled nothing so much on earth as an aged but still active shrew-mouse.

When they had done looking at each other, Lesley repeated her incantation.

"I want someone who can do all the rough work, Mrs. Sprigg, and if possible cook a little. Do you think you could manage it?"

"*Plain* cooking I can," admitted the shrew-mouse warily. "But I wouldn't want to be 'ere at dinner-time, because I got my own lot to give it to. But I could leave it ready p'raps, and then come back afterwards to clear."

"What time would that be?" asked Lesley, with a lift of her eyebrows. One didn't want her there at all hours!

"Oh, not more'n two o'clock or so," said Mrs. Sprigg surprisingly. "My boy, 'e gets 'ome at 'alf-past twelve; and in the morning I could get 'ere just before eight."

"And your wages?"

Behind the bright shrew-mouse eyes passed a flicker of speculation.

"A shilling an hour, Miss Frewen, according to how long I work."

Lesley hesitated. In all her life she had never before been in the position of directly employing labour. Taxi-men, of course: but that was different. One hired taxis by the fraction of an hour, not for two or three hours a day; they did not cook one's meals or handle one's crockery. A question suggested itself.

"When could you begin, Mrs. Sprigg? Could you stay now and wash up?"

"I'll just run back and get my apron," said Mrs. Sprigg, rising to her feet; and with a slight shock of surprise Lesley realised that everything was settled. Already, indeed, the old woman looked remarkably at home: her glance travelled frankly round the room, but rather to recognise it, it seemed, than to discover.

"You've been here before, perhaps?" hazarded Lesley.

"Deary me, yes!" said Mrs. Sprigg. "My cousin Annie died 'ere. What time will you want breakfast, Miss Frewen?"

"Half-past eight," Lesley told her: and was about to give detailed instructions when they were interrupted by a loud galloping sound outside the window. It was young Patrick, mounted on his bean-pole: and with a ridiculous tremor Lesley took the plunge.

"This is Patrick Craigie, Mrs. Sprigg, who lives with me."

Just as Uncle Graham had done, Mrs. Sprigg glanced swiftly from Lesley's black to Patrick's flaming hair.

"Sturdy, ain't 'e?" she said approvingly. "There's nothing like the country for children. I s'pose that means porridge?"

"Porridge or cereal, bread-and-butter, jam or honey, a glass of cold milk," said Lesley expertly: and felt herself for the second time go up in the other's estimation.

"And tea for yourself, Miss, or will it be coffee?"

"Black coffee, a glass of orange juice and very thin toast— that's all."

Mrs. Sprigg nodded intelligently.

"Half-past eight then, porridge and the usuals for Patrick, coffee 'n toast for yourself," she recapitulated. "It don't seem much, do it, to get through the morning? But there, I s'pose each stomach knows its best." She gathered herself together and rose to go, opening the door on such a blaze of sun that Lesley too stepped out and accompanied her to the gate. On the way they were again crossed by Patrick, lusty on his hobby horse.

"It's my belief, all men are villains at 'eart," said Mrs. Sprigg.

Chapter Two

I

One spring morning about three weeks later an odd thing happened. In spite of the difference in their *menus* Lesley and her young charge generally finished breakfast about the same time: at which point Patrick disappeared into the orchard and Lesley pushed back her chair to continue looking at *The Times.* On this particular morning, however, and while she was perusing the third leader, her left and unoccupied hand absently reached out across the table and took a piece of Patrick's bread-and-butter. With equal absence of mind, she then proceeded to eat it.

The slice and the leader finishing together, Lesley shook out the paper and turned to Drama: in a few seconds the same thing happened again. The plateful had been a large one, the slices thick, for Mrs. Sprigg believed in cutting a good lot of bread-and-butter first thing in the morning and then letting Patrick go at it all through the day: but even so, before she came to the end of the book reviews, Lesley had appreciably altered the massive outline.

It was pure absence of mind, of course, no more and no less: with a slight self-consciousness Lesley rearranged the pile to something like the original symmetry and went out into the garden.

Two mornings later there was a strong smell of bacon.

On the threshold of the sitting-room—for she had just been tak-ing a short pre-breakfast stroll—Lesley paused and sniffed inquir-ingly. The smell seemed to be strongest near the table, and on the table was a covered dish.

"Mrs. Sprigg!" called Lesley.

Like a weather-beaten but still cheerful cuckoo the head of Mrs. Sprigg appeared through the hatch.

"Mrs. Sprigg, why have you been cooking bacon?"

"Because it never seemed to get eaten," said Mrs. Sprigg.

It was one of those answers whose logic, though so palpably absurd, is almost impossible to invalidate: and Lesley let it pass. She even ate the bacon. For though the old woman's shortcomings were many and various, a second visit to the Post Office had revealed a complete dearth of female labour for a radius of ten miles. (The Postmaster, as it happened, was Mrs. Sprigg's cousin by marriage; but this of course Lesley did not know.) The old woman, moreover, was not without her points: she didn't mind Patrick—in fact she seemed almost to like him: she drew any amount of water; and she was also able, without apparent effort, to drive Walpole pigs in any required direction.

"But I'll just step in on my way 'ome, all the same," she promised, "and give that old 'Orace a piece of my mind. If 'e can't keep his pigs on 'is own ground you can 'ave the law of 'im, Miss Frewen, and that's what I'll say you're going to do."

"I'd rather not have a serious row if I can help it," said Lesley distastefully.

"Oh, 'e won't think you *mean* it," explained Mrs. Sprigg, "but it'll just show 'im we won't stand no nonsense. You leave it to me, Miss Frewen. I've known old 'Orace since afore 'e was born."

On principle, and from a cultivated horror of gossip, Lesley never encouraged her to talk, but no one could be in the same house with Mrs. Sprigg for three hours daily without insensibly gathering a good deal of information, much of it libellous, about the inhabit-ants of High West-over. There was Mr. Pomfret the vicar, with his

wife and four children: Mr. Cox at the Post Office: young Arnold
Hasty, whom Lesley already knew, and Mr. Walsh the postman, who
drank like a fish, said Mrs. Sprigg, but was always all right once you
got him on his bicycle. ("It seems to bring 'im to life," explained Mrs.
Sprigg. "'E can ride that bicycle, Miss Frewen, when 'e can't stand up.
I've seen it with me own eyes. But as 'is wife says, what's the good
of that to 'er? You can't take a bicycle to bed with you. . . .") There
was also, looming trout-like among sprats, the majestic figure of Mr.
Lionel Povey, landlord of the Three Pigeons and property-owner on
a large scale. It was he who had caused to be built, a year or two
after the War, the new line of cottages called Beatty Row: erecting
them on a site so notoriously damp and aguish that the shivering
inhabitants (said Mrs. Sprigg) might be seen nightly streaming forth
in search of warmth and refreshment in the Three Pigeons itself. A
Napoleonic trickiness, indeed, seemed to be Mr. Povey's chief characteristic. In 1918 he had palmed off on the War Memorial Com-
mittee a secondhand goddess, wired for electric light and picked up
cheap at some local Great House sale. . . .

"But—but couldn't anyone *tell?*" interrupted Lesley, who had
been listening in spite of herself.

"Tell? Not them. It was the old Vicar, not Mr. Pomfret. Blind as
a bat 'e was: and Sir Philip at the Hall—a proper old rip if ever there
was one—'e didn't care one way or the other. . . . Laughed fit to burst,
'e did, when they found the pair to 'er in Povey's backyard. She's got
'er 'and lifted above 'er 'ead, d'you see, to carry an electric torch, and
Povey, 'e'd taken away the light and put in a great big Union Jack, as
big as what the Scouts have. It looked real fine, Miss Frewen, you
wouldn't believe: and they set 'er up opposite the Post Office with all
the names on a step underneath."

"Do you mean in the square?" asked Lesley. "I've never noticed it."
Mrs. Sprigg shook her head.

"Ah, you won't find 'er there now. Couldn't stand up to the
weather, you see, 'er being only stucco. They 'ad to take 'er away
more'n five years ago, just after Mr. Pomfret came. And old Povey

'ad 'ad all the money, you see, so all we've got now's a tablet in the church."

II

With the passage of July, and being somewhat relieved from domestic burdens, Lesley's mind began to revert more and more frequently to the idea of a house warming. She had been cut off from her friends for nearly two months, and the out-of-town season was nearly upon them. With the approach of August bank holiday, therefore, and encouraged by a spell of brilliant weather, Lesley decided to issue the invitations for her first week-end party. The original project had been something in the nature, and on the scale, of a *fête champêtre*, but a closer acquaintance with an actual cottage had later decided her in favour of the intimate. By moving into the small room with Pat she could dispose of one best bedroom and a whole barn, the latter being furnished, to be sure, with no more than the large double bed she had found there on arrival: but two men could sleep there quite comfortably, and wash in the outhouse.

For more social purposes, indeed, there was only the one small sitting-room, oppressive though amusing with its crowded Victorianism; but the orchard was now quite agreeable, Mrs. Sprigg having by either fair means or foul (and probably the latter) obtained a signal victory over the Walpole pigs. The hordes had been withdrawn, the fences repaired: and Mrs. Sprigg returned from her embassy with permission for Miss Frewen and the little boy to walk wherever they pleased over Walpole grassland. In the orchard, then, the house-party would spend most of its time; if it rained they could play bridge; and if someone remembered to bring a gramophone, they might even try to dance on the level part of the barn.

With these considerations in view, therefore, the party was whittled down to three. They were Elissa: Toby Ashton, because Lesley owed him for a whole fortnight: and Bryan Collingwood, because he had once threatened to commit suicide, and she felt that her emotional life needed pepping up. By a singularly fortunate chance they were all able to accept, and Lesley at once sat down to plan menus out of a Fortnum and Mason catalogue. Elissa, indeed, had kindly offered to bring down her own provisions: but Elissa, though genuinely helpful, was notoriously absent-minded. And besides—thought Lesley, flipping over to the entrées—it wasn't going to be that kind of a party. Her position as hostess, with all that it implied of responsibility and distinction, was to be perfectly definite. She had no intention of being camped on; and if Elissa brought the gin it would soon be Elissa's picnic.

'I'll have to go up to Town,' thought Lesley; for the projected bi-monthly visits had not yet materialised. She had been too busy, too unhappy, and above all too tired: she had even washed her own hair, so that its thick natural waves now lay loose and uncorrugated; on one occasion, in Aylesbury, she had even risked having it cut. The result, indeed, might have been considerably worse; but it required more than the merely passable to eclipse Elissa, and on the Thursday before the party arrived, Lesley left Patrick in charge of Mrs. Sprigg and went up to Town by an early train. There she spent four expensive but profitable hours in the neighbourhood of Bond Street, emerging with an almost higher degree of fashionable polish than she had ever before attained. More obviously portable were a couple of brightly coloured table-cloths with napkins to match, and a pair of linen sheets to go on the double bed. The whole excursion, indeed, was highly successful, and in a final fling of good spirits Lesley paid extra on her ticket and returned first class.

Arriving at the White Cottage, however, her spirits were abruptly lowered. There had arrived during her absence a Fortnum and Mason van delivering provisions for the house-party: and the bill that came with them was so enormous that Lesley was shocked into the most purely domestic state of mind she had ever experienced.

It was incredible. With doubting eye she ran over the addition.

The addition was correct. Then she ran over the list itself. That was correct too. Food *was* expensive when bought course by course, so to speak, in attractive fireproof dishes: almost worse than the drinks, and God knew they were bad enough. . . .

In fact, one might almost say that it was the drinks that did it.

'After this week-end,' thought Lesley, looking at the row of bottles, 'I shall have to shop in Aylesbury. It's almost enough to make one marry Toby Ashton.'

The thought took her by surprise: half sardonically she followed it up. It was true that he had never asked her: but she had a pretty shrewd idea that if, the next time he made one of his dishonourable proposals, she were to reply, 'No, Toby, but if you like I'll marry you'—he would quite probably accept the change of procedure with at least equanimity. For he was a man, thought Lesley quite seriously, on whom marriage would weigh very lightly: and with an income on which one fairly conscientious wife would really make practically no impression.

'I could leave Pat down here, with a good nurse, almost out of my own income,' thought Lesley.

In such glowing colours did the vista unfold: more than ever was she glad of her visit to Bond Street. Elissa could amuse herself with Bryan or, if Bryan proved refractory, could get on with her Yogi. She always *said* she was longing for solitude: and for once she should get it. Lesley's brilliant scarlet lips curved in a rare smile: really it was going to be rather amusing! And if Bryan brought down another revolver, that would be rather amusing too. He would never actually pull the trigger, but the attempt at any rate should be pleasingly picturesque. . . .

'I shall take Toby over the Walpole meadows,' thought Lesley suddenly. 'Elissa loathes walking.' And thinking of those sunny, cow-inhabited slopes, she had a fleeting glimpse of certain lost advantages. For one could scarcely faint, nowadays, at the sight of an unexpected Alderney, nor was any credit to be got out of not having done so. With sense taken for granted, and sensibility at a discount:

with intentions unasked and mystery out of fashion—life was a good deal more complicated than one's grandmother imagined.

A step on the threshold—a pattering shrew-mouse scurry—brought her abruptly from her dream. Still faintly smiling, Lesley went down on her knees and began to sort the food.

"What things they do think of!" said Mrs. Sprigg admiringly. She picked up a bottle of stuffed olives and held it to the light: tomato-red spots on a cylinder of smooth green. "Now, if *I* 'ad that I'd want to keep it on the mantelshelf, not 'ide it away in me inside. If you'll pass them through the 'atch, Miss Frewen, I'll put 'em in the cupboard."

III

The final preparations proceeded smoothly to their conclusion. The larder was stocked, the linen aired. Lesley's hair lay like a skull-cap, her complexion continued perfect. It came inevitably as something of a shock, therefore, when late on the Friday evening Bryan Collingwood telephoned from Town to ask whether he might bring down with him a beautiful Russian. Her name was Natasha.

"But who *is* she, my dear?" asked Lesley, a trifle coldly.

"The daughter of an Imperial general, darling, only someone murdered him, and now she's taken up economics. She terribly wants to see the real English country, and I said I'd ask if you could have her. . . ."

"Well, now you have asked, my dear, and I'm terribly sorry, but there's no room. What time are you going to get here?"

"But, *Lesley*—"

"Well?"

"But, Lesley—I don't really know how it happened—but I've more or less *invited* her. I mean, she's *coming*. . . ."

At the other end of the telephone, by a notable effort of will, Lesley just restrained herself from swearing aloud.

"But my dear, there isn't a bed for her!"

"That doesn't matter. I'll put up at the pub, and Natasha can have mine."

"Well, she'll be sharing it with Toby Ashton, but I don't mind if they don't," said Lesley resignedly.

The following morning, of course, she went over to Aylesbury and brought back by car a divan bed. It was sheer waste of two-pounds-ten, but no hostess can properly exercise her charm with one guest at the local pub and another in compromising circumstances. Paying for the thing cash down with most of her ready money, Lesley was further and seriously exercised by the problem of its bestowal. To put it in Elissa's room would almost certainly annoy Elissa: but there seemed no other alternative to clean fun in the barn. The dining-table, too—it was fortunate that she had never had any intention of letting Pat feed with his elders, for it did not really accommodate more than three. Four would have been just possible, five would result in positive dovetailing. In these anxious considerations, and in a last run-through of the menus with Mrs. Sprigg, the intervening hours passed with astonishing rapidity: no sooner had she hung up the receiver (or so it seemed), than it was Saturday afternoon. Lesley made up her lips, smoothed her shingle, and went down to the gate to wait for Peter's car.

And now, as though suffering from reaction, time stood still. Elissa was always late, to be sure, and Bryan little better; but their reiterated promises to be down by two now threw a high light, so to speak, over what was really quite normal unpunctuality. After the first half-hour Pat, who had been hanging about the lane, lost interest and retired to the orchard. This Lesley by no means regretted, for he was definitely to be kept in the background: a rapid introduction as soon as the party arrived, and then no more sight or sound of him for the next three days. Pat might be slow, but he was very obedient: if one told him to stay in the kitchen, the kitchen was where he would be found. His presence, however, had afforded her much the same sort of companionship as one gets from a large dog, and without it the minutes passed more slowly still. Sunset would not have surprised her, nor the first stars: and indeed even by the kitchen cuckoo it was fully another hour before the big green car swung round the corner of Pig Lane. As far as could be seen, however, there were only three occupants. Toby Ashton driving, Elissa beside him with her head on his shoulder, and young Bryan Collingwood alone in the back.

"There she is!" cried Elissa shrilly: and a second or two later was clasped in Lesley's arms.

Chapter Three

I

When the first embraces were over, and with her arm through Toby Ashton's, Lesley said,

"I thought Bryan was bringing a girl friend?"

"So he has, darling," said Elissa, taking out her powder-box. "Natasha. She's at the Three Pigeons."

"We all went in for a drink, darling," supplied Bryan, "and she suddenly let out that she was afraid you didn't really want her, and wouldn't come on. She's so fearfully sensitive."

There was a brief silence, during which Lesley received the curious impression that though this was no doubt the complete truth as it appeared to Bryan, it was by no means the complete truth as it appeared, for example, to Elissa. Aloud she said,

"But that's absurd! Of course I want her. If you'll walk down the road with me, Bryan, we'll go and fetch her at once."

"Poor young lad!" said Toby Ashton compassionately. "He's exhausted already, Lesley, with exercising so much will-power. And I'm exhausted with driving, and Elissa's exhausted with heat."

"Then you'd better all lie down in a row under the apple-trees while I go myself. What's she like, Elissa?"

The powder-box closed with a snap.

"Extremely striking, my dear. Wears garters, but no stockings. To carry stilettos in. Or do I mean vodka?" said Elissa blandly.

II

It being finally decided that both Lesley and Bryan should return at once to the inn, the other two were conducted as far as the cottage door, introduced to Pat and Mrs. Sprigg, and there left to make themselves completely at home.

"We'll just get into country clothes, darling," promised Elissa, "and then play in the garden till you come back. It's all so perfectly heavenly I feel about ten again." With genuine emotion she gazed over the placid landscape. If anyone at that moment had offered her love in a cottage for the next twenty years, she would have answered: "No, freehold."

"We'll have tea or drinks or something as soon as I get back," said Lesley; and turning back with Bryan Collingwood, led him at a brisk pace down Pig Lane. He seemed vaguely uneasy, and even younger than Lesley remembered him: speaking nothing but the most trivial commonplaces, and hardly looking at her since the moment of arrival. They had kissed, of course, with the automatic enthusiasm displayed by all Elissa's friends on either meeting or parting: but the whole secluded length of Pig Lane was traversed without further incident. Outside the Three Pigeons stood a large American car, towards which her companion, however, though an amateur of the breed, cast no admiring glance; and no more, for the matter of that, did Lesley. She was merely reminded by it of the necessity of garaging Toby's.

"I think they're outside," said Bryan glumly.

Too preoccupied with her own thoughts to mark his unexpected use of the plural, Lesley followed him round to the back of the Three Pigeons, where the genius of Mr. Povey had created a small open-air pleasure-ground. It contained an arbour, a statue, three long wooden tables with benches on either side: at one of which, her chin propped between her hands, now sat the sensitive Natasha.

As Elissa had said, she was extremely striking. She was as striking as a leopard, or a panther, or anything else tawny, untamed and matchlessly graceful. Both eyes and hair were precisely the colour of amber, her eyes the clear, her hair the clouded: for the rest of her features, they showed a child-like perfection of contour completely unmarred by the ravages of thought.

('Economics, my God!' murmured Lesley under her breath.)

Nor was the creature's companion, in his way, any less spectacular. On the other side of the table, preposterously muffled in an enormous motor-coat, sat one of those magnificent young Americans usually encountered only in advertisements for underwear. He appeared to be a little over six foot or so, he had a kind and trustful face, and a mouth formed by nature for the very phrase on which Bryan and Lesley now entered.

"You poor little girl!" said the American tenderly.

The great amber eyes were misty but brave. As though unable to trust her lips, Natasha nodded.

"Just all alone, the way I am, and no place to go," said the American, more tenderly still.

Lesley was extremely annoyed. The vamping of the wealthy was a natural and recognised occupation, but there was no need to libel one's hostess in the process. Stepping promptly forward, therefore, she held out her hand and said briskly,

"But of course you've somewhere to go, my dear. I've just been scolding Bryan for not bringing you by force."

It sounded to her own ears so unpleasantly like a rebuke that for an instant she half expected a leopard's claw full across the face: and for an instant, indeed, felt the whole graceful body tense with fury. The next moment Natasha had swung round in her place, hands outstretched and eyes dim with tears of gratitude. Emotion, it appeared, overcame her very easily indeed: or perhaps she felt that as she had tears in her eyes already, gratitude was what they might just as well be of.

"How good you are!" she murmured happily. "But I think everyone is good in England. Even the Americans."

Thus admitted, so to speak, among the persons of the drama, the young American rose to his feet and bowed all round. From the general Natasha now descended to the particular.

"This," she explained, "is Mr. Teddy Lock. He has been very, very kind."

The kind Mr. Lock bowed again.

"I understand you have to go some little distance," he said. "I could run you over in my car—"

"A bare quarter-of-a-mile," said Miss Frewen crisply. "We couldn't think of troubling you. Ready, Bryan?"

With considerable alacrity Bryan dived under the table and brought forth a dressing-case. It was largish, old and quite remarkably battered: but there was still visible, upon its weathered side, the ghost of a monogram under the hint of a coronet. The American seized his chance.

"See here, sir, it may be only a quarter of a mile, but that's a pretty heavy article to carry. Now, my car's right outside, and it'll cover the track in two minutes: won't the lady reconsider her verdict?"

Overwhelmingly deferential, he turned once more to Lesley: and indeed with Bryan like a thundercloud and Natasha in tears her single impulse was now to terminate the incident as quickly as possible. With an absolute minimum of warmth, therefore, she withdrew the veto; and a moment or two later found herself being handed by Mr. Lock into the seat next to the driver.

"I'll want you to show me the way," he explained. "If I'm left to myself round here I just overshoot the objective and land: way out on the coast. . . ." He glanced over his shoulder to see if the others were ready: they were quarreling audibly, but had hauled in the dressing-case. With a superbly modulated purr the car shot past the Post Office, edged round a corner, and in one mighty gulp had swallowed up Pig Lane.

"That's all," said Lesley.

From her seat in the front row, so to speak, she could see straight through the open gate and into the orchard, where three unaccustomed figures were now discernible. Two of them were of course the other members of the house-party, and it was at once plain that they had got into their country clothes.

Elissa wore a bathing-suit and some bracelets. The suit, which fitted far better than most gloves, was grass-green, backless, and embroidered about the thighs with a row of little frogs. The bracelets were plain heavy circles of yellow wood, closely resembling curtain-rings. Beside her on the grass lay Toby Ashton in a pair of very wide white cotton trousers, a red-and-blue striped vest, and a hat like an American sailor's. They were making daisy-chains.

The third figure, standing a little apart by the cottage door, was dressed entirely in black, with one touch of white at the neck, and a wide black hat. As a matter of fact it was the Vicar.

". . . *Where*, Bryan?" whispered Natasha, peering about as though for a rare bird.

"There, by the door! It is, isn't it, Lesley?"

Passing through the gate, she would have given a good deal if it hadn't been. As a legitimate source of clean fun he would naturally be invaluable; but her two months at High Westover, on the other hand, had just begun to give her the slightest of insights into the mentality of those who have to stay behind after the week-end party has gone. At the sound of approaching footsteps Elissa looked up.

"Hello, darling," she called shrilly, "we're being children of nature. You don't mind, do you?"

"Not in the least," called back Lesley, "only you'll probably get rather bitten."

"Nothing bites me, darling, I'm too hardened," shrilled Elissa. "We put our things in the little sitting-room-place. Oh, and Lesley, darling"—she dropped her voice a tone or two—"*il y a quelqu'un à la porte*—do let's ask it in to lunch, and let Toby and me be heathen converts!"

"Quelqu'un à la port," chanted Toby Ashton.

"quelqu'un à la port',

   qui frappe et frappe et frappe et frapp'

"et frappe-e à ta port'!"

Even as she laughed, even as she hurried forward, a sudden doubt checked Lesley's course. It was funny to be so rude, obviously, but what about the converse? *Was* it rude to be so funny, or had her sense of humour got, as it were, rusted by disuse? Laughter on her lips, doubt in her mind, Lesley paused: and during that moment's indecision the situation was unexpectedly simplified. For the Vicar disappeared. Neatly as a professional illusionist, completely as through a trap in the turf, Mr. Pomfret vanished from view.

III

Not altogether unexpectedly, Mr. Lock stayed to tea. They had it at once, under the apple-trees, with a cocktail or two immediately afterwards: and between one cocktail and another Lesley drifted over to Toby Ashton and inquired whether he would like a walk. She had had to watch her opportunity: he appeared to have developed, during the previous two months, the completely new habit of sitting with his arm round Elissa. Lesley said,

"What about a walk, Toby? Everyone else looks exhausted. Shall I take you over a meadow or two?"

"A walk?" shrilled Elissa, refilling her glass from the tray by the well. "A lovely long walk? I'd adore it, darling. . . ."

With admirable generalship Lesley altered her plans.

"You come too, Mr. Lock, and observe the English scene." It was her best move, for Mr. Lock would come out of politeness, and Natasha would come for Mr. Lock, and Bryan for Natasha. They would all, in fact, go for a lovely long walk together: Natasha and Bryan in shorts and cricket shirts, Elissa with the addition of trousers like Toby's and a little red monkey jacket. Toby went just as he was.

"I don't think we'll go through the village, after all," said Lesley, as they started out. "It's terribly hot and there's nothing to see. We'll cut over the fields."

"I don't mind where we go, so long as it's trespassing," said Elissa. "Who's the local magnate, darling?"

"Sir Philip Kerr, I believe, but unfortunately he hasn't any land to trespass on. I'll take you over some farms, though," said Lesley, with her hand on the latch of Horace Walpole's gate. "The man here, for instance, is a perfect brute."

"Really brutal, darling? With horsewhips?" persisted Elissa. "He must have a horsewhip or it doesn't count."

"No, really, darling," said Lesley seriously, "he's got rather a tough reputation." The mild shade of Mr. Walpole—kindly giver of permissions—hovered rebukingly before her eyes: but Elissa had to be kept happy somehow. "We'll go straight up to those trees, but don't talk too loudly. . . ."

Under the spur of terror, therefore, they struck up a footpath and covered a mile or so across the grass in little over an hour. Both Lesley and Elissa were extremely good walkers, except that Elissa was always wanting to sit down and smoke; while the three men, and especially Bryan in his running shorts, were loud in their praises of the twenty-five-mile day. The real trouble was Natasha. As a child she had walked half across Russia to escape from the Bolsheviks, and the experience had left her with a rooted distaste for all forms of self-propulsion.

"But why did you come, darling, if you hate it so?" demanded Bryan miserably. "You know I'd have loved to stay behind with you."

"And you could have worn your shorts just as well in the garden, darling," pointed out Elissa, who at that particular moment happened to be wanting to walk.

Like a dumb but beautiful animal Natasha lay coiled under the hedge. Golden-brown and strong as a sapling, she nevertheless gave the impression of being mortally wounded. Quite probably she would lie there till she died. Her tawny eyes, now the exact colour of

Russian tea, were already fixed in a helpless gaze. It was only by the mercy of Providence that they happened to be fixed on Teddy Lock.

He saved her.

"Listen, Miss Frewen, I guess we're not more than two miles from your cottage right at the moment. That'ud take me, if I hurried, not much more than ten minutes. In the car, coming back, I can do it in five, and pick up Natasha right at that gate. How would that be?"

It would be splendid. With real gratitude Lesley saw him leap athletically over a stile and bound away towards West-over steeple: and leaving Bryan (who had also decided to return by car) to keep Natasha company, the diminished party resumed their road.

"I suppose we are coming to *somewhere*, darling?" asked Elissa, carelessly. "If I don't have a drink soon I feel as though I might melt."

With a fictitious confidence Lesley scanned the horizon. She had not the faintest idea where they were, and was merely hoping to disguise the fact a few moments longer: but suddenly, beyond some trees, her eye was caught by a scattering of red. Roofs! thought Lesley gratefully: roofs for five or six houses: and five or six houses, in Buckinghamshire, almost certainly meant that one of them was a pub. . . .

Elissa having temporarily lost all desire to smoke, the conjecture was rapidly proved correct. They made a bee-line for the trees, undid a gate, and a minute or two later found themselves approaching the humble George and Crown. Unfortunately, it was closed, and this, when Elissa and Toby at last believed it, upset them very much indeed.

"But, darling," protested Elissa, "one can *always* get a drink if one knows how. I've *never* had to go without . . . Can't one bribe a potman?"

Lesley looked up and down the sunny road and wished with all her might that she could. But there was no potman in sight.

"If I don't get a drink inside five minutes, I'm going to die," said Elissa. "Try banging on the door, darling."

With an elaborate imitation of a dying man making a last effort, Toby Ashton picked up a convenient piece of wood and obediently began to hammer. He had (as even the highbrows admitted) a strong natural sense of rhythm, and with the first phrase of 'Loving My Girl' had soon roused every dog within earshot. Before he had time to try them with a second, however, an upstairs window opened directly over the door and there appeared at it such a snake-like head of curling papers as would have silenced Cerberus.

"What the 'ell d'you mean by kicking up that racket?" said the head grimly. "Can't you see we're closed?"

With marked absence of mind Toby produced a handful of silver and looked at it reflectively.

"Oh, so that's what you were thinking of," said the head. "Well, you can bleeding well think again. And if I 'ear so much as a pin drop, I'll give the 'ole lot of you in charge."

It was curious, but without a word spoken, and almost before the slamming of the sash had ceased to echo, they found themselves moving at a good brisk pace towards the next turning.

"My *God!*" said Elissa at last. "The *country!*"

"I know it is," said Lesley apologetically.

"Oh, but darling, it isn't your fault! Of course not! Only— really"—words failed her, and with a sweep of her bare arm she indicated the sun, the sky, and the Vale of Aylesbury—"it all seems so ridiculous."

"Perhaps we'd better turn back," said Lesley. "There's plenty of stuff at the cottage." She spoke with the regulation lightness, but her heart was heavy. To keep one's guests supplied with drink was almost the first law of hospitality: that she had never before had to connect it with a knowledge of opening times might possibly explain the present fiasco, but could hardly excuse it.

"Let's go back to the cottage," repeated Lesley brightly.

In silence they turned their faces. Fearful of losing her way, Lesley now kept them to the road, where a cloud of whitish dust scuffed with every step round the folds of her companions' trousers.

Though nearly half-past five, it was still exceedingly hot; the skin round her nose felt sticky with sweat, and the skin round Elissa's was obviously feeling the same. They both walked with their heads down, as though in a futile effort to avoid the sun; and it was therefore Toby who first observed, on the fringe of a second hamlet, the inconspicuous hostelry of the Two Ploughmen.

It was open.

Like moths to a flame they hastened forward, Elissa leading and Lesley in the rear. She had never before entered any of the local bars, and was now experiencing a most curious reluctance to do so; but the others were at once the life and soul of the party. They were now four again, having been rather surprisingly overtaken, just inside the door, by Bryan Collingwood.

"I thought you were going back in the car?" said Elissa uncharitably.

"Well, I didn't," snapped Bryan. "I wanted some exercise. You're exactly the colour of your jacket, darling."

And now—the irony of it!—just as they had settled down to be thoroughly happy and get a little tight, it was Lesley's ungrateful business to get them away. Six o'clock passed, and seven: already the supper—the carefully-thought-out, Fortnum-and-Mason supper—would be waiting on the table: the *bortch* was being heated, Mrs. Sprigg was wanting to go home: when Patrick would get to bed had become a matter for speculation. And then Teddy and Natasha— 'Damn!' thought Lesley—there were their suppers too to think of, beside the Russian salad Mrs. Sprigg didn't know about. . . . Yes, certainly they must go at once, before Toby could order another round. Lesley pulled herself together.

"Supper, darling?" said Elissa vaguely. "Why can't we have dinner here? It's a *lovely* place. . . ."

As briefly as possible Lesley referred to the other guests, to Mrs. Sprigg, and even to Patrick's bedtime. Elissa heard her with every appearance of interest, and as soon as she had finished began to talk rapidly and well about the late Serge Diaghaleff. With a feeling remarkably near dislike, Lesley turned her back and appealed to the others. They too were happy, but not quite so happy as Elissa; who, at Lesley's suggestion, was now lifted bodily from her stool and carried outside. Once in the open air, however, her mood changed: so long as Toby had his arms round her, she didn't care where she went.

IV

The evening being now comparatively cool, and the way back a little over two miles, the party that arrived at the cottage was almost completely sober. The gain on the moral roundabouts, however, was a loss on the social swings, and Lesley was extremely glad when the sight of Mrs. Sprigg at the gate gave her an excuse to leave her companions and hurry on.

"So there you are!" the old woman greeted her. "Well, you've 'ad a lovely day for your walk, and I've give Pat 'is supper, and put 'im to bed."

The placid good sense of her was so like a physical relief that Lesley drew a deep sigh.

"Ah! you're tired out, Miss Frewen, and I don't wonder. If only you'd told me you was goin' to 'Ambly I'd 'ave sent you a short cut. Did you see the church?"

"Only from the outside," said Lesley.

"Ah! You ought to 'ave gone in. My granfer's buried there, and a proper old villain 'e was," said Mrs. Sprigg. "I s'pose you didn't go in the church at Woodey neither?"

For half-a-second Lesley's brain sought vainly for the proper, the dignified rebuke. It was no use. Not with Elissa in those trousers. So instead, and with a sudden feeling of relief, she said exactly what was in her mind.

"I suppose it *is* rather a conspicuous party. Have we been spreading alarm all along the route?"

With a great understanding the shrewd eyes travelled slowly from Bryan to Toby Ashton, from Toby to Elissa, and so from Elissa to Lesley again.

"Now don't you go worrying about that," she said. "Everyone thought they was 'ikers."

Chapter Four

—— ✼ ——

I

In rapid succession Lesley now made up Natasha's bed, gave Elissa the hot water intended for the coffee, and put on another kettleful in its place. She then lit the sitting-room fire, gave the second lot of hot water to the men, put the kettle on again, helped Mrs. Sprigg carve the chicken, and finally made the coffee. The Russian salad she temporarily abandoned, but even so the clock had struck nine before they sat down to eat.

It was then, for the first time, and reminded only by the number of places, that she remembered Natasha and Teddy Lock.

"But darling, you don't expect them *back*, do you?" asked Elissa innocently. She had one eye on Bryan Collingwood, and Lesley mistrusted what she was going to say next.

"Don't be absurd, darling, of course I do. They've probably gone out again. Mrs. Sprigg! Has the big white car been back this evening?"

But Mrs. Sprigg put her head through the hatch and shook it violently.

"Not it, Miss Frewen. The gentleman's staying over to Thame, at the Yellow Swan."

"There you are!" said Elissa, returning to her *bortch*.

They were both wrong, however: about halfway through the meal a light shone in Pig Lane, someone laughed in the orchard, and Teddy and Natasha knocked at the door. They had just dashed up and had tea in Town, they said, and was it really as late as nine o'clock?

"It doesn't matter if it is," said Lesley, disguising as best she could a faint quiver of disappointment. "Sit down, both of you, and find something to eat."

On the other side of the table Elissa set down her glass.

"And then tell us all about it," she said brightly. "Where did you have tea?"

"At the Carlton," said Natasha, reaching for a plate.

Elissa opened her eyes.

"Darling? In shorts?"

"No. In a frock and things," explained Natasha vaguely. "We found a shop open. . . ."

With sudden violence Bryan pushed back his chair and said he was going for a walk. From a certain familiarity in his expression Lesley judged that he might be going to commit suicide; but really she was too tired to bother.

"But, darling," Elissa was saying. "How selfish of you to change in the car! Never mind, we'll make you display afterwards. Won't we, Lesley?"

"I have the stockings now," said Natasha obligingly; and pushing back her chair slid unexpectedly into the splits.

"I learnt that when I was a little girl," she explained, apparently admiring the effect as much as anyone else. "It is very nice, if you have good legs. . . ."

II

The meal proceeded. Shortly after the cold capon, however, and under the pretence of speaking to Mrs. Sprigg, Lesley left the supper-table and went for a short walk. She went only as far as the tool-house and back, and smoked about two-thirds of a cigarette: but it was like a foretaste of some beautiful universe inhabited by one person to a world. Then she went back to the kitchen and found Mrs. Sprigg on the point of departure.

"I got to go now, Miss Frewen, but everything's stacked ready for washin'. It won't take long if you all lay an 'and to it."

Lesley looked towards the sink and concealed her emotion.

"You couldn't do it in the morning, Mrs. Sprigg?"

"I could if I did nothing else, but it looks like it's going to be an 'eavy day. Besides, there's the breakfast, and not a clean crock in the place."

With a feeling near despair, as though at losing a last ally, Lesley watched the old woman pin on her hat and go. There were dishes in the sink, dishes on the table, dishes on the kitchen chair. Some had been used to cook things in. Nearly all bore traces of cigarette-ash. At that moment, in the room overhead, Patrick awoke and began to call.

To reach the stairs she had to pass through the sitting-room, and with her hand on the door-knob Lesley's mind rushed forward after some light but convincing explanation. "This is where I tell the bedtime story, my dears!"—something like that. 'And then I'll send them into the orchard,' thought Lesley rapidly, 'and run upstairs to Pat—and then come down and get started. . . .'

The knob turned under her hand, her lips parted on the chosen phrase: but her pains might have been spared, for there was no one there to hear it. The door stood open, and from the shadowy orchard came a confused sound of voices: just as she had told them to, her guests were making themselves completely at home. . . .

With a distasteful glance for the uncleared table Lesley shrugged her shoulders and ran upstairs to the little bedroom. If not actually cooler there, it was at least free from cigarette-smoke, and pausing in the doorway she took a deliberate chestful of the clean, unscented air. Then a spring creaked, a pillow fell, and she switched on the light.

"What is it, Pat?"

Hot, rumpled, but mercifully tearless, he sat up in bed and sighed loudly.

"I want a drink of water."

Lesley glanced at the chair by the bed and saw that Mrs. Sprigg had forgotten to put his glass. There was one in Elissa's room, however, over the carafe; Lesley went and filled it and brought it back to Pat. He drank in a series of small, steady pulls, never shifting his lips and breathing rhythmically into the glass.

'Now I'll have to wash that too,' thought Lesley.

With an increasing consciousness of fatigue she turned his pillow, drew up the cool sheet: then went over to the window and knelt a moment against the sill. Far down the orchard four giant glowworms told her the whereabouts of four of her guests—two under the elm-tree, two by the shed: Elissa and Toby Ashton, Teddy and Natasha: all smoking hard to keep off the midges. As for poor Bryan, he was probably out looking for a pond to commit suicide in, and with all her heart she hoped he wouldn't find one. Lesley sighed: they didn't mean to be inconsiderate, but . . . in another minute she was going down to deal single-handed with the supper things. It was her own fault, of course, for saying Mrs. Sprigg did it, though how on earth they imagined that one old woman . . . Lesley sighed again: they couldn't imagine, that was the whole trouble. No one could imagine, who hadn't actually to do it.

"Frewen?"

She turned back to the room and saw Pat sitting up like a rabbit.

"What is it, Pat? Lie down and go to sleep."

"Have they come to *live* here?"

Startled out of her fatigue, Lesley hastened to reassure him.

"Of course not, Pat. Only for three days—only two, now. They're going home on Tuesday." An involuntary optimism warmed her voice. "I'll put the light out, and you must go to sleep."

With a great sigh of appeasement Pat at last curled up into his customary ball; but for a moment or two longer Lesley waited beside him.

It was their first faint glimmer of a fellow-feeling.

III

As has been previously stated, the members of the house-party—among whom Lesley had now apparently to number Mr. Lock—were due to remain until the Tuesday after Bank Holiday. That they all went home on Sunday night was therefore no preconceived design, but merely a happy accident.

The midges, however, had possibly something to do with it. At some time or other during the Saturday afternoon or evening Bryan Collingwood had been bitten all up his legs, Toby Ashton all up his arms, and poor Elissa simply everywhere.

"They're getting worse, too," she complained bitterly; "my left shoulder's gone all pimply. I thought midge-bites didn't."

"They do down here, I'm afraid," said Lesley: not because she believed it, but to keep their minds off harvesters. "Eat lots of salad, darling, and try not to scratch. Mrs. Sprigg! Where's the oil?"

"The young lady 'ad it yesterday to put on 'er sores," replied Mrs. Sprigg, appearing suddenly at the hatch. "The young lady in the bathing-dress."

"Oh, so I did, darling," said Elissa, almost before the pause had become noticeable. "I always oil all over for fear of blistering. You don't mind, do you?"

"Not a bit," said Lesley. "Was there enough?"

"Oh, yes, darling. I used it all, but there was enough." She reached out for a fork and helped herself to some smoked salmon; it was the first meal of the day, and so much too late for breakfast that Lesley had sacrificed all the rest of the week-end's *hors d'œuvres* to a sort of Russian sandwich-bar. There was also, for those feeling sufficiently bucolic, eggs and bacon and a pot of Oxford marmalade, both provided by Mrs. Sprigg in defiance of her employer's orders. In this case at least, however, the employer's instinct had been the right one; and the only person to feel bucolic was Lesley herself. Elissa looked at her in amazement.

"You *will* get fat, darling! . . . or don't you mind, now?"

"Personally, I don't think food has anything to do with it," said Lesley, who was feeling both hungry and pugnacious. "I've been eating bacon for nearly two months, and I don't believe it's made the slightest difference."

"You should look at yourself sideways, darling," said Elissa idly.

It was rather the tone of the whole party. They had not actually come to blows, but on the other hand they could not truthfully be described as enjoying themselves. It is almost impossible to enjoy oneself in the country while feeling dead tired: and for some reason Sunday morning found every member of the house-party, from Lesley to Pat, feeling very tired indeed. Neither Elissa nor Natasha had slept a wink, each accusing the other of snoring; but Natasha also accused Elissa of talking in her sleep, and said that to any student of psycho-analysis it was all far too dreadful to repeat.

("My dear," said Elissa, "I'm not really responsible for Bryan, but I feel I owe you an apology. Surely he could have *seen* . . .")

But that, at the moment, was the one thing Bryan would not do. All through the long Sunday morning—and in spite of the lateness of breakfast, it was very long indeed—all through the longer afternoon, he behaved as though there were no one in the orchard but Lesley, Elissa and Toby Ashton. It was a difficult thing to do, for Natasha and Teddy had stretched themselves in the middle of the grass, where they had almost to be stepped over in passing to and from the well, and where Lesley was constantly forced to disturb them with a request for water. This Teddy drew with a pleasant alacrity, and even carried as far as the kitchen before going to lie down again: but in the second pailful there bobbed a large grassy sod, which Lesley rightly interpreted as a symbolic Russian method of requesting to be let alone.

"Oh, well, it'll do for them to wash in," said Mrs. Sprigg philosophically. "Now you go along outside, Miss Frewen, and leave the rest to me."

With an unusual sensation of gratitude Lesley put down the milk-jug (she had just returned from a hasty trip to the Walpole's back door), applied a little more lipstick, picked up a sherry bottle, and followed this advice. It was time, she felt rather strongly, that someone began to make love to her; preferably Toby, of course, but at any rate someone. What else (hell take them!) had she asked the poor fish down for? The energy of her thought marked a sudden return of spirits (completely inexplicable unless by reference to a very fair number of cocktails consumed during an extremely wearing lunch. At the time they had had no more effect than water, so that she had been compelled to listen, in complete sobriety, to the wranglings of Elissa and Natasha over a missing tube of face cream. Belated but potent, however, the gin was at last in action: to box Natasha's ears would have been but the enjoyable work of a perfect moment. And as for Toby—*darling* Toby!—he should take her right off in the car somewhere, and if the others didn't like it, it would serve them damn well right. . . .

The afflatus, in fact, had descended; but it had descended too late. As Lesley stepped on to the grass a shrill cry of dismay rang under the apple-trees; and from the centre of an agitated group rose Elissa with a telegram.

It was a perfectly genuine one, which she happened to have received just before leaving Town, and which they now declared to have arrived while Lesley was fetching the milk. The contents were alarming and Elissa made no secret of them.

"It's Henry, darling, he's just broken his leg and implores me to go up to Town. And as we *are* more or less engaged, darling, I'm terribly afraid I'll have to humour him."

"What a hellish shame, darling!" said Lesley, at the same time wishing she could warn them that the boy who took round telegrams had just been serving her with milk. "Does that mean at once?"

Elissa tore her hair.

"I'm most frightfully afraid it does, darling. Or at any rate after tea. Toby's promised to run me up in the car. He *is* rather adorable, isn't he?"

"Oh, no, I'm not," cut in Toby mournfully. "I am a man with an ulterior motive. The same as a secret sorrow, only worse. The fact is, darling, I've just remembered a man from Paris."

"The man you had to go over about while I had your house?" prompted Lesley. The afflatus was rapidly leaving her again, but she could still carry the thing off.

He looked at her with real liking.

"That's the one. He's in London for the week-end, and I've got to give him a damned good dinner and play him five new songs. So if by chance I *can't* get back, *tout comprendre* will be *tout pardonner.*"

"We'll have tea at four, then," said Lesley. "You don't mind it early, Natasha, or did you and Bryan want to go another walk?"

"I never will go a walk again," said Natasha sullenly. She was upstairs at the bedroom window, retouching her eyebrows and thinking it very foolish of everyone to keep on pretending. If one wanted to go away, why not say so plainly? "Common courtesy," Bryan had said, when he was making up his own story about an uncle's birthday: but surely it was more courteous to speak the truth than to tell lies? And with a feeling of carefree righteousness—the same feeling that used to come over her, as a child, just before she broke her sister's hideous and therefore unpermissible doll—she leant a little farther out of the window and said simply:

"I am tired of here too."

IV

When the time came to go, however (and tea that day was very early indeed), a sudden wave of mutual affection lifted them buoyantly over the parting. Elissa kissed Lesley, Lesley kissed Elissa, and was herself kissed by Bryan and Toby. Natasha, it is true, did not kiss anyone, but the gratitude of Teddy Lock ran almost to blank verse. He had gone down to the village and fetched up his car, so obviously ready and willing to take charge of Natasha that Lesley at once carried out the big coroneted suitcase and dumped it in the back. Beside Toby's Talbot she found the luggage already piled and young Bryan Collingwood in an attitude of despair: at the sight of Natasha's suitcase he turned his back, and pretended to be examining the dashboard.

Suddenly touched, Lesley went to his side, and regretting her tactlessness.

"Look here, my dear," she said impulsively, "if you'd like to stay on a day by yourself—I don't mind."

With an elaborate start he turned and saw her.

"Darling, how sweet of you! But I think I'd better be getting back with Toby. As a matter of fact, my uncle's got a birthday to-morrow. . . ."

At the open gate the voices of Elissa and Toby, of Teddy and Natasha, could already be heard. Lesley yielded to temptation.

"My poor Bryan!" she said gently, "was she going to Warsaw with you?"

For answer he pulled open the door and slumped into a back seat. The next moment Toby and Elissa were settling themselves in front, while the Packard, already in motion, had begun to purr gently into Pig Lane.

"All right behind?" inquired Toby, letting in the clutch.

Bryan grunted. He was not all right, he was deplorable, and didn't care who knew it. From the car in front Teddy Lock turned and waved vigorously.

"Good-bye, Miss Frewen!"

"Good-bye, good-bye!"

"See you again soon, darling!"

"Soon, soon, soon!" shrilled Elissa.

When at last they were out of sight Lesley pulled-to the gate and went back through the orchard; where the first thing that met her eyes was young Patrick Craigie curled under an apple-tree and sleeping like the dead.

Chapter Five

I

As the wind, said Larochefoucauld, puts out candles and kindles fire, so absence will diminish a slender affection and increase a great. His words, passed on to Lesley at a Chelsea bottle-party, had somehow been remembered (it was a trick his words often had) a great deal longer than the rest of the conversation: and during the first week in August they were constantly in Lesley's mind.

'Candles every one of them!' thought Lesley, in her first bitterness. Mere flickering dips, unstable to the lightest breath! For she had forgotten, naturally enough, how fast things changed, how swiftly emotions developed and relationships changed, when their change and their development were the chief recreation of largely unoccupied persons. In a couple of hours, at one of Elissa's parties, one could be fallen in love with, fall in love oneself, lose interest, recover it again, and at the last be driven affectionately home by a person who two hours earlier had still been a perfect though interesting stranger. And if so much in two hours, how much more in two months! Elissa and Toby, when they came to the cottage, were already at their second and penultimate phase: from Lesley to Natasha had been more, for Bryan, than a single emotional stride. All these things, indeed, Lesley's intelligence, had she called on it, could probably have guessed at; but for once in her life she was giving rein to pure feeling. And in her feelings she was sore, disheartened, puzzled, shocked. To one almost professionally disillusioned, disillusion came very hard.

In this mood, and about half-way through August, Lesley Frewen called on the Vicar.

Her motive was frankly interested, being simply to obtain for Patrick the society of the young Pomfrets. At the moment the bulk of his time was being spent with Mrs. Sprigg, who, though in many ways a sound and suitable companion for youth, was also the possessor of a strong local accent. Pat had lately, in fact, began to drop his h's, a practice which annoyed Lesley considerably, and he was also forming the habit of constantly concealing himself behind fences to watch for the young Walpoles. One day soon he would quite probably climb over, and if some social intercourse were absolutely inevitable Lesley found herself with an instinctive bias in favour of the Pomfrets. They were considerably cleaner, they had impeccable accents, and above all there were at least two of them old enough to send Pat out alone with.

In spite of these advantages, however, it was a resolution to which Lesley proceeded at least with distaste. She had no desire in the world to enter into relations with the Vicarage, and deeply resented the threat to her isolation. There also remained to be cleared up that unfortunate business of the Vicar's call.

'I shall have to go and see him, I suppose,' thought Lesley: and thereupon spent a good deal of time and effort in trying to remember whether Elissa's behaviour had been bad enough to call for an apology. Right up to the last she was still undecided: right up to the finishing touch of rouge and the last dusting of powder. In obedience to an unexamined instinct, she had made up rather more thoroughly than usual, employing a new tangerine lipstick in place of her usual scarlet: between a tailored white walking dress and a tilted white hat, it took on an extraordinary vividness. Thus embellished, and complete to every detail, Lesley drew on her gloves and set out for the Vicarage.

She went by the short cut, across Walpole pastures: but less from an impatience to reach her destination than from a deep reluctance to pass through the village. The inhabitants of High Westover had none of that shy rural courtesy so rightly extolled by those who have presumably experienced it. They stared. They might be trying to dissemble their interest, but if so they dissembled it very badly. And behind their stares lay a dumb, sullen, and intimate antagonism. Or so felt Lesley: and she walked across the meadows.

Arriving at the Vicarage gate, the first objects that met her eye were none other than the four young Pomfrets in person, happily and usefully occupied in painting a garden roller. Lesley scrutinised them carefully. Except for a short hiatus of about fifteen inches they all looked almost exactly alike, with short sandy hair, freckled noses, white cotton cricket shirts, long brown legs, and the stoutest sandals she had ever seen; but between waist and knee some extra yard or so of grey flannel differentiated between the sexes. Two of the painters wore skirts, two knickerbockers. The whole four appeared uniformly healthy, hardy and unintimidated. With a slight stirring of satisfaction Lesley pulled at the bell.

It was answered, after a certain hesitation, by an odd little maid with untied apron-strings. Her eye was startled, her speech non-committal, but on hearing Lesley's name she let her come inside and scuttled away down an echoing passage. Lesley waited obediently. Through an opening door came the strains of the Brandenburg No. 5 played on a goodish gramophone; then silence, a short pause, and Miss Frewen was shown into the Vicar's study.

II

The first thing that caught her eye was a white china saucer standing in a patch of sunlight towards the centre of the carpet. It was lined with flannel, and to a more experienced eye would have suggested the small-scale culture of kidney beans. In Lesley's view, however, it was merely a kitchen saucer left lying about.

"Miss Frewen?" said the Vicar.

She looked up quickly, and saw him standing by the gramophone; tall, powerfully-shouldered, about forty-five, and with really quite an intelligent face. She decided for frankness.

"Yes. I live at the White Cottage. You called on me there about a fortnight ago."

"I remember perfectly," said the Vicar. (With or without malice? She couldn't tell.)

"I was out—or rather, just coming back—but some friends of mine were in the garden. They were in very high spirits, and I'm afraid rather rude to you. I must . . . apologise for them."

"That's all right," said the Vicar simply, "I thought they were drunk. Have you come to live here, Miss Frewen?"

"For four or five years," said Lesley, a little surprised to find the incident so quickly over. (Elissa probably hadn't been drunk, of course, but there was no point in going into that now.) "I'm not married, but I have with me a small boy," and she glanced swiftly up to see how he was taking it.

"Your own, or adopted?" asked the Vicar mildly.

"Adopted."

"And how old, may one ask?"

"Four-and-a-half."

Mr. Pomfret looked at her with interest.

"A great and fascinating responsibility. You must be very fond of children, Miss Frewen."

"On the contrary," said Lesley, "I dislike them."

As well he might, the Vicar looked slightly puzzled. This defiant young woman with the peculiar-shaped mouth—had she come with a genuine apology, or simply to relieve her mind?

'Confession!' thought Mr. Pomfret suddenly, 'what a need that fills! And what nonsense to say we can't hear it! If a woman wants to unburden her soul, the absence of a confession-box won't stop her. Secrecy, absolution—that's not what they're after. They simply want to tell someone. . . .' And glancing with slight apprehension at his new parishioner, Mr. Pomfret was relieved to find her looking distinctly uncommunicative.

"You want a cigarette," he said suddenly. "I haven't any myself, but if you want to smoke, do."

"You refrain on principle, no doubt?" said Lesley, opening her bag. The Vicar shook his head.

"I don't buy cigarettes," he explained, "because I can't afford to. But when people give me packets, I smoke them."

Lesley looked at him with a faint but obvious distaste.

"Isn't that rather inconsistent?"

"Why?" asked the Vicar. "It's all a form of alms-giving. And people give me cigarettes who wouldn't give me anything else. They feel it's a manly habit that ought to be encouraged. I feel the same about alms-giving."

Without a word Lesley took out her long gold cigarette-case and emptied it on to the desk: eleven slim brown Russians, and one intrusive Turk. Mr. Pomfret counted them with frank interest.

"Let's have one," he said, "and I'll go and fetch my wife. You ought to know her."

Alone in the study, Lesley drew at her cigarette and resigned herself to the inevitable.

The Vicar and his wife! Well, it might make an amusing incident for her next letter to Elissa . . . if there ever was one: and with a keen eye for the ridiculous she rose at the opening of the door and permitted herself to be shaken warmly by the hand.

"Miss Frewen! How nice of you to come!" cried the Vicar's wife. Her voice was warm too, like her hand and her colouring and everything about her. Dark of hair and eye, very much sunburnt, she carried herself with a complete lack of reserve that somehow avoided being a lack of dignity: though whence that dignity was derived Lesley could by no means decide. It was certainly not from her clothes.

"My husband has just told me that that dear little boy isn't yours at all!" she continued heartily. "I call it perfectly splendid. Is he in the garden, or have you left him at home?"

"At home," said Lesley.

"What a pity! He could have made friends with the children. They're just painting the roller, because it's Alec's birthday," said Mrs. Pomfret, her eye straying to the saucer of beans.

Lesley took the opportunity.

"That was really what I came to see you about. He doesn't get enough companionship."

"Then send him up here, my dear, any time you like. Is he used to other children?"

"I really don't know," said Lesley. "I shouldn't think so. But he seems quite normal generally."

Between the Vicar and his wife there passed a swift, mutually-inquiring glance. Then Mrs. Pomfret stooped and picked up the saucer.

"Well, that's settled, then," she said. "You'll stay and have tea, of course?"

But Lesley would not be detained. The whole thing had passed off better than might have been expected: but a Vicarage was no place for her.

III

About ten o'clock the following morning, and while she was making the beds, Lesley became aware of a sort of decorous trampling on the path from the gate. It sounded like a herd of very small and polite elephants, and looking out of the window she saw that Mrs. Pomfret's benevolence was not losing any time. The four children from the Vicarage were advancing in close formation: they were still bare-legged, but in recognition of the first autumnal nip had exchanged their cricket shirts for grey jerseys. Lesley hastily withdrew her head, automatically applied powder, and went down-stairs. Pat was somewhere in the orchard, but before she could go and seek him the visitors had arrived. They knocked carefully on the door and then drew back in an expectant semicircle, all counting under their breaths in order to know how soon they could knock again. At thirty-one, however, the door opened, so that the elder of the two little girls had to leave off her counting and take a step forward. She said politely:

"Good-morning, Miss Frewen. Please may Pat come up and play in our garden? We've got a swing."

"I'm certain he'd like to very much," replied Lesley with equal courtesy. "But just at the moment I'm not sure where he is."

The four children looked at each other, as though faced with a sudden social problem. Then—

"He's hiding behind the tool-house," said both the boys together.

Lesley followed their glances, and saw the dark scut of Pat's knickers bob down behind the fence. The situation was ticklish. How shy he was, or whether he was shy at all, she had not the least idea; but it did now strike her that in view of his unusually secluded life he might quite possibly be extremely shy indeed. And to call and call, with no great hope of his ever coming, was not a procedure that appealed to her dignity.

"Pat!" said Lesley: just once, and scarcely raising her voice. There was no answer.

Thus faced with the anticipated crisis, Lesley had a sudden inspiration.

"Listen," she said to the Pomfrets, "he's only about five, and rather shy. Would you mind playing down here this morning, in the orchard, just to make it easier for him to join in?"

Again the mute family council sat in rapid judgment, the small boys in particular casting a critical eye over the offered ground. Then the elder little girl, as before, took the votes of the meeting and delivered the verdict.

"Yes, thank you, we'll stay. I'll just go back and tell them at home."

"And bring the bows and arrows and my snow-shoes and the North Pole," added the elder of the small boys swiftly. . . .

A second later, they were all over the orchard.

IV

For a woman who disliked children, Lesley Frewen now saw a great deal of them. Her orchard had apparently unsuspected attractions; and reading from time to time, in the Sunday *Observer*, of the depredations of the muskrat, Lesley often put down the paper and thought of the Pomfrets. They were not nearly so destructive, of course; but they would probably be just as difficult to evict.

In the meantime, however, they were taking Pat off her hands for about six hours a day, and she grew quite accustomed, whenever she passed through the orchard, to seeing a child or so tied to an apple-tree. Unlike Mrs. Pomfret, she never felt any impulse to go and undo them: rationally presuming that if the experience were really painful they would cease to let themselves be tied. This attitude was deeply appreciated, especially by the young Pomfrets, who on their home ground would as often as not find the prisoner released and being pampered with a dough-nut. The first time they captured Pat, indeed, there were two experienced scouts to spy out Lesley's movements: but she merely glanced towards the stake, looked at her watch, and went straight on down the lane. After that they tied him up quite a lot.

"Do you like playing with the Pomfrets?" Lesley asked him, about a week after their first visit.

"Yes," said Pat.

Like all his other statements, it carried conviction; there was evidently no need to pursue the matter further. Crossing Mrs. Pomfret by the duck-pond, however, Lesley came to a halt and completed the inquiry.

"I hope your children don't find Patrick too much of a nuisance?"

"Good gracious, no!" said Mrs. Pomfret. "They're only too pleased to have him. And they *love* your orchard. But there was just one thing I wanted to ask, Miss Frewen—has your well got a cover?"

Lesley thought.

"There's a plank or something, I believe, that Mrs. Sprigg shoves across the top. But the water always seems very clean."

Less reassured than might have been expected, Mrs. Pomfret pressed for details.

"But is there any actual fastening, Miss Frewen? Or can the children just push it aside whenever they want to?"

"You mean they might fall in?" said Lesley intelligently. "I'll get a lid made." She drew out her list—for she had kept to her resolution and now shopped in Aylesbury—and made a marginal note. "Is there anything else?"

"I don't think so, my dear. Really, you *are* good—"

"Not at all," said Lesley. "I don't want them drowned any more than you do." And with considerable satisfaction she then terminated the interview and continued on her way.

As far as she could see, and with the exception of Mrs. Sprigg, there was now no one she need speak to for the next four-and-a-half years.

Chapter Six

— ❋ —

I

During the first winter at High Westover Lesley Frewen was probably the only person in England to keep abreast of current literature. Twice a week the Mudie's parcels arrived by van: twice a week Lesley revised her list. It is true that she made no attempt to cope with fiction: but she did read, roughly speaking, all the biography, all the history, and all the criticism published between October and March.

And meanwhile, to her considerable surprise, the weeks continued to pass with at least their normal rapidity. She was realising, in fact, though as yet unconsciously, that a constant routine, however dull, does at least get one through the day. The extreme regularity, the multiple divisions of each twenty-four hours, carried her almost insensibly from morning to night. At eight o'clock she got up, washed and towelled Patrick, helped him into his clothes, and dispatched him, according to the weather, into either the garden or the barn. She then made her own toilet, turned down the beds, and joined him below for half-past eight breakfast. After breakfast Mrs. Sprigg washed up, Pat amalgamated with the Pomfrets, and Lesley made the beds; for it had long been apparent that Mrs. Sprigg's responsibility for the cottage was one of those polite fictions that so often hold good between employer and employed.

The old Woman did her best: but her standards were not those of Beverley Service; and confronted by the alternatives of either relinquishing those standards or turning-to herself, all Lesley's inborn capability thrust her towards the latter. Slowly but doggedly she learnt first the names and then the uses of Vim, of Ronuk, and of Sunlight Soap. She learnt to put soap-flakes in the washing-up water, but not the same soap-flakes as she used for Pat's vests. She learnt to iron her own handkerchiefs and hang stockings by the toes. Once, on waking, she caught herself with the thought, 'This is a good day for drying,' and with wry humour made a note of the fact in a letter to Elissa. She was writing to Elissa again, after a long silence: the address on the envelope seemed a link with Town. Only on second thoughts that letter was never posted: and when Lesley wrote it again it was all about a very amusing volume of theatrical memoirs. Elissa did not answer, but she probably read it, and would realise that even in the depths of the country one didn't necessarily go to seed. . . .

With such occupations, and many others, Lesley was busy in the house until almost lunch-time. This she had to get herself, for Mrs. Sprigg had her own brood to attend to. After lunch, while Mrs. Sprigg washed up, she sat in the orchard and saw to her own and Patrick's sewing, or else read about two-thirds of a book. Then came tea, and at five o'clock Pat had to be read to out of *The Tailor of Gloucester*, given his supper, washed again, and put to bed. Mrs. Sprigg having by that time finally departed, Lesley looked round the kitchen and got herself what she still thought of as dinner. She then finished the afternoon's volume, and began on another. At about eleven o'clock she felt sleepy. Sometimes she felt sleepy even earlier, but she gritted her teeth and sat resolutely on until at last the clock struck for half-past and the day might fairly be considered over.

There was one feature of their routine, however, so extraordinary that only by a detailed and methodical relation can it be made in the least credible.

II

Every evening at five o'clock, Lesley, as has already been described, took down *The Tailor of Gloucester* and read Pat eight pages. Since she always began where she left off, and since the quota never varied, a night's allowance might quite easily consist of the last four and the first; but Pat never seemed to mind, and Lesley had long ceased to couple the words with meaning. Just as she had got the whole by heart, however, and about half-way through November, Pat suddenly asked for something new.

The request, though unexpected, was so reasonable that Lesley had shut the book in assent before she had time to remember that there was not in the cottage so much as half a line of reading matter which could possibly take its place.

It was a predicament in which a woman might have been far stupider and yet less at a loss; for there are few nursemaids, however incompetent, who cannot at a pinch produce the Three Bears. But though Lesley certainly knew the story in its main outline, the idea of telling it never entered her head; and indeed neither her turn of phrase nor manner of delivery was exactly suited to the adventures of Goldilocks. As luck would have it, the day was Saturday: at least two more evenings must elapse before she would be able to go to Aylesbury and buy a Hans Andersen: and more in despair than hope Lesley turned and looked along the bookshelf. *Ulysses, South Wind*, Lawrence and Julian Green, an odd volume of Pepys's and the poems of John Donne . . . and then right at the end of the shelf, wedged against the wood, Pat's own Family Bible.

'Noah's Ark,' thought Lesley thankfully.

Some little difficulty in finding the place was all that delayed the beginning: but just before the flood began to subside, and in view of Pat's extreme interest, a sudden scruple brought her to a halt. Whatever else her shortcomings, she had no intention of saddling the child with a religion before he was old enough to think for himself:

and what form, behind those enraptured eyes, might not the Lord God Jehovah be even then assuming? Or what if that delicious two of each procession should turn out to have been an insidious form of Anglican propaganda? Putting the book down on her knee, therefore, she said firmly,

"It isn't true, Pat. There isn't really anyone who can send down rain whenever he feels bored with the population."

Pat looked thoughtfully up.

"Were there two snails?"

Lesley tried again.

"Not really, Pat, because there wasn't really an Ark. It's just a story."

"In the story were there two snails?"

"There were two of everything, but they weren't *real*. It's a story, Pat, like—like *The Tailor of Gloucester*," said Lesley, suddenly inspired. "Now you understand, don't you?"

With a child's instinct for the right answer, Pat nodded. Only by his standards anything as true as the *Tailor* was as true as the heat of the sun or the cold of the floor, and having a perfect five-year-old memory he subsequently won several prizes for Scripture in the lower forms of Christ's Hospital. But of this Lesley naturally had no knowledge, and with a conscience at rest she proceeded, as the weeks went by, to the stories of Jonah and the Whale, of David and Jonathan, of the Infant Samuel, and many others. Pat seemed to like them, while for herself there was the occasional pleasure of a felicitous metaphor or mouth-filling cadence. It was not, in fact, nearly so boring as she had at first anticipated; and at any rate it was probably less boring than Hans Andersen.

And that was how it came about that Lesley Frewen read the Bible aloud at least four evenings a week.

III

So the days slid into weeks, the weeks grouped themselves into October and November, and still the weather continued mild; but with December came wind and rain, blowing across the Vale in such mighty gusts that a fortnight before Christmas the big wooden sign of the Three Pigeons was blown from its pole and battered beyond recognition. It was the event of the winter, and all High Westover went to have a look at it; even Lesley Frewen (though not until after lunch) turned aside on her way to the Post Office. The battered framework had been propped on a bench, leaning against the wall, and opposite she found Pat and the Pomfrets paying their second visit of the afternoon. They had already spent most of the morning in exactly the same positions, but the interest was still unexhausted.

"Well, as it's *got* to be done again, perhaps they'll have a change," Lesley heard one of them say hopefully.

"I wish they'd have a George and Dragon. . . ."

"Let's come and watch the man doing it. . . ."

"I wish they'd let *us* paint it. It hasn't got to have shading, or any-thing." The speaker—it was the eldest Pomfret boy—stretched out a small dirty hand and passed it over the weather-beaten surface. "I can't think why everybody doesn't paint on wood. It's ever so much nicer than canvas."

"I don't want to paint pictures, I want to paint doors," said his brother yearningly. And then, as though suddenly pulled by the same string, they all turned round and watched Lesley coming towards them.

A trifle self-conscious, as usual, in the matter of juvenile small-talk, she nodded over her shoulder and halted by the bench. The Three Pigeons, thus magnified into a close-up, revealed no unsus-pected beauties: the man who drew them—not even the landlord knew how many years ago—had evidently known what a pigeon looked like and been content to reproduce.

"We've got a cousin who's an artist," said a Pomfret child suddenly. "He painted a zebra, a teeny wee one. He did it—"

"And some sheep he painted," added another child quickly, "with two dogs and a shepherd."

Lesley's lips curved. How well she could imagine them! Woolly and twilit in a highland glen. . . !

"Only they weren't so good as the zebra. That was lovely, all stripes," said the eldest Pomfret. "Mother took me to see it when we went about my teeth."

"At the Academy?" hazarded Lesley.

"Oh, no. That's lovely, isn't it? This was quite a small place, with hardly any people. But we had tea at the Corner House."

"And now Pat must come and have tea at home," said Lesley. Suddenly, between one breath and the next, she was bored beyond endurance. With his usual docility, Pat stepped out of the ranks and fell in by her side: and from the boredom of the road they returned to the boredom of the cottage.

IV

About ten days later a sudden unnatural hush settled snowlike over the orchard; for a man had turned up at the Three Pigeons and was repainting the fallen sign. His studio was an empty stable, and according to Mrs. Sprigg he was likely to take his time: the terms of the bargain being five bob down and his keep while working.

"And from the amount 'e put away yesterday," added Mrs. Sprigg cheerfully, "I lay old Povey wishes 'e'd only got one pigeon instead of three. Eat! 'E's worse nor the Walpole pigs."

"Well, I hope he doesn't mind an audience," said Lesley. "The children spend half the day there."

"Mind! Not 'im. 'E told Florrie Walpole 'e once used to 'ave a pitch in Trafalgar Square, till the Police moved 'im off it. 'E said they're terrible hard men, them London bobbies." The shrew-mouse eyes flickered with alarm; like a proper weasel-run it must be, or a field under the reapers! And suddenly the shrew-mouse squeaked with laughter.

"I'd like to see young Arnold move anyone along!" said Mrs. Sprigg. "The only thing 'e can move's 'is vittles."

"If you want any water, there's some in the barn," said Lesley; and having finished clearing the table went out into the orchard.

The change was scarcely for the better. Here and there, under the apple-trees, an occasional tussock of grass heaved itself through the slush: but wherever, in summer, there had been a path, the mud was stretched smooth and undisturbed.

It was a cloak under which a good deal of rural beauty might safely lie hidden, and Lesley's was scarcely the eye of faith. From the sky downwards, moreover, all was grey: the smoke from the chimney, the bark on the ancient trees; the wood of the gateposts, the bucket by the well: even her own soft tweeds, in which she had so successfully decorated, at one time or another, so many different cars. Toby's yellow, and Bryan's scarlet, and the great green Packard that had belonged to that American. . . !

". . . And as cars go, they went!" said Lesley aloud; but no ripple of appreciation arose above the cocktail-glasses. The cocktails were all in Town, with their drinkers and shakers and cherry-stick-makers: with Elissa and Toby Ashton and Hugo and Tommy Bliss: with the people who made witty remarks and the people who appreciated them: and all at once, under those bare and colourless trees, an unendurable homesickness drove the tears to her eyes. 'The wind!' thought Lesley, 'the wind's like a knife!' and knotting her scarf higher she turned blindly through the gate and out into Pig Lane.

V

And curiously enough—for of the three alternative routes it was by no means the cleanest—she presently found herself in a narrow pathway skirting a disused stable. The door was open, but completely blocked by a handful of children, among whom, however, neither Pat nor the Pomfrets were for the moment discernible; and suppressing her normal impulse to hurry by, Lesley moved a pace or two nearer and stared frankly over their heads.

The screever was at work.

Familiar as Hyde Park Corner, shabby as the Strand, he squatted on the floor with the sign flat before him: and neither Bond Street on a fine morning, nor the theatres emptying at night were as much a part of the Town as the dusty and upturned cap that lay so conveniently to hand. Lesley thought,

'If those little brutes would go, I could ask him how he got here.'

And as though only waiting for that concrete and hostile thought, the children, who had already stopped their chattering, now began to turn and drift away. Lesley waited until they were all gone, then took out a sixpence from her bag and tossed it neatly into the centre of the cap. The screever turned.

"Good luck, lady!"

His face was like his voice, his voice like his greeting—all three pure cockney.

"This is a long way from Trafalgar Square," said Lesley.

"I sh'd say it is, Miss. You from Town too?"

Lesley nodded: the man put down his brush.

"Ah! Kensington, would it be?"

"No, Baker Street. Do you know it?"

"Do I know it! I once 'ad a pitch there, along o' the church railings. It's a nice part, Baker Street, but the people in too much of an 'urry. Not enough shops, y'see, though I believe they're putting 'em up."

"If you want shops, you should try Bond Street," said Lesley.

He looked at her compassionately.

"Shops? Yes. *Shops wiv commissionaires.* Give me Baker Street, any day. D'you ever know the 'Field of Hops,' Miss, in the Marylebone Road?"

"Only from the outside. Did *you* ever know—"

"Ah, that's a fine pub, that is!" said the screever. "What wouldn't I give to be there now!" He spoke with passion: like Lesley's Bond Street, his 'Field of Hops' had taken on the unearthly beauty of mirages. "And St. Martin's Church—you know St. Martin's Church?"

"Of course I do!" cried Lesley.

"Best pitch in Town," said the screever reverently. "I used to know the feller what 'ad it—not what you'd call intimately, o' course, but enough to pass the time o' day. I used to 'ang about just opposite, see, so's if ever 'e was called away or took ill or anything I'd be able to nip over and look after it for 'im: but 'e never was, and the coppers they took a down on me; 'n now I don't suppose I'll ever get such a chance again."

"What about Hyde Park Corner?" said Lesley, "where the buses stop?"

"Ah! now you're talking. 'Yde Park Corner!" Slowly, luxuriously, his tongue caressed the enchanting syllables. "'Ave they finished that new Underground yet, Miss?"

"They hadn't six months ago," she told him. "But you've been in Town since then?"

"You're wrong there, lady; I 'aven't been in Town since Wen'sday fourth of April last." He spoke with the ready precision of the experienced witness; and as though overcome by a sudden *malaise*, or at any rate by a painful memory, politely but firmly brought the conversation to an end.

"Well, I best be getting on with these 'ere chickens," he said regretfully. "It's been nice talkin' to you, Miss, it brought it all right back: but business before pleasure, as the sayin' is."

With a deep sigh he bent over his work: muttered a complaint or two over the state of the wood, then fell altogether silent: and only as Lesley was departing down the lane did she catch what might have been the voice of her own heart.

"'N a plucky long time it seems!" said the screever.

Chapter Seven

I

So the days, weeks and months slid monotonously by, and even Christmas scarcely disturbed her trance: for the Pomfrets invited Pat not only to partake of all the Vicarage festivities, but also to sleep there. He went rejoicing, and Lesley procured from Fortnum and Mason, and sent up with his belongings, a two-dozen box of extremely expensive crackers. He was gone for five days, but though Lesley could thus have locked up the White Cottage and departed for Town, a curious lack of initiative kept her where she was. She had received, as it chanced, no actual invitations, and although nothing would have been simpler than to telephone round till she found a party, the days slipped by in deliberation until suddenly it was too late. Frocks, 'phone calls, somewhere to stay—the effort was beyond her; and her final preparations consisted of Tolstoy's *War and Peace* (which she had often attacked but never read) and two hundred Russian cigarettes.

From first to last, indeed, the White Cottage added remarkably little to Mr. Walsh's burdens: Lesley's being a circle which customarily celebrated Christmas by getting out of the country for as long as it could afford. Elissa sent an Algerian paper-knife, Aunt Alice a butterfly-wing pen-tray which she had probably taken out from Sutton to post on the Italian Riviera. There were also a good many cards, a number of them (self-executed) from the artists who had tried to let Lesley their cottages; but this prolific and hitherto-untapped source apart, the total bag was about one-third of that usually addressed to Beverley Court.

Nor was the out-going post much heavier. Along with the crackers Lesley also obtained one dozen Christmas cards, and when those were disposed of bought no more. The cynicism was quite unconscious: with her customary intelligence she had simply accepted the facts. And the facts were these: that to keep any memory green in Chelsea, over a period of either four or five years, was beyond the power of an annual halfpenny stamp. And as for 'keeping up a correspondence'—those days were over. Chelsea 'phoned, wired or cabled: dashed off a note, sent a card with some flowers: but never sat down to the writing-desk from one year's end to the other. Letters were out, together with sentimental friendship and two-month visits: in fact, if one couldn't run a private road-house, all other effort was a sheer waste of tissue. Better be forgotten outright, thought Lesley, than haunt the public conscience as someone who ought to be written to. . . .

The facts were faced. For four more years—for that was the period of exile to which she now acknowledged herself condemned—drop out altogether: drug mind with print and body with work: wash Patrick's vests and save on the housekeeping. Drop out altogether . . . and then come back with a splash. . . .

The facts were faced: or at any rate as many as Lesley had noticed.

II

Of the others, the ignored, the chief was this: that for the first time in ten years she was getting a steady eight hours' sleep. Her body moved, though ungraciously, in clean air, was adequately fed, had almost ceased to ask for alcohol. And with the gradual return of physical poise the bitter mental irritation of the autumn passed into something so much less positive that it might almost be termed acquiescence. It was like a hibernation, a hibernation of all the faculties, in which even her relations with Patrick lost much of their bitterness. She no longer hated him. Occasionally, at the sight of his steadily increasing sturdiness, she even felt a faint satisfaction. But in general their intercourse continued to be marked by an oddly formal politeness: a dispassionate attention, on Lesley's side, to food and clothing, and on Pat's an almost startling exhibition of best behaviour. He was not an unhappy child: he spent too much time with the young Pomfrets for that: but he was silent, self-contained, and with Lesley at least, extremely undemonstrative. The society of one adult and four bigger children was making him older than his years, a boy instead of a baby; whatever he did was rational, and he had Scots blood on both sides.

III

His return from the Vicarage was naturally a cause for regret, which an increasing equanimity, however, enabled Lesley to bear with rather less annoyance than she anticipated. Her own simple festivities had passed off without a hitch: she had smoked her cigarettes, read *War and Peace* in a little under three days, and was now fully prepared to defend her original estimate. Some of her points, indeed, were so remarkably good that she was almost tempted to waste them on Mrs. Sprigg: but common sense prevailed, and the small-talk at the cottage continued as laconic as ever. Pat and Mrs. Sprigg, indeed, used to converse with each other in the kitchen, where they exchanged detailed lists of everything they had eaten for the last five days: but this Lesley did not know, and as far as she was concerned Patrick brought back from the Vicarage exactly as much conversation as he had taken with him. He did occasionally, however, volunteer some clean-cut statement of fact, especially at luncheon, where Mrs. Sprigg's waiting made the pace a trifle slow: and a day or so after the New Year broke a post-pudding silence to say that the Three Pigeons' signboard was once more in position.

"They put it up this morning," he explained gravely, "with Mr. Walpole's ladder. But the man's gone away."

From the other side of the hatch an aged voice hastened to corroborate.

"That's right, Miss Frewen. Went off last night, 'e did, and Florrie Walpole crying 'er eyes out." Mrs. Sprigg sniffed contemptuously. "'You just wait another nine months,' I said to 'er, 'and then you may 'ave something to cry about.' But they're a leaky lot, them Walpole's, an' always 'ave been."

"If you look under the bureau upstairs, Pat," said Miss Frewen swiftly, "you'll find a pair of heavy outdoor shoes."

IV

For another odd habit which had imperceptibly grown on her was that of going for long solitary walks. The weather was abominable— Pat and the Pomfrets spent most of their time in the barn—but despite a permanent treacly slush, and often in the face of a heavy rain, Lesley set out day after day to tramp across to Wendover, turn by the church, and fight her way up to the slope of the Chilterns. They gave her no pleasure, these excursions: it was simply that her healthy body now needed more to pit itself against than the handle of the well-crank, and in this daily battle with the wind found a deep animal satisfaction. Her mind, on these occasions, rarely wandered farther than the puddle beneath her foot or the bramble catching her coat: she thought from minute to minute of a rut to be avoided, of shelter under a hedge. Pausing only for extreme fatigue, she had grown familiar with the road while knowing nothing of the country;

and it was a rare chance indeed that held her, that afternoon, just long enough motionless to observe, with a faint stirring of disapproval, how far Nature was lagging behind the modern landscapist. Everything in the Vale was pure Royal Academy: all dark intersecting hedges and snow-coloured sky.

"Pure Academy! Pure Jigsaw!" said Lesley aloud; and continuing for another five yards or so came upon a heavy bucolic figure leaning over a gate. It was Mr. Pomfret.

He had not heard her, however, but appeared to be lost in contemplation. A long and oddly-cut overcoat muffled him against the wind, a soft grey fisherman's hat descended well over his ears: in their big woollen gloves his hands gripped resolutely at the wood. He might have been praying, or thinking, or composing his next sermon; but in spite of his stillness he was almost certainly not asleep.

The molten slush deadening her footsteps, Lesley moved cautiously on until the broad stooping back was safely rounded and she could once more quicken her pace. At that moment the Vicar turned.

"Good-afternoon," said Lesley at once. His children took Pat off her hands for six hours a day.

"Miss Frewen?" For a moment he stared at her almost stupidly. Then turning back to the gate, and with a wide, clumsy gesture, he said,

"Come here and look at this."

Still thinking of Pat, Lesley picked her way through the deeper mud till she stood beside him. The field before them dropped sharply down: below lay the Vale of Aylesbury. It was flat, dun-coloured, and just as she had seen it a few moments earlier.

"I could stand here all day," said the Vicar.

He was staring straight ahead of him, as though at something beautiful; and sideways glancing at his rapt and stubborn face, Lesley decided not to waste the simile of the jigsaw.

"My God!" said the Vicar suddenly. "If I could paint!"

Lesley glanced again. In spite of the oath, it sounded almost like a prayer. . . . And all at once, her perfect social memory, so many months unemployed, supplied the right tag.

"Haven't you a nephew who paints, Mr. Pomfret? You should get him down here."

The Vicar detached his gaze and turned to face her.

"I see the children have been telling you about Hilary. He once painted a zebra which they've never forgotten."

"It ranks," Lesley assured him, "with a visit to the dentist. By the way, where *is* it he exhibits?"

"Somewhere off Cork Street, I believe, with a group of several other young persons. They call themselves the London Reds."

Involuntarily Lesley looked her surprise. The London Reds! But wasn't that Hugo Dove's gang, and really rather brilliant? Exclusive, too, which was more than most of them were! And aloud she said,

"Then you certainly ought to get him here. It would be terribly interesting to see what he'd make of it."

"A mess," said Mr. Pomfret.

For a moment the placid stupidity of it exasperated her beyond words. Everything was a mess, no doubt, in his view, that did not closely resemble a tinted photograph! Controlling her voice to a decent civility, Lesley took up the cudgels.

"I thought you said he had a picture in the London Reds?"

"Oh, yes," said the Vicar simply, "but it was done on lavatory paper." And turning back to the gate he resumed his contemplation.

Lesley, however, remained where she was, experiencing to the full a most curious sensation. It was almost—(*God*, what a fool!)—as though she hadn't been quite quick enough. . . .

A second later her face changed: amusement had surprised her. So *that* was why the zebra lived so long in infant memory! And as a sidelight on the London Reds—really at least as entertaining as anything one picked up at Elissa's. . . .

With lips still curved she glanced towards the gate: he was still absorbed, she could easily get by. Directly before her, in a series of wide and winding sweeps, the Westover road descended to the Vale: there was a wind at her back if she wanted to take it. And then suddenly, inexplicably, her lips moved and the words formed themselves:

"Do you know Tolstoy's *War and Peace?*" asked Lesley of the Vicar.

Chapter Eight

I

With the first days of spring, like some busy little animal, Patrick began to dig. He dug squatting on his behind, patching with brown the seats of two pairs of knickers before Lesley observed and restrained him: but since it was beyond all others his preferred position, and since he must apparently dig or burst, she gave him an old square of carpet that was lying in the barn and made him carry it about like a Mohammedan his prayer-rug.

It was while he was thus engaged that he found the crocuses.

One was yellow and one was white, and they were growing far down the orchard at the foot of a pear-tree. Called out to wonder, Lesley emerged from behind *The Times* and picked her way distrustfully over the still-damp grass.

"They're crocuses, Pat," she said, one eye still on the Foreign News.

"Can I pick them?"

"I shouldn't. They'll only die in the house."

"Alec has them," said Pat. Alec was the eldest Pomfret.

"I think Alec's are in bowls," said Lesley.

"Can I have them in bowls?"

"No," said Lesley, "it's too late. And don't sit down on the wet grass, Pat; if you must kneel, get your mat."

It was still, for them, quite a long conversation; but he had lately grown far more communicative. This change Lesley attributed solely to the influence of the young Pomfrets, and never for one moment connected it with herself; but an impartial observer would possibly have hesitated. It was almost as though, in some way or other, she had become slightly less forbidding to the young. For the Pomfrets had begun to talk to her too. They told her what they had for dinner, and when they were going to have their hairs washed, and many other details of an increasingly intimate nature. And they also, sometimes indirectly, told her a good deal about Pat.

"He wishes his name was Frewen too, you know," a Pomfret child once observed casually.

The prettiness of the sentiment took Lesley aback. It sounded more like little Lord Fauntleroy than her stolid young Scot.

"But his own name is such a nice one!" she exclaimed.

"Not so nice as yours. Yours is *lovely*," said the Pomfret child enthusiastically. "It's almost like Bruin."

Lesley was struck by a sudden notion.

"Did Pat think of that too?"

"Oh, yes. For a long time, you know, he thought it *was* Bruin. Like Bobby Bruin the Bad Bear," said the Pomfret child. . . .

Such flights of imagination, however, were comparatively rare. By far his most outstanding trait was an extreme tenacity. Whatever he undertook—the digging of an earth-plot, the unknotting of a string—he carried through to completion. What he had not finished at bedtime, he returned to in the morning. In the matter of crocuses, though, he bided his time and returned in two days.

"Alec," he observed at breakfast, "says it isn't too late."

"Too late for what?"

"Crocuses," said Pat. 'You get a bowl, 'n fill it with fine earth, and you put the bulbs just underneath."

"Pat," said Lesley.

He stopped at once. She wasn't cross, like Mrs. Sprigg sometimes got, she was just . . . up there.

"I'm not going to have any bowls," said Lesley, "they're too much nuisance." She spoke purely by instinct, her previous experience of domestic horticulture being limited to the couple of window-boxes at Beverley Court. But her tone was final.

Patrick ate some more bread-and-butter and shifted his ground.

"If I had a penny, d'you know what I'd do?"

"No," said Lesley.

"I'd buy some nasturtium seeds."

Fully expecting to feel exasperated, Lesley drew up the paper and erected it into a screen; it was against her principles to be constantly scolding, especially at breakfast-time. But to her natural surprise, no irritation arose. Instead of annoying, Pat's wary and indefatigable hopefulness suddenly amused her. It was so very Scotch! With the flicker of sympathy, moreover, came a flicker of understanding. After all, what could be more natural? He had dug, now he wanted to sow. And moved by one of the oddest impulses of her life, Lesley took him down to the Post Office and spent a shilling on seeds.

They bought nasturtium, mignonette, sweet pea, sunflower, variegated candytuft, and the irresistible coryopsis.

II

The weather towards Easter was so exceptionally good that Lesley was forced to notice it. Her emotion, to be sure, was purely amateur: no passionate nature-worship suddenly filled her heart. She merely observed with appreciation that a series of clear sunny days had made everything green. Even the Walpoles' oak was coloured, and her own exhausted apple-trees, while the chestnuts in Pig Lane would have done credit to May. The air was warm and sweet, the grass in the orchard showed every blade brand-new: from the south side of the cottage, where Pat had planted his seeds, came the clean and definite odour of newly-dug earth. He had made the bed himself, with the help of the eldest Pomfret. Alec cut the sods, Pat dug, stoned and sifted: but Pat alone put in the seeds. It was a good big bed, and he put them all in together, sunflowers at the back, then sweet peas, descending through coryopsis and mignonette to the lowly but variegated candytuft.

"A fine sight it'll be!" said Mrs. Sprigg, when they told her what they had done. She had seen Pat bury his sunflowers a good six inches down; but she never went out to meet trouble.

The need to plant things at least temporarily assuaged, the need to feed things now took its place. He turned to live stock. The Walpole farm lay conveniently at hand, the Walpoles themselves offered no resistance, and for days together the orchard lay silent. It was almost like the sign-painter time, thought Lesley, the time when every-thing—how to put it?—when everything had seemed so much worse.

Seduced by the charm of solitude, she strolled idly between the trees and reflected on nothing in particular. Odd shreds and pieces floated through her mind: the sad case of Florrie Walpole, to which Florrie herself seemed so remarkably indifferent: Mrs. Sprigg's partiality for whist-drives: that extraordinary walk home with Mr. Pomfret, and its no less extraordinary culmination in Vicarage tea and toast. The oddest part of all, of course, being that she had actu-ally enjoyed herself. One day, in the distant future, she might even go again. Being so long cut off from civilisation had doubtless made her less critical, but she had also intelligence to realise that even at Elissa's Mr. Pomfret would have held his own. After two hours' conversation there was nothing Lesley could think of as being in the least likely to shock him. She had also discovered (though without for the moment regarding it as anything but an independent fact) that he was a great reader of Smollett.

Lost in these musings, she made a leisurely circuit of the orchard and at last came to a pause at the corner by Pig Lane. A great bough of chestnut swung down across the path, thrusting itself proudly upon her attention; and looking more closely Lesley saw that at the end of each long and upward-springing branchlet had sprouted either a clean white bud or a green and fawn tassel. Every miniature leaf was exquisitely and crisply pleated, the buds were like magnolia buds in their first week; and each most delicate line of tassel, bud, and branch contributed its part to the vigorous upward movement of the whole aspiring tree.

Involuntarily as a blackbird, Lesley sang.

III

The five children in the lane heard her and looked at each other. 'She's in a good temper!' the look said, and they hurried their steps. But even so the pace remained slower than usual, for the eldest were carrying between them a couple of February lambs; and by the time they reached the orchard gate Lesley had broken off her song and was walking back past the well, where, at the sight of the caravan, she came to a sudden halt.

"Look at the lambs, Frewen!" shouted Pat, clasping the nearest round the neck like an Infant St. John.

Lesley looked.

They had long legs, black noses, and were in fact just like the creatures she had seen photographed in *The Times* every February or March. Set down upon the grass they at once began to frisk, also in a very conventional manner, with much kicking up of their black legs and a tendency to come down in the middle of a jump. Without really seeing anything very funny in it, Lesley laughed.

The eldest Pomfret child at once took a step forward.

"If you don't want to have them, Miss Frewen," she said politely, "we're to take them back."

"Have them?" echoed Lesley, for the moment uncomprehending.

In spontaneous antiphon the children explained.

"Have them here, Miss Frewen, for a month, for Pat and us to look after. They have to be fed out of bottles, because their mother's dead, and Florrie Walpole has all the poultry, so she'd be only too glad. Pat's got the bottles."

"And they'll leave the milk every morning, with yours, Miss Frewen, so it won't cost anything, and they have to be fed five times a day—"

"Six—"

"Or else six, but we'll go back and make sure, and the milk has to be at blood heat, just a minute or so, and they can live in the shed, Miss Frewen, with netting over the door at night—"

"And they are not destructive like goats, Miss Frewen—"

"They don't dig up bulbs—"

"They get awfully affectionate—"

Lesley clasped her hands over her ears and retreated into the doorway. An inexplicable lightheartedness still possessed her, so that for the moment the inevitable nuisance of the thing seemed almost unimportant. Really they were rather charming! She said,

"If I let you—you'll have to look after them. The first time you don't I shall send them straight back."

They agreed passionately. They would have agreed to anything on earth: and scrutinising their five faces, Lesley saw that they all looked slightly startled, as though bliss had taken them by surprise.

And so indeed it had, for they never expected her to be so reasonable. With youthful adaptability, however, they adjusted themselves to the new and pleasing situation, jettisoning in the process a whole cargo of arguments. Nor were the lambs far behind in *nous* or *savoir faire:* without a moment's hesitation they frisked off through the orchard and displayed in the most natural manner possible their willingness to feel at home.

"They're not to come in the house, mind!" cried Lesley. "I won't have them. You understand, Pat?"

"Oh, *yes,*" said Pat radiantly. Always a little slower than the rest, his astonishment still lingered. But the excitement, the joys and fears of the afternoon, had quickened his spirits beyond their usual flow. Gratitude overwhelmed him, and seeing Lesley so near he flung himself at her knees and hugged them hard. It was all over in an instant, so that she scarcely realised what was happening; but when he had run off, she became aware of a curious silky sensation just fading from her palm. Instinctively she put up a hand to smooth her own smooth locks: they gave just the same feeling.

'Very odd!' thought Lesley. . . .

The rest of the afternoon was spent in christening the newcomers (rather arbitrarily, perhaps) with the names of Alice and John; in airing the tool-shed (which fortunately contained no more than an old spade or two and a broken mangle); and in constructing a detachable wire door from the remains of a Pomfret rabbit-hutch. Mrs. Sprigg, with her usual resource, also acquired a couple of sacks and a double armful of straw, under which she scurried up the lane like a mouse with a wheat-ear.

"I've never seen better lambs in my life," she said cordially. "That John'll turn out a proper champion."

Like Pat and the Pomfrets, she at once began calling them by name, and moreover displayed a most reassuring familiarity with their habits and requirements. Not all her observations, however, were equally welcome; it was she who first pointed out that in spite of all promises the last feed of the day must inevitably fall to Lesley. It was due at ten o'clock, and though the eldest Pomfret honourably proposed that he should slip nightly out of bed, the offer could scarcely be accepted.

"You'll soon get used to it, Miss Frewen," prophesied the old woman cheerfully. "Meself I like a breath of air before I go to bed, same as I like a bite o' cheese or something before I take me teeth out."

But Lesley listened unconvinced. Already she was a little regretting her impulse: and that night, in the pleasant fireside warmth, she regretted it even more.

IV

'Those blasted lambs,' thought Lesley, hearing the cuckoo slam his door.

The fire glowed, the clock ticked; she had never in her life felt less desire to move. A lamb, however, was obviously a highly perishable object: one which might easily be found dead in the morning; and for all Lesley's knowledge to the contrary such would be the fate of both Alice and John unless she now took them their milk.

With a final sigh of resentment she pushed back her chair, went into the kitchen, and there found both milk and bottles put ready by Mrs. Sprigg. Blood heat, they said—and what the hell was that? Mrs. Sprigg, earlier in the day, had simply dipped her finger after about a minute's heating: she said thermometers were too tricky. . . . Lesley waited about the same length of time, then filled the bottles and put in the rubber teats.

Outside it was so dark that she had to take a candle, sheltering it with her fingers against the soft fresh-smelling airs. In the crook of her arm the milk-bottles generated a faint warmth, almost as though she were carrying a child: it was impossible, so lighted and so burdened, to move un-gently.

And mind following body, her humour changed. Night, motion, errand, all combined to soothe her. From the little outhouse, black and ark-shaped among the apple-trees, a tiny cry now came to guide her, and over the half-door, quilted by the netting, two soft rough muzzles pressed up against her hand. Lesley bowed her head under the lintel and thrust a way in.

An importunate nose pushed gently under her elbow. It was Alice, with the ribbon. Lesley seated herself on an upturned box, the candle beside her, and offered the first bottle. At once John came nuzzling too, so that she had to hold him off with her free hand. His wool felt thick, springy, just touched with grease, but not unpleasant.

Alice was drinking in short steady pulls, never shifting for an instant her grip on the teat.

'Just like Pat,' thought Lesley.

Through the open door she could see the cottage, compact and dark and with a line of light showing under the rim of the barn thatch. It was the effect Toby or someone had likened to badly-joined scenery, but she was not just then thinking of him. The first lamb moved away; it was John feeding now, the lamb that was going to be a champion.

Mechanically Lesley tilted the milk to his needs. The atmosphere in the shed—of candlewax, old sacking, earth and growing wool—was making her sleepy. Rhythmic between her knees came the steady pull at the warm bottle: close above her head bent the shadowy curve of the roof. She felt quiet, protected: solaced of her troubles; acquiescent; assuaged.

PART III

Chapter One

I

The early summer opened eventfully. Half-way through May, Lesley dined with Sir Philip, and on the very same date Mr. Povey began trying to sell her his bird-bath.

"You *want* a bird-bath, with an orchard," explained Mr. Povey, waylaying her one morning outside the Three Pigeons. "It's just where the birds come. Once you get 'em into the habit, they dabble about all day. Your little boy 'ud like that, Miss Frewen."

"Thank you, but they dabble about already," Lesley told him, "in an old seed-pan."

He looked at her with pity.

"A seed-pan?" said Mr. Povey. "A *seed*-pan? You come in here, Miss Frewen." He moved majestically down the path; and fascinated as always by the sheer spread of his personality—the whale-like form and small hypnotic eye—Lesley too turned aside and followed him into the yard.

"Look there," said Mr. Povey.

With unwilling astonishment, Lesley looked. It was a piece 'of importance,' as the collectors say. Birds could have bathed in it, and babies as well. The nucleus of the thing was a shallow rectangular trough, very much resembling a small kitchen sink, but enriched

here and there with a good deal of fancy beading. It was supported
at one end by a rock, at the other by a Bacchante: but as though to
preserve the balance of interest, the rock was covered with frogs.
There were also frogs along the rim of the trough, and one frog,
rather unfairly, at the Bacchante's feet, the whole being executed,
with unbelievable persistence, in some sort of Aberdeen granite.

"Striking, isn't it?" said Mr. Povey.

Lesley nodded. She had a good critical vocabulary, but not good
enough for that.

"It would look nice," he continued thoughtfully, "over against
your big pear-tree. It would look natural."

Apprehension restored her. She seized on the first objection that
came to hand.

"It's too big. . . ."

"*Just* what I say. There aren't many places round here," conceded
Mr. Povey, "where it *would* look natural. It's too big, and too artistic.
That's why I sh'd like to see it in yours." He paused, impressively.
"And *because* I sh'd like to see it, Miss Frewen—you can have it for
six-pound-ten."

Lesley moved hastily towards the gate. She was aware how
swiftly, how unexpectedly, in the village of High Westover, things
could happen to one. Mrs. Sprigg, for example, and bacon for breakfast, to say nothing of two lambs who for the last month had been the
virtual occupiers of the White Cottage. (The weather had changed,
during their visit, from a forward spring to a belated winter, so that
they spent most of their time gambolling uncontrollably before the
sitting-room fire. It meant removing most of the furniture and taking up the carpet: but as Pat pointed out, the lambs did splendidly.)

"Thank you," said Lesley, "but I couldn't *possibly* afford it."

Mr. Povey waved his hand.

"Puttin' money in a thing like that," he explained, "isn't spen-
din' it, Mis Frewen, it's investing it. A thing like that, why you could
always get your price back, and maybe a bit over. There's a lot of
work in it, Miss Frewen."

Lesley backed a step farther.

"I'm sure there is, Mr. Povey, but I'm afraid I haven't got time to examine it." She was now at the outer gate and could see up and down the road: if only Mrs. Sprigg would pass by, or Pat, or the Vicar! And at that very moment, like an answer to prayer, the Post Office door opened and Mrs. Pomfret came out.

"*There's* Mrs. Pomfret!" cried Lesley: and with the alacrity of a favourite Girl Guide she pushed open the gate and ran across the yard.

Mrs. Pomfret too was pleased at the encounter: there was a little hitch, a little alteration, in the evening's plans. The maid at the Vicarage—one of the Coxes, not the village Coxes, but the Aylesbury Coxes—was showing symptoms of feverishness: it might be nothing, but again it might not: and if at half-past seven the issue was still undecided, would Miss Frewen very much mind going alone with the Vicar?

"Not in the least," agreed Miss Frewen, quite calmly. "But I'm sorry you're so doubtful."

"Oh, I'm sorry too," said Mrs. Pomfret, with a sigh. "It's always such lovely food. When Henry and I go by ourselves he and Sir Philip do all the talking and I just tuck in." She sighed again. "But you'll be quite all right with Henry, my dear, and he'll come and fetch you in Sir Philip's car."

Lesley asked what time.

"Eight o'clock. I shouldn't like my own meal so late, of course, but it does give you a chance to get up an appetite. What are you doing about Pat?"

"Mrs. Sprigg's coming in again from half-past seven," said Lesley. "It's really her whist-drive night, but fortunately they altered the date."

The Vicar's wife nodded.

"Mrs. Povey's new dress wasn't finished, because Milly Cox, who was making it—the sister of my girl, you know—is down with sore throat; and that's really the reason I'm staying at home to-night," explained Mrs. Pomfret allusively. They had now reached the turning in Pig Lane, where her path branched to the right; but still she lingered a moment as though there was something on her mind. And so indeed there was: nothing less, in fact, than a Social Hint, which for the last ten minutes had been causing her considerable embarrassment. She said,

"Oh, by the way, Miss Frewen—I don't know if Henry told you—but Sir Philip always dresses. For dinner, you know."

"Jacket or tails?" said Lesley.

"Oh . . . dinner jacket, my dear. But of course you needn't put on anything really *low*. I always wear my black lace, and that's got sort of sleeves."

Lesley thanked her politely; and continuing up Pig Lane put out in readiness the backless white moiré she had worn new to Elissa's.

II

Dressing that night in the tiny bedroom, she was assailed by memories. For it was almost exactly a year since that gown had last seen the light: a year which—now one came to think of it—had somehow passed with remarkable swiftness. 'And I've done nothing,' thought Lesley, rubbing at her nails; 'I haven't even been up to Town!' She looked again towards the bed. Like her shoes and her powder-box—like her own nails reddening under the stain—those gleaming yards of silk seemed part of a previous and dreamlike existence. That she had once worn such garments almost nightly was of course an established fact; but so also, in some households, is the angelic plumage of the unborn babe.

Lesley slipped off the dressing-gown and reached for her feathers. Fine and gleaming still—though with certainly no hint of the cherubic swansdown! With extreme precaution she dropped the stiff white folds over her head, felt the narrow shoulder-straps settle snugly in place, and so stood gazing a moment in the ill-lit glass. The

dress still fitted. Then she sat down again to look more closely. The
dress still fitted; but was there not, at the same time, a slight—how
to put it?—a slight falling off from perfection? The dress still fitted: but was that all? With a wrinkle between her unplucked brows
Lesley leaned closer. It was so long since she had really sat down
before a mirror that the image therein was almost unfamiliar—the
likeness of a brown-skinned woman with hair very like her own, but
longer and thicker, and set in less formal waves. It was an illusion,
no doubt, or something to do with the glass; for surely that smooth
oval was broader and softer than she remembered it? Rounder in
the cheeks, fuller in the lower lip?

'I shall have to pull myself together,' thought Lesley; and shrug-
ging her shoulders was aware of a peculiar sensation—night air on
the small of the back. She thought, 'No use powdering in patches:
better leave it!' There was Mrs. Sprigg down below: but rather a fresh
falling off from elegance than those gnarled and roughened hands,
catching, perhaps, in the grain of the silk. . . .

A sudden and natural pang changed the current of her thought.
Eight o'clock—as Mrs. Pomfret remarked, one had time to raise an
appetite! Lesley picked up her cloak, looked out of the window: and
a second or two later saw a very old Rolls at the end of Pig Lane.

III

If of her effect on the Vicar Lesley had very little idea, of her effect
on Sir Philip there was no possible doubt.

"You've been on the stage, I believe?" he said hopefully, as they
went in to dinner. The question was underlined by a slight but
definite pressure of her arm: and looking down from an extra two
inches Lesley saw a pair of light and goatish eyes glinting under
their lids. . . . Extraordinary eyes, in colour, even to the whites, a
clear pale agate, and in shape like the narrow slits of a paper mask:
very odd eyes indeed for a retired J.P. with antiquarian leanings. . . .

"No," said Lesley, "I'm afraid not: but I know quite a lot of dirty stories about actresses."

Sir Philip at once looked extremely alert.

"Not now," he said, "after dinner. My butler has a thoroughly salacious mind, and it would only distract him."

"What about yours, Vicar?" asked Lesley over her shoulder.

"Pomfret! My dear young lady, he needs nothing but Smollett and the Bible.—We dine, you see, by candlelight," said Sir Philip; "it belongs to the same period and spares all the blushes."

Taking her seat before a bowl of tulips, Lesley felt rather than observed, and with a deep and sensuous pleasure, the glowing harmonies of Sir Philip's table. The wood was walnut, old and luminous as the sherry in her glass: between the two in tone came the pink of the tulip petals, lustred yet soft above pale bright silver: while the highest note of all, the clean and shining glass, shone subdued by candlelight to an accordant glow. Lesley lifted her spoon, and was oddly surprised by the scarlet of her finger-nails.

'That stuff—usen't it to go darker?' she thought suddenly; and with a faint uneasiness saw that Sir Philip's glance was following her own.

"For what we are about to receive," said the Vicar abruptly, "thank God. The 'we,' Kerr, refers to Miss Frewen and myself: I haven't insulted you." He turned to Lesley, surprised at her soup. "Sir Philip won't thank anyone but his cook and his tradespeople—about two dozen all told. I go straight to the source. If ever I forget and take him with me, it offends his principles."

"What about mine?" asked Lesley.

"Oh, you don't care one way or the other," explained the Vicar quite correctly, "and you're nice enough to humour my weakness. The first time Miss Frewen ever saw me, Kerr, she gave me twelve cigarettes—all good ones."

Sir Philip looked at her again: 'Cigarettes,' the look seemed to say, 'Cigarettes, egad!' And again Lesley experienced that curious emotion. It was almost like nervousness; yet to feel nervous at a dinner-party—a dinner-party of two old men—the thing was absurd! But absurd or not, the sensation persisted: it even increased: and as a matter of fact, it was not absurd at all.

For Sir Philip was judging her—had indeed already done so—by a standard which was rapidly becoming obsolete, and which he himself had preserved only through the accident of circumstance. The outbreak of War found him in the late forties, and therefore too old, by the optimistic standards of 1914, for anything more active than quill-driving in the War Office. There he stayed five weeks, taking real pains with a naturally deplorable handwriting. At the beginning of the sixth week, however, he was missing from his desk; no questions were asked and he was next heard of in Greece. It was a country he knew well, there was very little office-work, and in Greece he remained until a year after the Armistice. The change from pre-war to post-war England was thus unsoftened, for Sir Philip, by any period of transition; returning home in 1919 he took one look at London, disliked it exceedingly, and went straight down to High Westover. There were changes even there, but not so many; in his own house and garden none at all. With the avowed intention of staying there till he died Sir Philip modernised his kitchens (retaining of course the coal fire) and made two or three trips to Town to suit himself with a cook. That done, he kept his word and strayed no more from his garden, his library, and his excellent cellar; consorting chiefly with the Vicar, eating seriously but with discretion, and having no more idea of the modern young woman than of the lost poems of Sappho, or the other side of the moon. Lesley Frewen was the first of the genus that had ever come his way; but far from being at a loss, he knew exactly what to make of her. By the standards of 1913, there was indeed no possible room for doubt: she lived alone, had an unexplained child; painted her face, dressed like an actress, smoked cigarettes and was free with her tongue. And very cautiously, under the walnut, Sir Philip put out his foot and touched her shoe.

Lesley did not even notice him. The food was good, the wine excellent, but she did not notice them either. She was too troubled.

And the thing that troubled her was a growing conviction, that her host, having been promised a dirty story, would expect to have one.

He kept looking at her with a sort of quiet anticipation, lending only half an ear, she felt sure, to the Vicar's really amusing remarks. It was rather disconcerting: as though after the conventional defence of promiscuity all the men present should invite one to bed.... And with a sudden flicker of pure dismay Lesley wondered what would have been the result if, in that hasty choice of retorts, it *had* been promiscuity, and not the actress, that her tongue laid hold of. '*No, not on the stage, Sir Philip; but I quite often let men make love to me. . . .*' The phrase slipped ready into her mind: and what would her host have done then?

'Sent a maid up with a warming-pan,' thought Lesley.

Still paying lip-service to the conversation, she tried with all her might to remember something really gross. And not only gross but lengthy, circumstantial, and if possible connected with the stage: for in Sir Philip's eyes—and as Lesley was too intelligent not to realise— she had, by that first casual piece of brightness, put herself definitely into the smoking-room: where she could fancy him urgent as Shylock and insatiable as the sea.

The wine passed, the Vicar talked, and Lesley racked her brains: only to discover, with no little dismay, that the conversation at Elissa's must have been a good deal purer than anyone intended. With the coming of the dessert her discomfort grew: it was like the last few minutes before a viva, in which the unprepared student feels his palms clammy with horror. For Lesley, though she had laughed at dirty stories for years, had never made a habit of passing them on: holding the retail of smut, like the conducting of orchestras, to be an almost purely masculine gift. The principle was of course an æsthetic, not a moral one: but the results were just as unfortunate.

"Coffee in the library, I think," said Sir Philip.

With a sinking of the heart Lesley rose from her chair and obediently traversed the long wide corridor. As never in life before her spirit yearned and thirsted after the sanctuary of drawing-rooms:

but there was no escape. Her white moiré fishtail swished over the carpet, her smooth white back gleamed in a succession of dim round mirrors: at the door of the examination-chamber a silver coffee-tray exactly preceded them. For the chamber itself, it was less aggressively masculine than her fancy had painted; being many-windowed, white-panelled, and lit and coloured by a sumptuous painting of a woman in evening dress.

"Early Sargent," murmured the Vicar, "the late Lady Kerr."

Lesley looked curiously at the woman who should have been her hostess. Superb, refulgent, tiny head above a stately bosom—Sargent and the Edwardians both at their best. One hand toying with her pearls, the other half-hidden in a billow of amber silk: pearls again in the auburn hair, pearls again at the ears. What had happened to them all, wondered Lesley?

"The only coffee fit to drink," said Sir Philip suddenly, "is made by worthless nations. Turks, Arabs, Greeks, Armenians—all make excellent coffee."

"I like Turks," said the Vicar thoughtfully.

"Where did you meet any?"

"At Gallipoli. Though they didn't have time to make much coffee. And what about the French?"

"They can't make coffee," returned Sir Philip simply.

The Vicar turned to Lesley with a gesture of mute appeal; and a little piqued nevertheless at not being offered Arabia (to which country she had once had serious thoughts of going), she took up his cudgels.

"But surely the coffee on the boat-train is almost the last reason for crossing by sea? It tastes of a new civilisation."

"*Anything* drunk on dry land, immediately after a channel cross-ing, tastes like a new civilisation," said Sir Philip. "Have you ever drunk greasy cocoa immediately after a shipwreck?"

Lesley was forced to confess that she had not.

"That tastes like a new heaven and a new earth. A cigarette, Miss Frewen?"

Automatically she accepted it: and was at once aware of Sir Philip's happy interest now focused on her long jade holder. . . .

"Extraordinary," said Lesley (to whom the subject appeared as innocuous as any they were likely to reach), "the difference between cocoa and chocolate. The real chocolate, frothed—there's nothing more delicious. Damnably fattening, of course, but delicious all the same."

"It's a question of milk," observed the Vicar, almost as though divining her thought. "Most common of household cocoa is made with water. Now chocolate—"

Sir Philip looked up.

"Chocolate? My dear fellow, there's only one place where they can make chocolate, and that's Paris. I once, in the days before you reformed me, used to know a young lady there who made probably the best chocolate in the whole world. One would even get out of bed for it. She was a dancer at the Opéra. . . ."

He paused: he offered the opening. Lesle looked at her slipper, and said,

"Opera—I wonder if we shall ever acclimatise it? At present it seems to be one of the few luxuries that the English are genuinely eager to give up."

"Exactly," said the Vicar. "We're a practical and a moral race. And quite a large section of the community would still like to see a 'Danger' sign outside all playhouse doors."

Sir Philip's eyes glinted.

"Speaking of road signs," he said, "this young woman I was telling you about—she hit on a most ingenious use for them. Her bedroom had two doors, you see, and there was a sign over each. One came from outside a National School, the other from outside a hospital. The first said—"

"God bless my soul!" exclaimed the Vicar, "it's ten o'clock! My dear Kerr, I hate to break up the party, but I promised my wife to be home in good time." He rose: his eye sought Lesley's: but Sir Philip was too quick.

"Well, if you must, you must," said Sir Philip, with every appearance of resignation. "Miss Frewen and I will endeavour to console each other. . . ."

His eye glinted again, and Lesley at once stood up. Now that the Vicar was actually going, her one dominant emotion, stronger than pride, dignity or bravado, was the simple dread of being left behind. She must go too, she said, and relieve Mrs. Sprigg; nor could Sir Philip find blandishments wherewith to shake her. Like the properest Miss-in-her-teens, Lesley smiled and said nothing: and keeping extremely close to the Vicar, fought a rearguard action out.

IV

As the car stopped at the gate the door of the cottage opened and let out a long beam of light for Lesley to see by. Mrs. Sprigg had been listening for her, and there was a plate of biscuits on the sitting-room table.

"I just put them out in case," she explained, "but maybe you won't need 'em, not after the Hall. Did you get a good dinner, Miss Frewen?"

"Very," Lesley told her, advancing into the warmth. "I won't eat anything, but you have one yourself, Mrs. Sprigg."

The old woman shook her head.

"Oh, I won't neither, thanks, I've just taken me teeth out." She was looking, indeed, about a hundred years old; but her powers of speech were quite unaffected, and after a moment or two's silence—

"I seen old Povey trying to sell you 'is bird-bath," she observed conversationally. "I was right next door at the Coxes, lookin' out of their window. But don't you have it, Miss Frewen, it's not worth the money."

"I'm not going to," said Lesley, with a suppressed shudder. "Where on earth did he get it?"

"At a house over to Tring, nigh on three years back. It was the last day of the sale, and old Povey 'e bought 'er for fifteen shillings.

Seems a lot for the money, don't it? But they couldn't get rid of 'er nohow, d'you see; and now 'e can't get rid of 'er neither," said Mrs. Sprigg relishingly.

She picked up her hat and began skewering it on with the two long hat-pins which were also employed, as need arose, for probing the insides of cakes. Miss Frewen too bestirred herself, drew back the curtains, opened a window: she felt unusually tired, as though after prolonged mental effort. Mrs. Sprigg scuttled off home, the fire was out: but still Lesley lingered, glancing round the room with more than usually friendly eyes. It was small, ugly, inadequate, but it was also safe.

It wasn't exactly a drawing-room, but at least there were no spittoons.

Chapter Two

I

Even in the first few days at Yellow House Lesley had never actually purchased a blue suede album with 'What Baby Says' in repoussé-work; and this was fortunate, for in all the years she was to know him young Patrick Craigie never said anything in the least worth repeating about either God or the fairies.

He was an ordinary child.

He would probably have to go into the Police.

In the meantime, however, they were getting on quite well, and about the middle of the month an incident occurred which finally dissipated the last of their constraint. It arose, superficially at least, out of the simple human fact—which Lesley had nevertheless taken about six months to assimilate—that children really do need something to eat in the middle of the morning. A glass of milk, with two plain biscuits, was accordingly instituted for the hour of eleven; and the biscuits were Lincoln Creams, a brand chanced on by hazard, but proving so much to Pat's taste that he ever after resisted all talk of change. A natural conservative, he presumably saw no need to strive after the better when the good lay already at hand.

On the fifteenth of June, however, the tin was bare, the grocer's van overdue, and eleven o'clock striking: so Lesley cut instead a piece of currant cake and bore glass and plate into the orchard. There was no Patrick in sight, and setting them on the wooden table she sat down herself to finish the paper.

When she glanced up again, Patrick was there. He stood staring silently at the plate, his hands in his pockets, and on his usually placid face an expression of extreme stubbornness. He was holding it, Lesley felt, until she looked and saw him.

"Where are my biscuits?" asked Patrick.

"They haven't come yet," Lesley answered calmly, "so you've a piece of cake instead. Drink your milk, Pat."

He looked at her sulkily, but still without any overt sign that he had definitely stopped being good and was now going to be bad.

"I don't want cake. I want biscuits."

"I'm afraid you can't have them," said Lesley.

"Then I don't want anything," said Pat.

Lesley picked up her paper again. It was the first time in all their acquaintance that he had ever really been naughty; and she hoped to goodness she would be able to deal with him. She said quietly,

"You needn't eat the cake, but you must drink your milk. At once, please, Pat."

Slowly, very slowly indeed, he began to walk away. Lesley lowered the paper.

"Pat!"

He stopped. ('Thank God for that!' thought Lesley.)

"Drink your milk at once, please."

With a quite disproportionate relief she saw him stretch out his hand to the table. He picked up the glass, advanced it half-way to his lips: then with a sudden change of motion emptied it on the grass.

The next instant he was over Lesley's knee being soundly spanked with the flat of the hand.

How exactly it happened she could never afterwards make out; but for a lifelong opposer of corporal punishment her reactions must have been in surprisingly good condition. Nor did she, the spanking over, feel in any way brutalised: with Patrick, of course, it was harder to tell, for he merely gave one good loud bellow and then went off over the fence to play again with the Walpole pigs. It seemed highly probable, in fact, that should necessity arise she would spank him again; and with this knowledge in both their minds the relations between them took on a new ease. They knew exactly where they stood with each other, and got on a good deal better in consequence.

II

A day or two later, Lesley went over to Aylesbury and bought new curtains. She acted on pure impulse; had she stayed to consider, the curtains would not have been bought. For the original and hideous rep had been retained for two definite reasons: firstly, because it was amusing, and secondly, because the whole outfit—cottage, curtains and all—was a mere temporary perching-place on which it would be foolish to spend money. Both these reasons still held good, though time had certainly elapsed since Lesley laughed aloud while opening the windows; but indeed she made not the slightest attempt to question their validity. The curtains remained established, so to speak, as adequate and amusing; she merely felt, as she sat over her coffee, that she could no longer stand the sight of them.

"I'm going into Aylesbury, Mrs. Sprigg," called Lesley through the hatch: "which is the best draper's?"

"Alfred Walpole, by the 'bus stop," Mrs. Sprigg called back; and before Alfred Walpole's chintz counter, about thirty minutes later, Lesley stood staring hopelessly at a bunch of pale-pink rosebuds on a Cambridge blue ground. It was all very difficult.

There was only one design that at all appealed to her, a broad diagonal stripe in black, white and red, which Mr. Walpole (though this of course Lesley did not know) had rashly stocked for the fancy-dress season and then been unable to get rid of. She could have had it, moreover, for sixpence ha'penny a yard; but a natural integrity of taste restrained her. At Toby's Yellow House, yes; in a genuine cottage in the actual country, no; the clash of styles would have been almost audible. Deliberately shifting her viewpoint, therefore, Lesley turned back to the pile of her first weeding-out—the pile of the frankly pretty; and from it selected, not without a certain perverse humour, the very prettiest of all. It had a pattern of blue and pink delphiniums.

"Ah, you'll like *that*," said Mr. Walpole approvingly. "I've got it up myself in my own drawing-room."

Lesley opened her mouth to countermand the purchase: but too late, for he had started to cut. As a sort of antiseptic, however, she bought a copy of the *Tatler* and a bottle of Cointreau, which latter, in her passage down the 'bus, she unfortunately dropped plump into the lap of Florrie Walpole.

"I'll take that for you, Miss Frewen," said Florrie obligingly; and since she had already got it Lesley was reluctantly obliged to sit down beside her. Florrie Walpole, with her masses of red hair, her beautiful, slightly dirty skin, was overwhelming enough at the best of times: in her present state of—of fecundity, it was like sitting next to a Venus Genetrix.

"I see you been to old Alfred's," she remarked, indicating Lesley's parcel. "I hate that nasty thin paper 'e uses, but 'What's the good?' 'e says, 'they only throw it away.'"

For the first time Lesley connected the names.

"Is he a relation of yours?"

"Rather! 'E's my father's cousin. 'E's offered me a job in the shop, too, but of course I can't just now take it." She broke off rather delicately, and changed the subject. "What sort of stuff you been getting, Miss Frewen? Chintz?" Lesley nodded. "Ah! Everyone goes to Alfred for chintz, 'e gets such lovely designs. Which one did you take?"

"Pink and blue delphiniums," said Lesley.

"Why, I believe that's what Alfred 'as in 'is own drawing-room!" exclaimed Florrie. "Pretty, ain't it?"

"Very," said Lesley, unfurling her *Tatler*. "That's why I bought it."

"The Walpoles 'ave got theirs with a plain border," proceeded Florrie. "But then of course it was all done in the shop, so you don't wonder. Mrs. Walpole she wants chair-covers as well, but the old man's too mean. You going to make it up yourself, Miss Frewen?"

Lesley hesitated. Curtains—curtains meant a sewing-machine: or at any rate needles and scissors, tape-measures and pins, all the impossible set-out of the home-dressmaker. . . .

"*Because*," said Florrie helpfully, "if you *should* want Milly Cox, she'll be over at our place this very afternoon."

"Milly Cox?" repeated Lesley, playing for time. "Isn't that the sister of Mrs. Pomfret's maid?"

"That's right, Miss Frewen, but it wasn't sore throat really, not the bad kind. If it *was*," said Florrie earnestly, "I wouldn't make the suggestion, not with your little boy there. But you'd find her satisfactory, that I do know. She makes for Mrs. Povey."

Lesley closed her paper again and prepared to employ, through the serviceable Miss Walpole, the efficient Miss Cox. The conversation lasted all the way to Westover, where, seeing her companion turn towards the road, Lesley at once announced her intention of cutting across fields. It was the longer way round, but she said she needed exercise.

("I'd come with you myself," said Florrie, "if it wasn't for the stiles. . . .")

Once out of sight of the road, however, Lesley sat down under a tree, disposed of her parcels, and opened the *Tatler:* where the first thing that met her eye was a photograph of Elissa. '*Seen at Ascot*,' she was captioned; '*Another of the many striking toilettes.*' There were seven on that page alone, but Elissa's was easily the best. Long, exquisitely-moulded, dead-white piqué—(Was it piqué? Or something else, stiffened?) tiny black-and-white tippet, long black gloves; hat out of a French Noah's Ark. And under that hat, so perfect that it must have been made up specially for snap-shots, Elissa's profile at its most successful angle.

For perhaps five minutes, while the cows grazed all about, Lesley's eyes took their fill of elegance. Then without looking further she put the pages together again and collected her parcels. It was a quarter to one, nearly time for dinner; and as she continued her path she thought how there was at least this to be said for landscape, that it didn't continually reflect the figure after the manner of shop-windows.

III

Late that same night, in obedience to the natural law of coincidence, Elissa telephoned. The time she chose was shortly before twelve, so that both Lesley and Pat were awakened out of their sleep.

"Lesley darling"—high and shrill as ever, against a background of dance music, Elissa's voice floated cajoling over the wire—"Lesley darling, it's just occurred to me—could Natasha come and stay with you while she's having a baby?"

"No, she couldn't," replied Lesley, with the uninhibited candour of the imperfectly awake.

"But, darling, why not? Would it shock the village?"

Herself only recently inured to the everyday conversation of Mrs. Sprigg, Lesley was forced to admit that it would not.

"But there's no room, my dear, and she'd have nothing to do. Why can't she have it in Town?"

"Oh, no actual reason," replied Elissa vaguely. There was a short pause, rhythmic with far-off saxophones. "She's very amusing, you know."

"It was sweet of you to think of me," said Lesley appreciatively. "Aren't they playing that Tango too fast?" And her feet being by this time unpleasantly cold, she hung up the receiver and went back to bed.

Chapter Three

I

Inevitably, Patrick acquired a dog.

Its name was Pincher, and he acquired it by sheer determination. For a dog was one of the things Lesley had consistently set her face against, and she did not attempt to conceal her sentiments when Pat and the Pomfrets returned one afternoon with what they confidently alleged would soon be a thoroughbred Airedale. But theirs was the eye of faith, for they had found him in the road and he had at once licked all their hands; to the eye of reason he was a mangy, carrot-coloured, six-months mongrel: flea-bitten, pugnacious, remarkably loud-voiced. Said Lesley from the doorway:

"Put that dog outside, Pat, and come and wash your hands."

And immediately, from the expression on his face, she knew there was going to be trouble.

"But, Frewen—"

"Outside, Pat. I've said before you can't have a dog, and you shouldn't have brought it."

There was a long, horrified pause. The children looked at each other, faith, hope and charity tottering under the blow. '*But over the lambs,*' that look seemed to say, '*she was quite reasonable!*' And Lesley, interpreting, consolidated her position.

"Outside, Pat."

"But he'll die!" cried all the children together.

Acutely conscious that she was about to be blackmailed, Lesley advanced a step from the doorway to take matters into her own hands. Pat shifted his grip from the pseudo-lead to the handkerchiefs round the animal's neck. Behind him the children seemed to close their ranks.

"Let go, Pat," said Lesley.

And then, looking down from her superior and adult height, she saw that he was in agony. There were no tears, but his face was somehow twisted and wrenched, as though a mask should try to express more than its designer intended. Lesley thought, 'It's no good. You can't force a child to turn out a starving animal. It's wicked;' and the adjective, so long a stranger to her mind, fell so naturally into place that she hardly noticed it.

"Very well, then," said Lesley, "you may get it some scraps from Mrs. Sprigg, and then you must put it out." She kept her eyes fixed on Pat's face; all at once it was round and childish again. The device had worked, then. He would feed and fondle the creature, see it go on its way relieved, and so leave his mind free to forget all about it.

But the five children exchanged glances. *They* knew, and the dog knew, that it was the thin end of the wedge.

II

In the morning the dog was still there; and for the next two days the blackmail continued. Not a word was uttered, not a tear wept: but like a brooding thunderstorm the sorrows of Pincher filled the air. He was not on the premises, for in obedience to her edict he had been ruthlessly put out: but Lesley had a strong suspicion that he was just on the other side of the fence. There was a disused woodshed of Mr. Walpole's, backing on to the cottage tool-house, which had suddenly begun to exert a magnet-like influence: and Pat, for the first time in his life, developed the extraordinarily messy habit of concealing food about his person.

"If you haven't finished, don't ask to get down," said Lesley, the second time she saw him.

"I have finished," said Pat, uneasily clasping the jersey over his stomach.

"Then don't take food away with you. It's rude and greedy," said Lesley, on whom the didactic was now beginning to sit quite naturally.

"I'm not," said Pat.

It was quite true; he *wasn't* greedy: but without admitting the existence of Pincher (at present still a sort of open diplomatic secret) the injustice could hardly be remedied. The situation, in fact—the ridiculous, childish situation—was rapidly becoming impossible; and seated that morning at her writing-table Lesley suddenly and fantastically wondered whether she had at last stumbled on the secret of that brooding Russian melancholy which has so long puzzled the Anglo-Saxon. Were the children of the Treplevs, the Voynitskys, the Karamozovs, all being denied a dog? Lesley looked out of the window. They were all there, Pat and the four Pomfrets, grouped in attitudes of listless despair under the biggest apple-tree. The strength of the June sun was like a personal gift, something undeserved and lavish from a bachelor uncle: beneath it the backs of their necks were warm but bowed.

Unable to bear it a moment longer, Lesley picked up her hat and went out for a walk. She wanted a long period of solitude in which to examine and reaffirm her already considered position; but in this she was not indulged, for hardly had she left Pig Lane than her way was effectually barred by the figure of Mr. Povey leaning thoughtfully on a gate.

"Warm, ain't it?" said Mr. Povey.

Lesley agreed. The dog-days!

"But not," said Mr. Povey, "close."

She agreed again. Looking inquiringly towards the gate, she added that however hot, the weather was probably not stormy.

"Ah! you're right there," said Mr. Povey, making no attempt to move. "*You* never had a storm here, not a really bad one. They get inside the hills, d'you see, and they can't get out. Just go round and round. My wife she gets all 'ysterical." He slightly shifted his position. "Now, about that bird-bath, Miss Frewen—"

"I've decided not to have it," said Lesley quickly.

"You haven't thought what it would look like, I s'pose, picked out in green?"

Lesley admitted that she had not.

"Well, I have," said Mr. Povey. "I've an eye for these things, and I can tell you, Miss Frewen, that it would look very natty."

With a tremor of apprehension she braced herself to resist.

"But I don't think—"

"Wait," said Mr. Povey. Extending his right forefinger he described an airy circle. "Just the beading round the rim, d'you see, and the bodies of the frogs, and the vine-leaves in 'er air. A piece like that in London, Miss Frewen, would cost you a ten-pound note."

"You couldn't *get* it in London," said Lesley. She had just remembered a perfectly genuine reason for leaving him at once and returning to the cottage. It was the day for going to Aylesbury, and Mrs. Pomfret would be calling for her. . . .

"And there's another thing I've thought of," said Mr. Povey, "it's getting on to be summer. Summer and autumn. . . . And after autumn you get the winter. And in the winter time what've you got, in a garden like yours? You got nothing at all, Miss Frewen."

The dying fall of his rhetoric affected her in spite of herself.

"I don't suppose I have," admitted Lesley weakly.

"Whereas with a nice piece of statuary," continued Mr. Povey, pressing home his advantage, "you'd have something to look at—something to fill the eye as you might say—the whole year round. And you can have it, Miss Frewen, for six-pound-five."

"Thank you very much," said Lesley, "I'll think it over. Only just now, Mr. Povey, I've got to hurry home."

He looked at her reproachfully, for he had just been getting into his stride. But Lesley had no illusions: it was a choice, and she knew it, between buying the bird-bath and taking to flight. She took to flight. She ran all the way back to the cottage (she quite often ran, nowadays) and entered by the kitchen door. Mrs. Sprigg was not there, but on the flap by the door stood a plate of freshly-chopped scraps suitable to a puppy six or eight months old.

With a feeling of being surrounded by secret and hostile forces, Lesley returned to her writing-desk and faced the situation. It was an extremely simple one. The animal Pincher, however long she might continue to disown him, was in fact already a member of the household: in which case the sooner they got him into carbolic the better for all concerned.

III

"You're perfectly right, my dear," said Mrs. Pomfret, observing this last item at the bottom of Lesley's shopping list. "People say dogs don't need washing, but they do when they're in the state your animal is." She looked about her, while Lesley put on her hat, and thought that the whole room seemed somehow brighter. There were new curtains!

"You've got the same stuff as the Alfred Walpoles!" exclaimed Mrs. Pomfret. "How nice it looks."

"And unlike Mrs. Alfred, I can have a chair-cover as well," said Lesley. "I bought four yards too much."

"My dear! But chintz always comes in useful. . . . Why can't Mrs. Alfred have them?"

"Because her husband's too mean," said Lesley.

Gathering basket, list and bag, she followed Mrs. Pomfret out. The Aylesbury 'bus stopped on the main road, a bare quarter-mile or so beyond High Westover proper, but in the early days of her taking it Lesley used to double the distance by going across the fields.

Mrs. Pomfret, however, automatically turned down Pig Lane; and walking through the village beside her Lesley suddenly realised that she no longer minded doing so. The thought was an odd one, and she completed it aloud.

"Do you know," said Lesley, "for months and months I used to avoid coming to the Post Office, because I fancied people looked at me. Just people in the street, you know. They were probably thinking exclusively about the crops, but somehow I always felt they were . . . hostile." She glanced sideways at her companion, fully prepared for amused astonishment; but Mrs. Pomfret, though perfectly cheerful, was not in the least surprised.

"But, my dear, they were hostile!" she exclaimed. "You got all your things from Town. Oh, I know it all evens up in the Balance of Trade, but here they can't see it. Going to Aylesbury is all right, because they all know each other, and half of them are related: the big draper there, for instance—Walpole, where you got your curtains—is a cousin of old Horace's."

"I know," said Lesley. "He offered Florrie a job there, but now of course it's no good."

Mrs. Pomfret sighed.

"Oh, dear! I do hope it won't mean more unpleasantness. Henry always christens them, you see, just like—like ordinary children, and then half the other mothers lie in wait for me and complain."

"I hope you pitch into them," said Lesley indignantly.

"Oh, no, my dear, it's very natural. They don't think it's fair, you see, when they've been through all the trouble of getting married, and putting up with their husbands, and slaving day and night—"

"—Keeping themselves respectable, in fact," said Lesley.

"Exactly, my dear—they don't feel it's fair. Like the parable of the Prodigal Son," added Mrs. Pomfret vaguely. "Henry never *can* make them see it. Martha and Mary, too—that's another difficult one. But you mustn't think they're brutes, Miss Frewen, because they're not. They're just a little jealous of their rights. It won't make a scrap of difference to the child really, or to Florrie either. Why, look at you and Pat—"

Her voice suddenly ceased: her earnestness had run away with her. With extreme ingenuity, she began to explain. . . .

"That's all right," said Lesley. "Of course they do. I don't know who Mrs. Sprigg fathered him on, but she's very resourceful."

"I don't know either, my dear, but I expect we're the only two in the village. And he does do you credit, you know: they all think he's a *splendid* little boy."

"So he is," said Lesley, signalling to the 'bus. "If I stay here much longer I shall join the Mothers' Union."

They climbed in and found themselves seats, suspending, in deference to Mrs. Pomfret's position, all further references to Lesley's potential bastard; and so proceeded to Aylesbury to buy Garibaldi biscuits; lard, bacon and corn-flour; two tins of shoe-polish; and carbolic soap for Patrick's dog.

IV

He was a good dog. Within a couple of weeks regular feeding and carbolic baths began to do their work, appearance and manners improving together. His coat grew thicker, though no less carrotty, the search for fleas became daily less urgent. He developed, moreover, into an intelligent watchdog, learning to know and pass all regular visitors, and holding the rest gently at bay until further orders. Towards Lesley he displayed a respectful attitude, towards Pat the unconscious intimacy of a twin-soul. Their characters were complementary. Pat walked, thought, inquired, considered: Pincher ran, rejoiced, cavorted, leapt. Crossing a meadow, Pat invariably took the straight line between two gates, while Pincher raced round in circles chasing the birds: but they arrived within a yard of each other. A yard, indeed, was apparently the maximum distance they could bear to be separated by; and the two days Patrick lay up with a bruised knee Pincher never left the orchard.

He was a good dog; but he was never an Airedale.

Chapter Four

I

All through the summer Lesley's household consolidated itself. It now included, besides Patrick, Mrs. Sprigg and Pincher, a fine ginger cat who was sometimes called Alice; and of this tiny universe—as variously inhabited, for all its size, as the island in *The Tempest*—Lesley herself was the natural and undisputed centre. Within it, whatever she said or did was of extreme importance: goddess-like in her meanest activities, she dispensed food, favour, justice and protection. She had scraps for a dog, milk for a cat, bread for a child, a wage for an old woman: she had a roof and a fire and a door to shut or open. She was beginning to be beloved, and she was already essential.

II

In her relations abroad, the outstanding factor was perhaps this, that she liked the Vicar.

She even liked the Vicar's wife.

The shock to a young woman of Lesley's temperament and habits was naturally great, and it must be allowed to her credit that—as in the case of Pincher—she kept her head and faced the facts. She liked the Vicar (and the Vicar's wife) because they asked no questions, genuinely loved music—on Mr. Pomfret's gramophone, indeed, Lesley was now hearing more Bach, Mozart and Beethoven than ever in her life before—and made no attempt to redeem her. More positively, she liked them for a quality which Elissa would have called their technique of living, and to which Mrs. Sprigg commonly referred as their easygoing ways. More than any family or group Lesley had ever encountered, they let each other alone. The Vicarage was a large one, and they spread all over it. Meal-times assembled them, but not for long; and the only place where three or four consistently gathered together was the schoolroom on a wet morning.

"The schoolroom?" repeated Lesley, when first ushered through the door. "Do they do lessons, then?"

Mrs. Pomfret stared in astonishment.

"But of course Alec and Joan do lessons! It's holidays now, but they've been doing them all winter. Hadn't you noticed there were only two about in the mornings, instead of four?"

Lesley shook her head.

"They get behind things," she explained. "Trees, and so on. It's only at meal-times, don't you think, that children can really be checked?"

"But didn't Pat tell you?"

"I don't think so. But it's only lately, you know, that Pat's begun to talk."

Mrs. Pomfret gave her a sudden clear glance. Henry, as usual, had been quite right. There was a change. Aloud she said:

"You don't make Pat do any, then?"

It was Lesley's turn to look surprised. The idea of giving Pat instruction had never entered her head; and indeed, now that it had, she could scarcely see herself bending above the infant scholar. And yet Pat was now six: with his new-found boldness he had no more than a fortnight ago, on August 12th, directed her attention to the fly-leaf of the *Tailor:* 'To Pat on his birthday,' it said, 'August 14th.' And Lesley had pulled herself together and bought him a cake and given a party for the four young Pomfrets. . . .

"Who teaches yours?" she asked.

"Why, Henry and I between us. Henry teaches them Latin and Arithmetic and French and History, and I teach them writing and spelling and easy things like English. But Alec's going to school in the autumn."

'School!' thought Lesley. There was school ahead of Pat too, and at the moment he didn't know a thing! She looked at Mrs. Pomfret's face: it was kind, intelligent, patient and firm. *She* could teach any child its alphabet.

"If I promise not to pay more than about fourpence a week," said Lesley persuasively, "would you possibly consider taking Pat on as well?" And she braced herself in advance for the inevitable argument, during which Mrs. Pomfret was slowly beaten up from twopence to threepence by way of twopence-ha'penny. She gave in at last, however; and at a monthly cost slightly below Lesley's old cigarette bills, Patrick Craigie started his education.

III

Complementary, as it were, to Lesley's intercourse with the Vicarage, was her intercourse with the Hall. It was a phenomenon in its way almost as strange as the first, the opening stages of their acquaintance having been characterised on the one side by acute disappointment, and on the other side by acute malease. After the first unforgettable meeting Lesley's one desire, with regard to Sir Philip, was never to see him again; yet within a space of about four months she had somehow formed the habit of dining at the Hall, and often alone, no less than two or three times a week.

It was odd, it was inexplicable; but between the first meeting and the second—which Lesley, after dodging as long as possible, was at last forced into by a thunderstorm—something had evidently occurred to alter Sir Philip's attitude. (The unknown factor, indeed, was neither more nor less than a sound talking-to from the Vicar's wife; and therefore much too simple for Lesley to guess it.) He was charming, intelligent, and slightly formal: displaying even, in momentary glimpses, the tender and delicate respect with which age sometimes pays homage to the youthfulness of the young. Lesley had never met such urbanity. Wooed in spite of herself, she instinctively responded, and all unaware presented a change of personality at least as striking as the one she marvelled at. For if Lesley wondered, so did Sir Philip: and though with both on such super-best behaviour the acquaintance was naturally slow to ripen, the mutual sympathy when they both fell from grace—when Lesley swore again and Sir Philip told the wrong story—seemed to carry them at one stride into the easy territory of life-long friendship. It was not, however, until considerably later that Lesley received, in the course of one of their long after-dinner sessions, a clear-cut exposition of Sir Philip's attitude towards women in general and herself in particular.

They had been discussing, as not infrequently happened, the peculiar awfulness of Mrs. Sprigg.

"Every time she opens her mouth," complained Lesley, "I have to send Pat on an errand. She gets bawdier and bawdier."

Sir Philip threw up his hands.

"You can't do anything about it, my dear. All the Spriggs are bawdy, and always have been. They got set in their ways under the Georges."

"And you?" said Lesley.

"Under Victoria the Good."

"She really was, then?"

"Good? As good as gold: we've gone off the standard," said Sir Philip. "Everyone was good in those days—either good or wicked. Things were a lot less streaky."

Lesley looked at him with interest.

"I keep forgetting how long it is since you were young," she said thoughtfully. "Were there still demi-reps?"

Sir Philip shifted in his chair.

"There were," he said, "and a young woman like you wasn't supposed to know about them."

"A young woman like me would probably have been one," said Lesley. "What were they like?"

"They were excellent company, and they never met one's wife. Some of them were also extremely expensive." He broke off, coffee-spoon suspended, and in his eyes the unmistakable expression of a man who is going to boast. "My dear Miss Frewen, I've spent fifty pounds and more on one day's entertainment of one young woman. We wound up, I remember, with a genuine champagne supper—champagne in the flower-vase, champagne in the finger-bowls: not a drop of anything else allowed on the table. It caused quite a sensation. And there's another thing I remember: the flowers were camellias, and after an hour or so in the champagne they went a deep ivory yellow. I'm possibly the only man in England," said Sir Philip, "who can give you that first-hand information."

"I should say it's extremely probable," agreed Lesley.

He looked at her over his coffee-cup.

"It strikes you as wicked extravagance?"

In something of a dilemma Lesley shook her head: the thing that did strike her was not the wickedness but the vulgarity. Astonishing that a man of such quick and delicate perceptions—of such wide and sophisticated experience—could still look back with pride on a leaf from a novelette! It was a vulgar period, of course, full of practical jokes and private menageries: but even so one would not have expected the illusion to last. . . . Aloud she said:

"I only hope the lady was worth it. Was she?"

Sir Philip considered.

"Not in herself, no. Because, of course, no woman could really be worth fifty pounds for one day. But as the excuse for a glorious burst, as an incitement to throw caution to the winds—she was worth every penny of it. In my experience it's a pretty general rule that no man can get really reckless of money unless he's got a woman with him. Drinking is different, of course: in fact, woman's more often than not in the way: but then drink never gave me the same feeling. *I* could only get it by throwing the guineas about." He drank off his coffee and took another look into the past. Women and wine, just as the song said! Both of them expensive, and particularly the women. "But take them all round," finished Sir Philip thoughtfully, "they gave deuced good value."

Lesley looked at her cigarette.

"And you didn't mind the—the obviousness of it?"

"On the contrary. One knew where one was. Nowadays, I believe, there's a fashion to have a bar in the drawing-room: personally it wouldn't appeal to me. I don't like to find either barmaids in the drawing-room or ladies in the bar: and under Victoria the Good one didn't."

"Form at a glance, in fact," murmured Lesley.

Sir Philip nodded.

"For instance"—his old eyes glinted humorously at her—"any woman in the kind of frock you wear for dinner, my dear—"

"Was at once assumed to have fallen from virtue." Lesley laughed.

"Exactly," said Sir Philip. "Especially if she used your language as well. It would have been taken as a direct invitation to dishonourable advances. As I said before, one knew where one was."

"But isn't it much more convenient," argued Lesley, "to have me just as good company, and socially correct as well? To be able to say what you like *and* introduce me to your aunts?"

"But I can't say what I like. I'm what you probably describe as inhibited," said Sir Philip. "My dear Lesley, let me explain. The first time you came to dinner I was completely at my ease: in fact I had only one regret, which was that you hadn't turned up a year or two earlier. That's what I thought you were. But now I know you're not— and in spite of your truly appalling language, I did know it very quickly indeed—that particular kind of ease is completely gone.

And the other sort—the drawing-room sort—can't take its place; you won't let it."

Lesley nodded intelligently.

"You mean the things that amused you when you thought I was a pros—"

"Please!"

"—A light woman, then—no longer amuse you now that you find I'm not?"

"Exactly."

"But why not?"

"Because knowing that you really are a lady, I'd like you to behave like one," said Sir Philip.

IV

Purely out of regard for his feelings, Lesley did so. It came more easily than she would have thought; it came almost as easily as being bright. For the qualities required by Sir Philip, in his definition of a lady, approximated very closely indeed to the qualities required by herself as the essentially modern characteristics of a young woman of the world; an intellectual integrity, the custom of polite intercourse, and in temper the aristocratic habit of never giving a damn. Their only real divergence was on the definition of polite, which to Lesley meant cultivated, amusing, or, quite simply, modish, and to Sir Philip unexceptionable. Unexceptionable, that is, to a person of slightly more than average intelligence. No more than Lesley had he an appetite for bread-and-butter; he only did not like raw meat.

Within these limits, however, his conversation was at least as interesting as that of Toby Ashton. He knew six European capitals, the countries of the Near East, and could remember as far back as the début of Yvette Guilbert. He had adored, with apparently equal fervour, a Duchess of Devonshire and Mlle. Demay—she who sang at the Ambassadeurs, in 1892, a song called '*Moi, je casse les noisettes en m'asseyant dessus.'* He had known George Moore as a painter and did not think much of him; he never did think much of the Irish, they were always harping on their ancestors. He himself had ancestors, naturally, but he didn't keep harping on them. Lesley, indeed, sometimes wished that he would; one or two of them, from the rare glimpses vouchsafed, seemed to have had some very odd traits indeed. There was a Sir Philip of the Civil Wars, who, throughout that most troubled period of England's history, had been chiefly distinguished by an extreme susceptibility to draughts. (He was also, it is true, an experienced and indefatigable soldier: but whenever the campaign permitted he at once returned to the Hall and to his special draught-proof chair, which to judge by contemporary description must have closely resembled the later sedan.) Another Sir Philip, a generation or so earlier, had such strong simplicity of character that he always took off his clothes when he felt hot. The mannerism was at least harmless (unlike that of Sir Giles, who threw daggers to express distaste), and beyond refusing all invitations for the dog-days, not even his wife did anything about it.

Descended from such a line, it was scarcely possible that Sir Philip should have been dull. And he was not dull. He was deeply interesting. So was Mr. Pomfret. Nor had Lesley ever been bored in the company of Mrs. Sprigg. In fact, it might almost be said that she was never bored at all. There was a constant intercourse, a continual deepening of acquaintance; instead of knowing a hundred people by sight she would soon know half a dozen by heart. An eventual return to Town was still, so to speak, the vanishing point of her perspective; but the lines were four years long, and in the meantime, for her consolation, there was this new and startling discovery: that the country is populated by really quite interesting persons.

Chapter Five

I

Running downstairs one morning in September, Lesley was halted at the door of the sitting-room by a brilliant and novel blaze of colour. For a moment she stood bewildered, as though before a floor and wall that had blossomed overnight; but the truth was not in fact so far to seek. It was only early sunlight pouring through the transparent blue and rose of unlined chintzes: she had forgotten, before going to bed, to pull back the new curtains.

The incident was a trivial one; not so its consequences. All through breakfast Lesley's thoughts kept returning to that extraordinary vision of a charming room. For the first time in months she consciously looked about her; and the Brixton décor, nearly eighteen months shabbier than when she first saw it, completely failed to amuse. It was hideously ugly, it would very soon be sordid: but until Sir Philip had recovered from the bathroom, there was obviously nothing to be done.

Lesley cleared the table and set back the chairs. They were made of some reddish, sticky-looking wood, by comparison with which the one chintz cover, its delphiniums notwithstanding, was a positive relief. Lesley plumped up the cushion, turned towards the door again, and as she did so noticed a three-cornered flap of wall-paper hanging loose under the ceiling. Almost without thinking she put up her hand and tore down a two-foot strip of buff chrysanthemums, crimson ramblers and variegated stocks: for the palimpsest was three deep.

Behind the stocks appeared a couple of cabbage roses, wrinkled hard over an uneven surface. Lesley seized a knife from the tray, and scoring at random felt the blade slip from plaster and bite on wood. She thought—

'Oak!'

It was a beam running crosswise the whole width of the wall; and having traced out its length Lesley stood still as Michelangelo before his imprisoned angel. She had received a vision. Her eye had penetrated through rep, maple and four layers of paper to a dwelling-place perfect in conception, harmonious in detail, and as much her personal creation as a child or a poem.

"Oak!" said Lesley, this time aloud.

The ecstasy passed, or rather was translated into action. Forgetful of all else she scraped furiously at the pink and mottled surface, powdering herself with dust until she had to stop and wipe her eyes. And pausing to do so, she heard voices without: voices, not angelic, but still of joy and amazement. She looked up, her lips moved to prohibit, and the next instant the children were upon her.

"*Frewen!*" cried Pat. "Why didn't you tell us?"

It was a great and memorable occasion. The prohibition died unborn: for to try and stop them would have been not only barbarous but also impossible. Within five minutes not a child was clean; while as to the room itself, it was already so coated in dust that there was no longer any point in taking care. Like artificial snow innumerable shreds of paper floated through the air: on carpet, chairs and table blossomed a sudden flora of stocks and roses. The children stripped, ripped and scattered, Lesley soaked, coaxed and loosened; until at last the two main walls stood boldly patterned with a triple stripe of oak on plaster.

Lesley stood back and looked at them with a deep satisfaction. It was *her* oak, *her* plaster, divined by her spirit and made visible by her labour; and she also decided, with her usual common sense, that the job would undoubtedly have to be finished at the hands of a professional.

II

A perfect house stands in a perfect garden; and while the professionals were busy, Lesley, for the first time in her life, came into personal contact with soil, sod and earthworms. She began with Pat's flower-bed, where the candytuft alone held ground against weeds; and here, a day or two later, Mrs. Pomfret found her in action from the base of Pat's prayer-rug.

"Give me a trowel and I'll help you a bit," said Mrs. Pomfret, plumping suddenly down on the grass.

In some surprise, for the Vicar's wife did not usually have so much time to spare, Lesley passed her a small fork. For a minute or two they worked in silence, the pile of weeds growing slowly between them. Then—

"I'm going to buy a mangle," said Mrs. Pomfret defiantly.

Lesley sat up.

"It's not extravagance," continued Mrs. Pomfret, "the one we've got now is dropping to pieces. Harry keeps mending it and the boys keep mending it, but the whole trouble is that it simply will not *mangle*. It's too old."

"Then you're quite right to buy a new one," said Lesley.

"Oh, not a new one, my dear, they're terribly expensive, but I've had notice of the sale at Elm House, at Thame, you know, and Mrs. Sprigg's daughter-in-law who used to work there told Mrs. Sprigg that if the mangle in the sale is the one she used to work with, it's just as good as new. So I'm going over on Monday," finished Mrs. Pomfret, "with the intention of buying it."

"And I'll come with you," said Lesley, quite carried away.

The Vicar's wife beamed with genuine pleasure.

"Will you really, Lesley? Then that will make quite an outing of it. And if you want anything yourself, I believe the furniture's quite worth looking at. Nothing old enough to fetch the dealers, you know, but good plain country stuff." She sat down abruptly and looked back at the cottage. "My dear, if you tackle it as you tackled Pat, it's going to be perfectly lovely."

"Oh, but this will be much more interesting than Pat," said Lesley seriously. "I know exactly what I want and I've just got time to do it."

Mrs. Pomfret shifted her gaze.

"But won't you be heart-broken to leave it all?"

"Heart-broken? Good God, no! I like to do a thing and finish with it and then do something else." The words rose mechanically to her lips. They were one of her pet gambits, and had been the opening phrase (usually with the addition of the word '*finito!*') for many a modern conversation. In the presence of Mrs. Pomfret, however, she forgot the *finite* and added instead,

"What I do want are chairs. Ladderbacks with rush-bottom seats. Do you think I could get any at the sale?"

"In the nursery and schoolroom you probably would," said Mrs. Pomfret.

"Then if I can I shall. And a gate-leg table and a corner cupboard. I shall go," said Lesley, "prepared to spend ten pounds."

And they looked at each other with genuine excitement.

III

Before any social excursion—even one of no more than three miles, and having as its objective the town of Thame—Mrs. Pomfret's natural impulse was to go to the kitchen and cut sandwiches. There Lesley, arriving early to deposit Pat, found her absently buttering a yesterday's loaf; and without standing on ceremony put both bread and butter back in their places.

"You're having lunch with me," she explained, "at the Yellow Swan. With rather a lot to drink, to improve our voices for bidding."

Mrs. Pomfret looked up with frank pleasure.

"I'd love it," she said. "I *love* eating away from home. Only nothing to drink, my dear, because it always makes me hiccup at once. That time we dined with the Bishop Henry has never forgotten."

She untied her apron and folded it over a chair-back: even when hiccupping at a Bishop's table, thought Lesley, she could never have been taken for anything but a thoroughly nice woman.

All the way in the 'bus they talked with enjoyment. They talked about the affairs of the village, and the characters of the children; discussing more particularly the rheumatism of Horace Walpole and the brilliance of Alec Pomfret. Old Horace was laid up and couldn't put foot to ground: young Alec had constructed, from a musical box and a nutmeg grater, a machine that played music while grating the nutmegs.

"Patrick," said Lesley, "has an amazing way with animals. Pincher adores him, of course, but so does the cat. And you know what cats are."

Without the least insincerity, Mrs. Pomfret nodded. She was waiting, though quite patiently, to tell about the other thing Alec had made, the thing for saving matches: but there would be plenty of time after Lesley had finished. Lesley, however, took longer than either of them expected, and with equal surprise (the matches barely touched upon) they looked out of the window and saw it was Thame.

"That's Elm House, behind the pub," said Mrs. Pomfret. She spoke with calm, but her eye was bright: like a war-horse smelling battle, she hurried impatiently forward. Lesley followed more demurely, but still with a certain excitement, it was her first sale, and she was prepared to spend ten pounds.

Their movements for the next hour are of no possible interest to anyone but themselves. They ascended stairs, looked into cupboards, opened drawers, thumped stuffing, and rang glass: they behaved, that is to say, precisely like any two women at any given sale. To the women themselves all these actions are passionately absorbing; but not to anyone else.

Within that hour, however, while thus lost to sight, Mrs. Pomfret succumbed to the mangle and Lesley discovered her ladderback chairs. There were four of them, not very old, but of agreeable design and in good condition; and she had noticed with alarm that more eyes than her own had been favourably attracted. The actual sale did not begin till two, so that she had almost an hour, during lunch, to decide on her price. The meal was a silent one, though they both enjoyed their food; for Mrs. Pomfret too was cogitating on the subject of mangles. At last, over coffee in the lounge, she came to a semi-decision.

"If you don't mind, Lesley," she said, "I think I'll just run over to the Stores and have a look at a new one. It's the last I shall ever buy, I hope, and I don't want to make a mistake."

A trifle startled by the allusion—for few people are really familiar with the fact of their own mortality—Lesley nodded acquiescence and moved to the window from which she could command the entrance to the Stores. A new car now stood outside, a great yellow tourer with a fawn hood; and walking up the path, chattering at the tops of their voices, were Elissa, Mrs. Carnegie, and two men whom Lesley did not know.

IV

Her first impulse was to tap on the pane and attract their attention; but before she could do so a second and a stronger had taken its place. Very quietly, as they passed between the geraniums, Lesley drew herself to one side and hid behind a curtain.

Elissa was being very spontaneous.

"Drinks, drinks, drinks!" she cried. "Preferably a Martini, darling, and see if they'll let you shake it. I feel like an unwatered pot-plant."

"*Cela se voit*," murmured Mrs. Carnegie. She herself resembled nothing so arid; a prize Maréchal Niel perhaps, reared solely on fertiliser. Like the flowers at her feet she was dressed in tight crimson; and after the manner of Frenchwomen continued to look cool.

Lesley slipped over to the mirror and looked at her face. It was not really shiny, but lightly browned all over to an even sun-burnt gloss; and with a tiny twinge of dismay she remembered that she had not yet renewed her lipstick. For the reflected mouth—after even a glimpse of Elissa's immaculate bow—had nothing to be said for it. Red enough to pass at a pinch, but sadly in need of pulling together. . . .

'Oh, well,' thought Lesley, 'it can't be helped'; and picking up her bag she moved across the room. At the door, however, she hesitated. A confused noise without—chattering, laughter, Elissa's scream— told her that they were all gathered in the hall. To fling open the door, step forth and declare herself—what could be simpler or more effective? But still she hesitated: it would mean seeing Elissa, of course, but it would also mean going to the bar and sitting and having drinks and being unable to get away while all the time someone else was snapping up her chairs. And thinking of those four superlative ladderbacks, Lesley's mind suddenly made itself up. She was fond of Elissa—very fond indeed; only just at the moment she couldn't be bothered.

Amid a good deal of laughter the footsteps passed on. From the other side of the road, Mrs. Pomfret waved a beckoning hand. Lesley pulled on her hat, picked up her gloves, and exercising a certain amount of caution emerged into the empty hall.

Just as she appeared, however, the bar-room door swung open and one of the men came out to get his coat. Tall, dark and lightly whiskered, she would have known him anywhere for one of Elissa's weaknesses: while he, by a certain fixity of gaze, seemed to reciprocate her interest. But Lesley knew too well how to interpret that look to draw any flattery from it. It was a look, in fact, of pleased recognition, such as may be seen on the faces of tourists when confronted with their first Arab; and it amused her to think how accurately she could supply the exact descriptive phrases with which he was even then regaling Elissa.

'I'm a Country Type!' thought Lesley, raising her eyebrows in silent amusement: and since the joke was too good to spoil, she went out by the back door and so avoided the bar-room windows.

Chapter Six

I

The sitting-room that night felt close; and it was one of the few evenings in the year when a fire could have been dispensed with. Fatigued with her unusual outing, triumphant in the possession of her chairs, Lesley propped open the door and walked slowly down to the gate.

In all the orchard not a leaf stirred. It was an extreme of stillness like an extreme of cold; one heard, not saw, the breath. And then suddenly out of the darkness, an apple-tree groaned.

Lesley turned and ran. With a single mighty clap, like the slamming of a sluice, the heavens had opened.

II

At eleven o'clock the storm was still raging. The Vale was a bowling-green where giants flung cannon-balls; they rebounded from the hills to meet crashing in the centre, or sidled round the rim with a sullen departing roll. The rain slashed, the wind blew; and behind them was more wind, more rain, enough to last till the day of judgment. It was a night to shake the Pyramids and astonish Noah; it was a bad night, in fact, for anyone who had to be out.

But the White Cottage crouched low and its walls were sturdy. Lesley ran up to look at Pat, found him still miraculously sleeping and returned to the sitting-room with a new book on Picasso. She could not read, however, she could only sit and listen. There were elephants in the orchard, trampling and trumpeting and stamping with their feet, reaching up with their trunks to snap off the branches; in the rare, moment-long lulls one could hear the rattle of boughs like the rattle of fighting antlers.

'It's the animals come back!' thought Lesley fantastically; and for a wild and astonishing instant she visioned a whole prehistoric fauna reloosed into Bucks.

'I must go to bed,' she thought, 'I'm asleep already.'

But an extraordinary reluctance held her where she was. With all that turmoil outside it seemed wrong to take off one's clothes and lie defencelessly down: better, like prehistoric man, to stay crouching on guard and build up the fire. . . . She listened again. The wind had hurled itself down the chimney and was now fighting to get out: the rain against the windows rattled like hail. From the direction of Pig Lane came a sudden mighty crash: then silence, and a second crash following the first.

'There'll be the telephone wires down to-night,' Lesley thought; and with a final effort she pulled herself together and went upstairs.

Pat was still asleep. Thanking her stars for his phlegm, Lesley passed into her own room and drew the curtains. Through the rain-blurred glass there was nothing to be seen save a couple of lights in the Walpole windows.

'They're up late,' thought Lesley, 'I suppose it's the storm;' and hoping to emulate Patrick's example, she hastily undressed herself and got into bed.

III

But now the thunder was worse. They were not giants, they were postmen, double-knocking on an iron door. Lesley opened her eyes. There *was* a knocking. Loud, erratic, and far nearer than any symbolic gates, it seemed to batter at the wall directly below her bed. It was a knocking at the cottage.

She put her hand to the switch. It clicked uselessly.

'Damn!' thought Lesley. 'The light's gone.'

She lay in the dark a moment, and heard the knocking continue. Through the open door came a faint rustling.

"That you, Pat?"

His voice came calm and matter-of-fact as usual: but she had the impression that he was glad to hear her.

"There's someone trying to get in, Frewen," he said. "They've been banging and banging."

'On a night like this, poor devils!' thought Lesley, feeling for her slippers. There was a candle on the chest; she jumped out of bed and cast a flickering match-light over the room. From the tail of her eye, as she thrust on her dressing-gown, she saw Patrick too preparing to rise.

"No, you stay here, Pat," she said. "I won't be a minute, and you'll catch cold." There was a draught on the twisting stair, indeed, that nearly blew her light out: she shielded it with her fingers and bore it safely into the sitting-room. A fresh volley of knocks had just begun: and her anxiety to stop the racket effectually swamping all other emotions, she went straight to the door and pulled it open.

Close under the thatch stood a small dark figure. It was the eight-year Walpole boy, hooded in an overcoat and dripping like a tiddler.

The wind blew him inside and slammed the door. By the light of the candle Lesley saw his lips part and move; and in that instant, directly overhead, thunder crashed back. The hot wax dripped on her fingers, she reached for his sodden cloak and tried to take it off. But he would not let her, he clutched it round him, and for an instant they shouted ineffectually at each other against a dwindling rattle. Then the last rumble died and in a sudden silence the child got out his message.

"Please, Miss Frewen, Mother says will you use your telephone and get Miss Cook?"

The blank irrelevance of it was so astonishing that for a moment Lesley stood tongue-tied. Then,

"Who in God's name is Miss Cook?" she demanded.

"District Nurse, Miss. They want her quick."

The light flickered, the wax dripped.

"Is it for Florrie?"

He nodded dumbly. With the strangest mixture of emotions— pity and repugnance, response and withdrawal—Lesley went over to the telephone and lifted the receiver. There was no response. The line was dead.

She tried again, clicking impatiently at the hook and calling into the mouthpiece. It was no use. The line was dead. She hung up the receiver and turned back to the child.

"Have you done it, Miss?"

"No. It's either a line down or the lightning, but tell your mother I'll stay here and keep on trying." She broke off to look at him and was suddenly aware that beneath his stolidity he was frightened out of his wits. Her words might have reached his ears, but he had certainly not taken them in. To put him out in the rain again would be not only barbarous, but completely futile. And seeing him stand so dumb, terrified and uncomprehending, Lesley came to a sudden decision. She said quickly, "I'll go back to your mother, Georgie, while you stay here. There's Patrick too, so you won't be alone."

The belated recollection of his name seemed to lend her words authority, and she ran back upstairs with the child stumping obediently after her. To Patrick she said with equal firmness,

"Georgie is going to stay here, Pat, while I run over to the Walpoles. There's someone ill there. Don't light the candle again, and try and go to sleep." She stooped for her shoes; he was taking it quite calmly. "And you, Georgie, get out of those wet things and roll yourself in a blanket. You can curl up on the end of Pat's bed, if you like, and tell each other stories."

As she spoke she was pulling on her clothes, the stoutest and simplest that came to hand. Her raincoat was downstairs and an old leather hat: it was no night for umbrellas. With a glance at the two children—they appeared reasonably wrapped up, and more excited than alarmed—Lesley ran downstairs again and out into the storm.

IV

The wind, on first meeting it, was like a buffet in the face. She put down her head and let her body think for her. The fence by the toolshed—that was the place to cross, where a couple of big stones made a rudimentary stile. The rain beat in her eyes, the mud sucked at her shoes; she reached the fence panting as though after a two-mile run. Up, now, and over! Her skirt caught on a nail, she ripped it free and hurried on to where the Walpoles' back door showed a crack of light. It widened as she approached to a yellow rectangle filled with a black figure: Mrs. Walpole was waiting, half out in the rain with a shawl over her head.

"Miss Frewen!"

Lesley got her breath.

"I've left Georgie with Pat," she said. "The telephone isn't working."

The old woman's face seemed suddenly to shrivel.

"I thought as much," she said; and in the silence between their words and the thunder, there came from within the house a long, despairing sound. It was neither cry nor moan, but something between the two; and it was completely uncivilised.

Lesley shuddered.

"Is that—?"

"Florrie. It's the storm done it."

The voice was dry, hopeless, and yet somehow appealing. 'My God!' thought Lesley, 'she can't be expecting *me* to do anything!' And as though reading her thoughts, the woman said,

"I daren't leave her, Miss Frewen, and Walpole 'e can't set foot to ground. Except for Georgie's young brother I've got no one in the house."

For an interminable moment Lesley stood dumb. But she was not, like Georgie, frightened out of her wits: her difficulty was far more subtle. In brief, the whole situation was so utterly hackneyed that she could not believe it to be really happening. It was like a very early movie. Childbirth in a thunderstorm, with Tom Mix on his wonder-horse to ride for a doctor! The image flashed through her mind; she thrust it away and took a fresh grip on reality. The rain poured, the wind blew, in a room upstairs Florrie Walpole laboured: Miss Cook—

"Where does the woman live?" asked Lesley, in a tone of pure annoyance.

"Second house on the Wendover Road. It's about two mile, Miss Frewen."

"Hasn't anyone got a car?"

"Only Sir Philip, and that's a mile back to start. But there's Florrie's bicycle."

'My God!' thought Lesley again. 'A bicycle!' It was the finishing touch, the last stroke of unreality; and she had almost laughed aloud when suddenly, at something in the old woman's eyes, the current of her thought was changed. And it set in a strange channel.

She was conscious, for almost the first time in her life, of being one of the gentry. The gentry, on whom people still at a pinch depended: who were still, it seemed, expected to rise out of their beds and career through a thunderstorm whenever an incontinent young woman saw fit to have a baby. Feeling extraordinarily akin to the Sir Giles who threw daggers, Lesley accepted her lot.

"Right," she said. "You'd better give me the thing."

With no word, but her whole face suddenly relaxing, the old woman took a step into the passage and wheeled forth a bicycle. Its lamp, Lesley noted, was already alight.

"I go straight down to the village—"

"And that's all you need go, Miss Frewen. As far as the village, and then knock up the Coxes. If you give 'im the bicycle, Tom can go on from there."

Lesley nodded. In spite of this considerable alleviation, she was still in an extremely bad temper. The action of lifting the machine, moreover, as she bore it across the threshold, had taken her straight back to the Upper Fifth. The Upper Fifth had bicycles, the Sixth looked down on them; and it was thus a dozen years at least since she had last mounted one. But cycling, they said, was like swimming—once learnt, never forgotten; and as she wobbled out at the gate Lesley sincerely hoped this was true.

At that moment, however, she had no need to do anything but balance, for by a piece of supreme good fortune the wind, against which she could scarcely have pedalled a yard, was now more or less steady at her back; it blew her down Pig Lane like a scudding leaf or a scrap of paper. At the turn into the village she not unexpectedly fell off: but the mud was at least soft, and she zigzagged into the square plastered but unharmed.

And now, across the mild glow of achievement, a doubt came troubling. The Coxes—did that mean the Coxes at the Post Office, or the Coxes next to the pub? Lesley put foot to ground and looked up through the rain from one set of windows to the other. Like all the rest of the village, they were dark: and standing astraddle over her mount Lesley swore like a trooper. And she had reason to swear: before Tom could be off she would have to hammer at doors, bawl explanations, knock into God knew how many thick heads the necessity and the errand: she would have to struggle back on foot and sit with Mrs. Walpole—sit with Florrie, perhaps—and wait and wait till the nurse arrived. All these things were good reasons for swearing: but the strongest reason of all was that she would not be doing any of them.

'Blast the Coxes,' thought Lesley, 'I'd better go myself.' Her foot, one instant ahead of her mind, had already returned to the pedal. She pressed down, wobbled forward, and let the wind blow her out of the village.

That the errand was one of mercy could never have been guessed from her language; nor did an occasional forktongued flash tend to soothe. For though to be struck by lightning is an ancient—nay, a primeval—mode of death, to Lesley Frewen it was death doubly horrible, death whose second and sharper sting would be a three-line obituary, between a champion cow and a hundredth birthday, in that provincial foot-of-the-column, From All Quarters. Should judgment also visit the herd, she and the cow might even be lumped together, sharing their modest half-inch in a ration of two to one. . . . '*During the same storm, a cow belonging to Mr. Horace Walpole—*'

"Blast Horace Walpole and blast all cows," muttered Lesley impartially; and from a sudden smoothness in her motion knew that she was on the metalled quarter-mile between the bridge over the canal and the Wendover road. The wind was now less friendly, so that rain and sweat ran mingling in her eyes; Lesley bent over the handlebars, topped a short rise, and found the gradient in her favour. Still drawing freely on her vocabulary, she bowled downhill, turned sharply to the right, and fell off her machine at Miss Cook's front door.

Like everyone else, Miss Cook had gone to bed.

The door had no knocker, but two electric bells. Lesley put a finger on each and held them there. On the slightest provocation— a minute's delay, for example—she would probably have broken a window. (Sir Giles would have broken the door, and on less provocation still.) Almost immediately, however, and directly overhead, a sash rattled. Lesley looked up through the rain and saw a kind and sensible gargoyle lean suddenly forth.

"Miss Cook?" asked Lesley. "I've come from the Walpoles'. They want you for Florrie."

"Who says so?" countered Miss Cook. "Florrie or her mother?"

"Her mother."

With a gesture of assent the head withdrew; and both temper and strength having suddenly evaporated together, Lesley leant patiently against the wall and waited for something to happen. It happened almost at once: the door opened, a light shone, and Miss Cook with her skirt on stood beckoning in the hall.

"Come in," she said, "and bring your bicycle. I'm going to take the Morris."

Like Georgie Walpole half-an-hour earlier, Lesley walked dripping and blinking into the strange lady's room. The bicycle was taken from her, she was told to sit, and obediently she did so. Meanwhile Miss Cook moved neatly about the room, dressing as she moved, and putting things together in a battered attaché-case. She then disappeared, with a word about the garage, and following as far as the door Lesley observed, in an incredibly short space of time, the rear end of a car protruding out of the dark. Cautious as a tortoise, it fidgeted its way out: then rain glittered in the lamps and a door swung open.

"Get in," said Miss Cook.

Lesley did so, and jerky as her thoughts the car lurched forward. It wasn't so bad. Within the circle of the hills, thunder still muttered: but the rain was abating, and they had only once to get out and wipe the windscreen. The greatest enemy was the gale, which, having blown Lesley there, seemed determined to prevent her getting back. But the old car laboured mightily, rattling louder than the thunder and tunnelling into the wind like an ancient mole in clayey soil. As a conversational background, however, its efforts were not happy, and they had covered nearly two-thirds of the distance before Miss Cook found a lull in which to ask her first question.

"Did you see Florrie, Miss Frewen?"

"No. But I heard her."

"Poor thing! Well, I hope this time she has better luck," said Miss Cook. "Where's your little boy all this while?"

For the first time since leaving him Lesley remembered Patrick.

"At home in the cottage, with Georgie Walpole. They're both in the same bed, to keep each other company," she explained; and against the next burst of thunder heard her companion shout something about Keating's. It was their only attempt at conversation, for the racket had recommenced; but as they turned into Pig Lane Miss Cook gathered her forces for one last remark.

Said Miss Cook, with a nod of her head towards the desolate universe—

"Well, I must say, Miss Frewen, I never expected to see *you* here."

PART IV

Chapter One

I

As on every Wednesday afternoon, Lesley Frewen sat in the orchard and darned Pat's shirts. Wash on Monday, air on Tuesday: at the Vicarage they left the mending till Thursday, but Lesley liked to get it out of the way. On the chair at her side lay a paper bag containing a quarter of a pound of chocolate almonds, which the Post Office now kept in stock for her along with Basildon Bond writing-paper and silk washing elastic. (Other people were beginning to buy them too, said Miss Cox: they hadn't any smell to them.) From the other side of the fence came the constant low grunting of Walpole pigs, but otherwise all was so still that Lesley could hear Pat and the youngest Pomfret conversing afar under the pear-tree.

"Gr-r-r—I'm a lion." That was Pat, conservative as ever.

"Well, I'm a bus—I'll put you in my radiator."

"No, you can't—this isn't a stopping-place."

"Yes, I can—I'm marked Private."

There was a short pause.

"Oh, well," said the lion philosophically, "I'll be a beetle."

Lesley heard them with pleasure, for most of the time they were off all day looking for motor bandits. The way they did it was to lie concealed outside road-houses and see that the same people got into cars as had previously got out of them; and though no bandits had actually been caught, enthusiasm as yet showed no sign of waning. To the recital of their exploits, however, neither Lesley nor Mrs. Pomfret lent a particularly sympathetic ear: for in the opinion of both it would have been much nicer and healthier to go on being lions.

'But they're growing up so!' thought Lesley, helping herself to a chocolate almond. The nut crunched agreeably between her teeth; and suddenly out of the shadow walked Alice the cat, newly elegant after the weaning of her five kittens. She was bound for the back door, nor did the sight of company distract her from her course: with a casual nod, so to speak, she waved her tail and sauntered purposefully on.

"Where's Pincher?" called Lesley.

Alice looked scornfully over her shoulder. There had once, it is true, been a time when the sound of that name would have sent her flying into an apple-tree; but that was long ago, and the joke palled.

'Oh, dear,' thought Lesley (concealing nevertheless her chagrin), 'it must be years since Alice has jumped!' And she began idly to calculate how long they had had her. Alice! There had been a lamb called Alice as well, but that was in spring. Alice the cat dated from a summer—from the summer, in fact, when Florrie had her baby; and the youthful Gerald (he had been christened after the eldest son of Princess Mary) was now two years old.

'Two years!' thought Lesley. 'And I'd been here more than a year already. Nearly four years. . . .' And she looked vaguely round the orchard as though to see what had become of them.

Well, there they were, at any rate in part. The grass was not yet a lawn, but there were some quite smooth patches: her two herbaceous borders, without actually blazing, at least gave out a glow. They had hollyhocks in them, lupins both blue and yellow, sunflowers, anchusas, a good deal of lavender, oriental poppies, phlox and tiger-lilies; so they would blaze all right in time. But the next bed she made—with the true gardener's instinct her mind at once ranged ahead—was to be for roses. . . .

Only chintzes first; for with the gardener there dwelt a house-keeper, and the two were occasionally at war. Well, chintzes first, then; and from the visionary Maréchal Niels Lesley's eye came affectionately and thoughtfully to rest on the cottage itself. Every-one said it was perfect, but she knew better. One might just as well call Pat perfect, or the garden, when to the eye of understanding they were all three of them very little more than hopeful begin-nings. From without, to be sure, the cottage was good, for behind the plaster there had been broad black timbers—no neat and superimposed zigzag, but the strong irregular pattern of upward heaving arms. That was good, that was very good, that was not to be bettered: but within! Without moving from her seat Lesley looked straight through the walls and saw her four spurious lad-derbacks, once a collector's triumph, now a daily reminder of the Tottenham Court Road. The fireplace, too, for instead of having it bricked she had temporarily lost her head to the quaintness of Dutch tiles. Well, that could be put right easily enough, as soon as she had the money; only curtains must come first, because even across the orchard the blowing pink-and-blue chintz showed lam-entably faded. . . .

'And towels,' added the housekeeper, 'those big new coloured ones.' Pat would love a pink towel! The picture was enchanting! And with grave, considerate eyes Lesley looked through one wall more to the boarded-off section of the barn that was now known as the bathroom. It was not very showy, for Sir Philip, while by the loudness of his complaints giving the impression that he was facing the walls with marble, had actually managed to make do at very small expense. The white enamel bath was fed by a pipe and tap from the copper, and unaffectedly voided itself into a flower-bed: nor was the simplicity of material, or the still greater simplic-ity of construction, in any way concealed. Though without frills, however, the place served its purpose; and in a smaller subdivi-sion still the genius of Messrs. El-San had made possible an indoor lavatory.

'Really,' thought Lesley, 'I could have anyone to stay now. . . .' And as the gate creaked open she smiled quite hospitably, though on no more of a visitor than the morose Mr. Walsh.

Taciturn as ever, and walking a little too straight, he advanced across the grass and placed the letters in her hand. Lesley felt suitably flattered, for he did not usually put himself out, even by so little as an extra ten paces. Her vanity, however, was not long in action before it gave place to surprise; for between the couple of seed-merchants' catalogues, and looking remarkably out of place there, was a letter from London.

Elissa? The last time Elissa wrote she was just going to Cairo, but that was—how long?—almost a year ago. And Elissa hadn't—or usen't to have—a typewriter. Aunt Alice, then, or old Graham Whittal? Except for the annual ninepenny Christmas card—to which Lesley now replied with a fourpenny—they held no communication with her. . . . And still childishly turning the envelope, Lesley's eye was suddenly caught by the extraordinary difference in appearance between her two last addresses. Miss Frewen, Flat J16, Beverley Court, Baker Street, N.W.1—it used to straggle from corner to corner; whereas Miss Frewen, High Westover, Bucks, sat squarely in the middle and gave the impression of someone far more important than the Miss Frewen of Baker Street. Lesley laughed, slipped a finger under the flap, and found herself in cordial communication with a gentleman called Teddy Lock.

'. . . *Your kindness to me that summer,*' he exclaimed, '*has always been one of my happiest English memories!*' and after a good deal more in the same strain went on to announce that he now had with him a wife, for whom he was naturally desirous of procuring similar joys. They were in London, at Claridges, they were staying a fortnight, and on any day Miss Frewen might select would just love to run down and renew old acquaintance.

Lesley stared at the signature, repeated it aloud; and casting her mind back and back to a long-ago summer, she did seem to remember, along with Elissa and Toby Ashton, a tall young American with very good manners. And he had a car, and there was another girl . . . and wasn't Bryan Collingwood somehow mixed up in it? But not the new Mrs. Lock, for the letter specially mentioned that this was her first visit to the real home-country of the American people.

'Bless their hearts!' thought Lesley. "They're on their honeymoon.' Well, she wished for a visitor, her wish had been answered: and not only answered but multiplied by two. Lesley smiled. For if Providence could be lavish, so could she: and returning to the house she wrote a brief but cordial note inviting Mr. and Mrs. Lock to come down on Saturday and stay the night.

II

Walking down Pig Lane on her way to the Post Office, Lesley met first Florrie Walpole and then Arnold Hasty. They were not exactly together, nor yet exactly apart: they were separated, that is to say, by a distance of about six yards, but there was also present Florrie's infant son, who strayed to and fro as he listed and to whom remarks were being shouted by both parties. He was a handsome child, the pride of his mother's heart, and at two years old had stout brown legs, gipsy eyes, and hair as dark as Lesley's own. "Looks like we got the wrong ones, don't it?" Florrie had said, the first time she saw him and Patrick together; and the remark striking her as particularly happy, she had gone on making it ever since. She made it now.

"It does, doesn't it?" agreed Lesley. Politer than her cat, she even raised a smile; but her impulse was to go back and offer Alice an apology.

Chapter Two

I

They answered by wire. They would arrive on Saturday, they were evidently in an ecstasy, and there was a reply prepaid form on which Lesley could think of nothing better to put than a meagre 'Delighted.' She was suffering, indeed, from a slight reaction in favour of peace and quiet, which the exuberance of the telegram did nothing to lessen: they seemed to be just the sort of people (reflected their hostess in alarm) who would want to see cathedrals.

With a shake of the head for her own folly, Lesley picked up a tape-measure and slowly unrolled it. One thing in any case the visit had settled: if she were going to have new curtains at all, she might just as well have them now.

'I'll get Mrs. Pomfret,' she thought, noting down the total measurements, 'and we'll go over to Aylesbury and find something with sprigs'! Sprigs! Very English! As English, in their way, as any cathedral! Well, she would do her best, and Sir Philip would have to help: he should invite the Locks to dinner and talk about Queen Victoria. And Mr. Pomfret, what could he be? An old county family, or the Vicar of Wakefield? With spirits a little risen Lesley picked up her bag, put on her hat; and was half-way across fields before the suddenly remembered (what nothing but approaching honeymooners could ever have made her forget) that her appearance at the Vicarage would almost exactly coincide with the arrival of a resident pupil and an electric gramophone.

Lesley paused. That meant Mrs. Pomfret would be busy—at any rate too busy to come jaunting; but having already turned aside from the straight route to the 'bus stop, it seemed a pity not to go and see what was to be seen. So Lesley continued along the path at a good swinging pace, heard a church clock strike eleven, and arrived pink-cheeked with hurrying to find Mr. Cotton and the gramophone five minutes before her. They had come, it appeared, by the same train, a happy coincidence which enabled the instrument and its fixtures to be surreptitiously conveyed on Mr. Cotton's cab. Mr. Cotton himself had no more than a rucksack and a suitcase, and but for the porter's promptness would undoubtedly have walked: which all went to show (as Sir Philip afterwards remarked) how the love of music can stimulate employment.

"How long are you going to keep him?" asked Lesley, when the young man had vanished upstairs.

"Until the gramophone's paid for, of course," replied the Vicar, rapidly unrolling a ball of flex. "If you'll wait one moment, my dear, I'll have this thing fixed. Put on the Brandenburg, and sit down."

With the fleeting reflection that she had just missed a 'bus in any case, Lesley obeyed. From the spare room overhead came the thump of Mr. Cotton's baggage, and she said idly,

"What are you going to teach him?"

"Modern Greek, Turkish, and the rudiments of sol-fa. He's still up at Oxford, with an eye on the Consular. Now shove that plug in, my dear, and let the old man rip."

Like a glorified harvest festival the first movement rushed joyfully upon the air: his knees white with dust, the Vicar stood translated.

II

In the ordinary course of events not a day could have passed without leaving Lesley in full possession of Mr. Cotton's personal appearance and general characteristics; but such were the exigencies of curtain-making that for the next forty-eight hours she never stirred from the cottage save on errands of domestic necessity. The Pomfrets came over, of course, and once Dennis Cotton accompanied them; but what with her billows of sprigged chintz and a wind that was blowing through the orchard, Lesley gathered merely a vague uncritical impression of extreme youth and fair hair. Mrs. Pomfret seemed to like him, and Lesley was of course glad to hear it: but what really gave her pleasure was the unexpected discovery of two dozen new curtain-rings. She stitched quite placidly, however, comfortably aware of the cottage in apple-pie order and two white piqué frocks hanging immaculate on their hooks. The visitors would have her room, now permanently furnished with the big double bed—a remarkably good one, its origin wrapped in mystery—that used to be in the barn; so that apart from putting the divan in with Pat there was really nothing that needed attention. Even the weather seemed almost reliable, displaying red skies at night and on Saturday morning the fine shimmering mist that means a day to be proud of.

And such a day it was, blue overhead, green underfoot, and all washed over with unlimited gold: a day, felt Lesley, to lie on the grass and read Hans Andersen—or, better still, to lie on the grass and read nothing at all. She did not, of course, really hope that the Locks would meet with an accident; but there was a spot under the pear-tree, just lightly dappled with shade, where one would almost wish to take root.

It was not to be. Punctual to the minute—she had vaguely mentioned noon and the cuckoo slammed its door as their car crawled up Pig Lane—the visitors arrived. They were out and at the gate as Lesley hurried across the orchard—Teddy just as she remembered him, tall, broad and handsome: a wife as high as his shoulder, dark-eyed and pretty: and every stitch they had on was brand and shining new.

"Miss Frewen!" cried Teddy joyfully. Emotion was too much for him, he shook her violently by the hand, and for the next few minutes all was joy and introductions. Joy unalloyed, moreover, for at the very first sight of them—both so pleased and happy in their beautiful new clothes—all Lesley's churlishness had melted like the mist. They were charming! And quite carried away, she said impulsively,

"Don't go to-morrow! Can't you stay till Monday?"

Their eyes started; from the look that passed between them she knew that they had been discussing just that possibility all the way down. Was there a chance, or wasn't there? Would she, or wouldn't she? And now she had. Teddy drew a deep breath.

"Do you really mean it?" he asked anxiously. "You're sure we shan't be in the way?"

"I do and you won't," said Lesley. "I shall make you draw all the water."

They did not actually kiss each other; but it was a very near thing.

III

In the face of such strong temptation, Mrs. Sprigg behaved rather better than might have been expected, neither mingling with the gentry in the orchard nor joining in their conversation through the dining-room hatch. This restraint, however, was less a matter of delicacy than a friendly concession to the short-sighted prejudices of her employer.

"All the same, it's a great waste," she lamented after Lesley had expounded those prejudices at some length. "I could ha' told her a lot of things that I only wish someone would ha' told me. Why, I remember plain as anything—"

"In any case, she probably knows them already," interrupted Lesley.

"Not she!" said Mrs. Sprigg. "She's a nice little thing. . . ."

The young Locks, meanwhile, were behaving rather as though they were in heaven, stepping cautiously over the grass and standing mute with admiration before all the commonplaces of Lesley's life. The thick old walls of the cottage, the thick new thatch on the roof, the well with the bucket you had to wind by hand, and from which they rapturously drew more water than Mrs. Sprigg could cope with—from all these things they got what can only be described as a holy kick. (Gina also got a blister, which she evidently intended to preserve as long as she could—unto New York, if possible, but certainly as far as the boat.) On the Saturday afternoon Lesley walked them across country to buy buns at Wendover: Gina carried the basket, Teddy opened the gates; and the mere fact of going on foot seemed to give them one kick more.

"You're the nicest guests I've ever had," said Lesley, during a momentary halt to admire the view. "You like everything."

"Like!" they echoed, one on either side of her on top of the gate. "We just adore it. It's the loveliest thing that's ever happened to us."

A cow in a field turned and looked at them; but for once Gina did not remark her. She had seen something else.

"Look behind you, Teddy!"

Lesley looked too, and beheld the placid figure of old Horace Walpole approaching slowly along the path. He wore, as usual, a grey flannel shirt without a collar, a check waistcoat, and very old breeches.

"My!" breathed Gina. "Isn't he just too cunning?"

Her eyes shone with enthusiasm, her husband's no less. If they'd only got a camera, lamented Teddy, what a picture they could have taken!

"It's Horace Walpole," said Lesley, "we'll have to get out of the way."

They climbed respectfully down, he touched his hat and passed through.

"Fine afternoon, Miss Frewen."

"Beautiful, isn't it?" said Lesley.

"Ah!" said old Horace.

As to the language of Shakespeare, the Locks listened spell-bound; and observing their expressions Lesley was conscious of a slight dismay. Such joy was gratifying indeed, but how was it to be kept up? Having begun with the superlative, to what could one proceed? So Lesley, in her innocence; but she need not have troubled. Her guests had reserves of enthusiasm as yet untouched: they were barely out of the positive, and for the next three days Lesley was to watch with steadily increasing wonder while they scaled peak after peak of genuine rapture. For they stayed until Tuesday, in order to dine on the Monday night with Sir Philip at the Hall, where they let off behaving as though in heaven and behaved instead as though in the British Museum. That they were actually allowed to sit on the sofas was more than a treat, it was an experience; one could see them (said Sir Philip afterwards) absorbing culture through their behinds. . . .

But Sir Philip liked the Locks all the same, and having learnt his lesson from Lesley made no attempt to pay Gina's appearance the tribute of a kiss on the stairs. She wouldn't have minded: she would probably have thought it an old English custom, like God Save the King or left-hand driving; but Teddy was not so liberal.

"He's going all Southern on me," Gina complained proudly. "Would you believe it, Sir Philip, when we were in London a boy from home wanted to take me dancing, and Teddy just would not let me go. He just put his foot right down."

"And it's there still," growled Teddy. "It feels like it's taking root." He looked at Gina severely: she was the first wife he had ever had, and he was making the most of her.

"Young man," said Sir Philip, "you're perfectly right. The woman's place is in the home, if not in the harem." He watched them with benevolence; like Lesley, he found them extremely engaging, as though a couple of love-birds should ruffle up their feathers and pretend to be tough old owls; and for the sake of Gina's great eyes talked all evening long about more Princes of Wales than she had ever known existed.

He did even more: when the time came to go, he gave her a wedding-present. A little eighteenth-century Shakespeare, very difficult to read in, and with the Kerr dove and dagger emblazoned on the back....

The pinnacle was reached.

IV

Late the next afternoon, when at last they tore themselves away, Gina stood powdering her nose before the bedroom mirror. She had thanked and thanked again, and so had Teddy; but a final rush of gratitude was not to be denied.

"You'll never know, Miss Frewen—you just *can't* know—how much we've loved being here. It's what we'd both just longed for."

"I'm glad you weren't disappointed, then," said Lesley. (That reply-paid telegram!).

"*Disappointed!*" Gina stared in amazement. "Why, I didn't think it was going to be a *bit* like this! From what Teddy told me, I expected one of those rackety week-end places like we have sometimes, with a lot of drink around."

'Dear me!' thought Lesley: how wild that sounded! And with a wrinkle between her brows she tried to remember back to a summer four years ago, a summer—how extraordinary!—when she was hardly into the place, and Teddy Lock had come dangling after—who was it?—after Natasha! A dreadful week-end! And hadn't someone been rude to the Vicar?

"Dear me!" said Lesley aloud.

"I hope you didn't mind me saying that?" asked Gina a little anxiously. "Teddy's great on getting hold of the wrong story. . . ."

"On the contrary," said Lesley, "he was perfectly right. It's nicer now."

Her guest nodded.

"I think it's just wonderful. And—and about the little boy too, Miss Frewen." (Lesley at once looked apologetic: for Pat, without being exactly rude to the visitors, had rather pointedly dodged them. Gina had kissed him on arrival, and he was afraid she might do it again.) "We think you're being just wonderful about him. And as for the place—it's what we read about all our lives, and then go back disappointed because we can't find it. You've no idea what your hospitality has meant to us, Miss Frewen."

The great dark eyes, so charming and earnest, gazed reverently out of the window; and indeed in the scene below—the old green apple-trees, the young green grass—there *was* something special, something—how to define it?—one didn't get out of England. And what an English time of day!—five in the afternoon, the heat of the sun already gone, but a soft golden light making all clear and luminous. From the thatch above their heads a soft grey feather floated slowly down; and Gina sighed.

"Wouldn't it be just perfect," she said softly, "if one could be here when ... when ..."

The sentence was never finished, but Lesley understood. And suddenly another memory of Natasha rose up out of the past. . . .

'Women are just like cats,' thought Lesley to herself, 'no sooner do they find a good place than they want to have a baby in it.'

Chapter Three

I

That same evening, after the Locks had gone, she at last made the acquaintance of Denis Cotton. Sir Philip had asked him to play bridge, with Mr. Pomfret for a fourth; and arriving rather late Lesley found them all three on the terrace watching a clear green sky.

"Sit down and look at that, my dear," said Sir Philip, pulling up a fourth chair. "There's a star just over the cypress, a little to the right. Got it?"

Lesley stood and stared. The colour of grapes, the colour of shallow water, the colour of jade hollowed into a dish! And watching her astonished eyes, Sir Philip suddenly threw up his hands.

The Vicar laughed.

"Yes," he said, "Lesley's a proper country-woman. She never notices the landscape, only the weather."

"Miss Frewen's a part of the landscape," muttered Denis Cotton; and then flushed suddenly crimson, as though in readiness to be laughed at.

But unfortunately neither the Vicar nor his host paid him any attention. They were both looking at Lesley, as she stood with her head thrown back and her body motionless: in a dress of honey-coloured silk that held all the last of the light: with her sun-burned throat and line of white shoulder.

Then the green faded from the sky, the yellow from her gown; and behind them in the lighted house a gong rang for dinner.

II

It is a commonplace of natural history that young men cramming at country vicarages always fall in love. To this rule Denis Cotton was no exception, and during the course of the following week—as soon, that is to say, as relations between the Vicarage and the cottage had resumed their natural flow—he paid tribute to convention and fell in love with Lesley. He did it so thoroughly, moreover, that the passage of one week more found him dogging her footsteps with the persistence of a detective and the expression of a spaniel. Whenever she mentioned a new book someone always sent it to him (a belated birthday present) by the next post from Town. He was exhibiting, in fact, every symptom of a classic case, and both the Vicar and Sir Philip were making a grievance of it.

"It's all very well, my dear," said Mr. Pomfret, "but I'm being paid to teach the young ass Turkish. If he gives his whole mind to it we may get as far as the pronouns: with the present one-third in action we'd better give up the Consular and try for Pitman's."

Sir Philip's attitude was even simpler: with the arrival of Denis he had at last been able to make up a bridge four, and now, after only two sessions, all was rapidly being marred by the young man's palpable inability to keep his mind on his cards.

"If he plays with you he can see your eyes, if he plays against you he can see your profile. *I* can't think of anything," said Sir Philip glumly.

Lesley put down her cup—they were taking tea together in the library—and sighed. It was all perfectly true, and the young man was swiftly becoming a perfect nuisance: but short of deliberate brutality there seemed to be no mode of behaviour from which he could not draw encouragement.

'And I *can't* be brutal,' she thought, 'it would be like being brutal to Pat.' And she sighed again, for, as was perhaps only natural, she herself saw Denis's case a good deal more sympathetically than either of the men. Young Cotton, however egregious in behaviour, was being badly hurt; and with the fellow-feeling of youth Lesley slightly resented Sir Philip's flippancy. To change the subject, therefore, she said idly,

"Pat had Ellen again last night. Do you know that's three times running?"

They both laughed; for the care of Pat, on the extremely frequent occasions when Lesley dined at the Hall, now devolved on one or other of the Hall maids, and the volunteers for this duty were so remarkably persistent that she was never much surprised to discover, on the following morning, a trace here and there of yokel-sized boots.

Sir Philip sighed.

"They use it, I fear, as what is technically known as a Love Nest; and short of calling for a second volunteer to chaperon the first, I can't see any way of stopping it. You don't really mind, do you?"

"Not in the least," said Lesley, "so long as they'll hear if Pat's being kidnapped and fish him out if there's a fire."

"Oh, they'll do that all right," Sir Philip assured her. "In fact, in either of the cases you mention, two pairs of hands would probably be far more useful than one. My under-gardener, for example— he was probably there last night—would deal with any number of kidnappers."

Lesley sat thoughtful a moment.

"It's so funny," she said slowly, "to realise that this time next year he'll be on the verge of school. Dear me!"

Sir Philip looked at her.

"Relief, or regret?"

"I don't really know. Both, perhaps. But the odd thing," said Lesley thoughtfully, "is that what relief there *is* isn't nearly so—so thorough as I expected it would be. In fact, it seems horribly likely that I'm going to go on feeling responsible for him."

"It's a very good school," said Sir Philip.

"I know. But if I don't think he gets enough to eat I shall quite probably write to the Head. And then Pat will find out and loathe me ever after. . . ."

They laughed together, but Lesley was serious.

"That's all very well, but at the moment he's quite fond of me. And it's not good for the young to be suddenly disillusioned."

Sir Philip smiled.

"You needn't worry about that, my dear. Pat will never stop being fond of you."

"Why not? It's very natural."

"Because you don't try to possess him," said Sir Philip with sudden energy. "You don't want to. You don't love him enough. He'll never have to bother about whether you're really going to commit suicide or are only bluffing him. He'll never have to go round the house removing ornamental weapons. And the older he grows the more grateful he'll be."

From where she sat Lesley could see the great glowing Sargent on the opposite wall. Superb! She said,

"You make love very . . . undignifying."

"Possessive love, yes. They say women can stomach it sometimes, but I know no man can. He just wants to bolt. And daren't, for fear of the consequences. My God!"

Lesley kept her eyes on the picture. The words were bitter: did he wish them unspoken, he might imagine them unheard. She thought: 'I've known him now nearly four years, and in all that time he's never once mentioned his wife. Surely he hasn't forgotten her altogether!' There were no children, of course; no kinsfolk, hardly, for the War had played havoc with the succeeding generation; the name would die out and the Hall itself go to some remote middle-aged connection whom Sir Philip had ferreted out on his return from Greece. He was a man named Brooke, at that time in the Navy, and the nephew, by a first marriage, of a cousin of Lady Kerr's. The connection was thus extremely distant—so distant, in fact, that Charles Brooke himself was probably not aware of it, and Sir Philip, after thus having satisfied the deep-rooted instinct to leave property in the family, had resolutely refused either to make his heir's acquaintance or to have him informed. The lad (for so, during fifteen years, Sir Philip had continued to think of him) would only go on borrowing on post-obits; for the rest, he was presumably a gentleman, had a wife and two boys, and could count his chickens at leisure as soon as they were hatched. . . .

". . . And if he isn't grateful, he ought to be," said Sir Philip.

With a start Lesley recollected herself. It was not Charles Brooke they were talking of, it was Patrick. . . . .

". . . No," she said slowly, as though that had been her thought too; "no I don't adore him. I'm not even sure that I love him. I'm not a bit maternal, really."

Sir Philip looked at her thoughtfully.

"You know, it's a curious thing, but I believe that's true. That good woman, Mrs. Pomfret, for instance, keeps saying how you've devoted yourself to him: but she isn't right. You've devoted yourself much more to me. You've devoted yourself to the cottage, and quite a good deal to her own Henry. And as a result of all this non-devotion you've brought Pat up damned well." The faunish yellow eyes were suddenly steady. "A child should be—how can I put it?—not too much concentrated on. That's the real advantage of a large family. An only child supporting the whole weight of the mother's emotions—and sometimes the father's as well—he leads the most exhausting life on earth. It's what might very well have happened to Pat, if you'd been another kind of woman. My dear Lesley—you know all this better than I do, of course—a child doesn't want to absorb a life, he wants to inhabit one. Make a happy life for him to inhabit, and you make your child happy too.—I've never tried it myself," admitted Sir Philip, "but that's the theory."

'And you had it all ready for them!' thought Lesley. She got up from her chair and walked over to the window. It was an abrupt breaking-off; but if she would hide her compassion, what else was there to do?

III

Walking pensively home, she encountered Denis Cotton.

"By the way," he said carelessly, "weren't you saying you liked truffles? My aunt's just sent me a box on her way through Town. . . ."

Lesley gazed at it hopelessly. How impossible he was, how touching; above all, what a nuisance! And with a shiver of dismay she felt stir within her something that might very well develop (only she sincerely hoped it wouldn't) into the uneasy emotion of feeling responsible for him too.

Chapter Four

I

About five nights later her instinct was confirmed.

It was warm but showery, and Patrick having been put to bed, Lesley settled down to one of her rare evenings alone at the cottage. She was knitting a cream and dark-blue sweater (design by Chanel) from printed instructions, and though now reasonably expert felt the need for concentration. The fact that eight ounces of wool cost no more than five shillings, whereas the finished article (at any rate as worn by herself) cost three to four guineas, had been one of the outstanding discoveries of the previous year. With extreme perseverance, she learnt first to knit, then to knit well; and as a consequence was habitually to be seen about the orchard in the last word of woollen elegance. The one at present in hand had broad diagonal stripes and a stitch like string gloves, and with a cream tailored skirt—she still got skirts from Bradley's—would probably be unrivalled even in the by no means unmodish county of Bucks.

So for two hours Lesley knitted steadily on, with no more accompaniment than the click of her needles; and at the end of that time reaching a certain previously-fixed point, folded wool and needles together and lit a cigarette. It had long stopped raining: the night was warm, for she had let the fire out, and with possibly a moon above the apple-tree, if she cared to go and look for it. But Lesley smoked her cigarette and stayed where she was: a proper countrywoman! It was twenty past ten, and already quiet as midnight: when the cuckoo cried the half she would dout lights and go to bed. And suddenly, in that perfect stillness, her ear was caught by the faintest possible sound from the path under the window. It was a tiny dull jar—no more than that: as though someone in rubber shoes, moving cautiously up the path, had knocked against the iron scraper. Lesley held her breath.

There was someone outside.

There was someone outside the window, trying to see in. How she knew she could not have told; unless a will to enter, a yearning to see, could be stronger to penetrate than walls to exclude.

"Who is there?" said Lesley.

But her voice scarcely carried the length of the room: of course there was no answer. She thought, 'If I wait another moment, I shall be too frightened to move.' And suppressing the first prescient tremor, she got up and opened the door. It was Denis Cotton, not daring to knock.

For an instant they stood motionless, ridiculously staring. Then she put up her cigarette again and drew a long breath.

"Don't be angry with me."

His voice disarmed her. It was husky, low, beaten. Instead of rating him, she said,

"I thought you were burglars. I've been shivering with fright."

Instantly his whole being was a vessel of contrition. He loathed, he cursed himself; he wanted to die for having alarmed her. The usual sunburn no longer coloured his cheek: health, strength and life seemed to be visibly departing. And Lesley, who had once or twice observed the same phenomenon in Pat, sat down by the hearth again and asked for another cigarette.

He gave it to her with a slight return to normality; took one himself and burned his fingers with the match. Carefully avoiding all reference to the object of his visit, Lesley asked if he would like coffee.

He shook his head. He had not again spoken. But speech was rising within him, and an instinctive desire for tranquillity prompted
Lesley to get in first. She began to talk about Pat, about Pincher,
about her plans for the garden: related, with a wealth of amusing
detail, the latest sally of Mr. Povey's and his repulse by Mrs. Sprigg.
When she had finished, Denis told her that he loved her.

He told her extremely badly. With a naïve astonishment, as
though at something rare and strange, he described the classic
symptoms. He thought of her constantly, and was unable to sleep:
revolted from all customary occupation, and had discovered new
beauties in the works of the poets. In the silence of the room, in
the greater silence of the night, the words fell now one by one,
now in a sudden burst, but always with the same inevitability. In
his longer pauses, Lesley could have prompted him. She could have
prompted him—twenty-one and romantic—even to the end, when
he employed the last cliché of all to ask her to marry him.

With the strangest mixture of emotions—pity and affection, a
touch of amusement—Lesley sat and looked at him. 'How young!'
she thought. 'How charming! How young and charming, and what
a nuisance!'

"Say something, Lesley."

She said the only thing that seemed at all apposite.

"My dear—I was thirty-one last birthday."

He regarded her with ingenuous surprise. He had been telling
himself, thought Lesley, that she was perhaps twenty-five. . . . She
followed up her advantage.

"So you see how absurd it would be. You've made me very proud,
my dear"—he hadn't really, of course, because given the circumstances his falling in love with her was practically inevitable; but she
lied out of kindness—"and I hate you to be unhappy." She looked at
him again: he was miserable! And as though to show how seriously
she was taking him, Lesley frowned hard, wrinkling her brow into
unaccustomed lines. "Absurd!" she repeated severely.

"Tragic."

She accepted the correction.

"But only from your point of view, you understand. Not from mine. I should simply hate to be twenty again, or even twenty-five. One has a good time, of course, but it's still the good time of a children's party. Lots of ice-cream méringues, and a bilious attack afterwards."

He wasn't listening to her. He was watching the movement of her lips. When they were still again, he became conscious of a silence.

"Lesley."

She looked at him kindly. The next moment he was on his knees at her side, his face buried in her lap.

II

Just as she would have done for Pat, she smoothed back his thick short hair and promised that he would soon be better. She told him a beautiful fairy tale about the glories of the Levant Consular Service. She invented an uncle, an uncle in the Foreign Office, who had always maintained that of all Government services the Levant Consular was the most important. She drew a rapid word-picture of Athens and the Golden Horn, lavishing roses and marble against an azure sea. . . .

The head in her lap stirred convulsively.

"Don't."

Lesley broke off. But her fingers continued to move, and under them the head stirred again.

"Don't you know that anything beautiful always makes me want you more?" He looked up: his face, no more than six inches from her own, was twisted with distress. "Even here, seeing you every day, I can only just manage. As soon as I wake up, I think, 'When shall I see her?' And until I do see you I feel as if—as if I hadn't had any breakfast." The words were coming more easily, so fast indeed that once or twice he stumbled and mis-pronounced: attitude and all, he might have been at prayer. . . .

"Lesley, darling, you—you don't know how beautiful you are. Beautiful and good, and everything you say. . . . With Pat and in the orchard . . . always with your head bare. . . . Your lovely hair. . . . When you say that about being older, you don't know how silly it sounds. I—I want you so much I can't sleep."

A deep compassion troubled her heart. She said gently,

"My dear, I can only tell you what you won't believe."

"That I'll get over it when I go away?"

"Yes. Or . . . even without going away . . . if you stay long enough."

"The last part . . . is what *you* don't believe," said Denis slowly.

And suddenly, with denial on her lips, she could not utter it. For deep in her being, in her body and in her heart and in her subtle brain, she knew that if she wanted him, he was hers to have.

But she didn't want him, poor Denis!

She thought, 'I must be careful. To him this is all real and ter-rible.' And like some expert craftsman before an important and delicate piece of work, she gathered all her resources of skill and experience.

She thought, 'I must not belittle myself. Before the ultimate vir-tues (which he obviously believes me to possess) one may bow down and worship without loss of self-respect. And as for beauty—since, after these two months we shall never meet again, it is perfectly pos-sible that he may die happy in the belief that I resembled Lady Ham-ilton. And to have loved and lost, in early youth, a mixture of Lady Hamilton and Florence Nightingale—that is no misfortune for any man.' The conjunction of these names did not intimidate her: for the boy was in love. 'I must be very good, and very beautiful,' thought Lesley quite calmly; 'and then however hard it is now, there will be no bitterness afterwards.'

"What are you thinking of, Lesley?"

She knew what to say.

"I am thinking how selfish I am."

"You!"

"Because I take happiness from you without giving any back."

"Lesley!" A returning flicker of life brightened in his eye. "You mean—you mean it really does make you happy, my loving you?"

She nodded.

"It would make any woman happy, my dear. As I say, we're selfish. But then when I see you being hurt like this, I feel I want to do anything on earth to stop it. Even to pretending love in return. Only that . . . that's the one thing I can't pretend, and I don't think you'd have me try."

Denis shook his head violently; and in this was unwise, for the tears, which he had hitherto managed to conceal, now ran free. But he was getting better, he was almost brave; he said gruffly,

"I'm not crying. Those have been there some time. I wish you'd tell me to die for you or something."

"I'd much rather you learnt Turkish," said Lesley.

"Well, I'd rather die," said Denis. He paused as though to consider the matter. "I've been thinking about it so long," he said.

Instinctively, as though she had seen him reach for a weapon, Lesley put out her hand and caught his arm.

"Denis!"

He stared at her with a sort of wonder.

"You look quite frightened. . . ."

"Of course I'm frightened!" cried Lesley. And it was frightening, it was terrifying, that this boy of twenty-one should for a month and more have walked and talked and played with the children, and always in his mind the familiar image of death. Terrifying in its incongruity, more terrifying still in all that it implied of the soul's isolation. . . .

"It's all right," said Denis gruffly, "I won't now, not now that I know you do care a little. I promise I won't." He soothed, he nursed, he comforted her! "And I'll learn my God-awful Turkish and pass my exams, and get into the Consular and uphold British prestige— anything you want, darling, so long as you'll just write to me sometimes. . . . You will, won't you?"

And seeing her nod, with a sudden gesture he caught at her fingers and pressed them against his breast. Under her palm the heart knocked.

"Feel there," he said, "it's quite steady."

And all at once, to her extreme surprise, she found that all she had been saying was quite true. He *had* made her happy. He had reminded her, with a sort of piercing sweetness, that man in his youth is a generous creature.

Chapter Five

I

There were several mornings, during that unusually fine September, when Leslie awoke to a feeling of ill-defined responsibility. She had to do something, but what was it? Wash Pat's hair, or buy marmalade? And then as she sat up in bed, as her brain cleared, the forgotten duty would gradually return. She had to be good and beautiful and remind Denis Cotton to write to his mother.

She was also making him roll the grass rather a lot, and the patch nearest the house improved visibly. When the ground was too dry to roll he dug in a new flower-bed, which Lesley was planning to fill with roses as soon as she could afford them. The sight of so much gratis labour sometimes disturbed her a little; it seemed heartless, a trifle opportunist, even, so to harness his passion to the garden-roller. But a deeper instinct carried her safely past such refinements, and Mr. Cotton's appetite began at last to improve. He slept better, too, and had once or twice to be called in the morning (but this Lesley heard of only from the Pomfrets; Denis himself never mentioned the fact, probably through fear of hurting her feelings). As for his mental activities, he was still completely incapable of playing bridge, but could just keep his mind on Turkish if the Vicar were there to help.

Thus, week by week, the delicate and important task went successfully forward: Denis openly adoring, but not without other occupation, Lesley conscientiously good and beautiful, but now with no greater anxiety than that he might be prevailed on by Mr. Povey to give her the bird-bath as a keepsake.

For in the Aberdeen bacchante Mr. Povey had at last met his match. She was going for thirty-five and six, and she was still unsold. He had even tried Florrie Walpole, who with her noted taste for the showy seemed at first blush a likely victim; but Florrie, though she would have been pleased enough to possess the object, drew the financial line (with her equally noted frankness) at ten shillings. She talked the matter over with Arnold Hasty, in one of their long-range conversations that Lesley used to hear every evening; and the policeman agreed with her. It was a handsome piece, no doubt, and had a lot of work in it; but to spend more than ten shillings on what was virtually a knick-knack! The reason rebelled.

"Myself," added Arnold judicially, "I wouldn't give more'n seven and six. And that's as much as a dog licence."

Florrie said he was probably right. Whatever her faults, she had nothing of the gold-digger, and the ten shillings in question had been scraped and saved out of her butter-and-egg money. For her career was not, after all, to be pursued behind a draper's counter; she had tried it for a week and returned rejoicing. It was not the hardness of the work that repelled her, it was the formality; Florrie was strong as a horse, placid as a cow, and could stand all day long: but to see someone she knew, and not be able to shout to them—that was too much. She was always seeing someone she knew, and sometimes, naturally, forgot herself. So old Alfred, with very great kindness, had waived his right to a week's notice and let her go at once. The story reached the cottage piecemeal, partly from Mrs. Sprigg, partly from Florrie herself, and partly from Mrs. Pomfret, who had been one of those shouted to while passing through the haberdashery; and Lesley never ceased to regret that no visit of her own had fallen during those remarkable six days.

The regret itself—had she not to a large extent lost the habit of introspection—might have struck her as remarkable also; she had not used to be disappointed by anything less than a Cochran first night. But so it was. And one thing at least could be relied on: that however successful the piece, however brilliant the stalls, in missing Florrie at the counter she had missed at least equal enjoyment.

II

At the beginning of October Denis returned to Oxford. The actual parting, which Lesley would have given a good deal to avoid, took place at the cottage. She did not avoid. Her delicate masterpiece was completed to the last stroke. But she did manoeuvre so that interview would be cut short after ten to fifteen minutes.

Immediately after lunch, then, on the last day, Lesley sent Pat up to the Pomfrets with a message that she herself would follow in an hour's time. Twenty minutes later, exactly when she expected him, Denis Cotton appeared at the gate. He had not brought her the bird-bath. Traditional to the last, he bore the manuscript of a sonnet and a photograph of himself. The latter, indeed, he did not so much bring as happen to have about him: but when Lesley asked if she might keep it, the relief was so great that he forgot to look surprised. His lips worked, but without sound, he folded paste-board and paper together and held them dumbly towards her. Emotion, it was plain, would soon overcome him; so in equal silence Lesley took his head in her hands and kissed him once, very gently, on his still-moving lips. The next instant there was a clatter of pans as Mrs. Sprigg returned to the kitchen.

"Good-bye, my dear."

He looked at her stupidly, his mind not yet recovered from its swoon: then perceiving that she meant him to go, he turned and went.

Chapter Six

I

With the departure of Denis summer ended. The fact was purely objective: Lesley missed him, to be sure, but the rain on the Chilterns found no echo in her heart. The autumn had simply come early, and if she watched its progress with unusual interest the reason had nothing whatever to do with Denis.

The reason was this, that it was the last autumn she ever expected to spend in the country. Next year would see Pat at school, and though they might still quite possibly spend summers at the cottage, from September to June she could live where she pleased. It was the end, in fact, of bondage.

'I ought to celebrate,' thought Lesley.

She thought it quite sincerely. The desirability of returning to Baker Street was an article of faith; she had always intended to go back, she would soon be able to go back, and back she would therefore go. So . . .

'I ought to celebrate,' thought Lesley again; and after a little rummaging through cupboards found out a dusty bottle of Cointreau. It was slightly corked, but more than half-full: she poured out a liqueur glass and with doll's-tea-party solemnity drank to approaching freedom. The ritual over, she wiped her lips, washed the glass, and as an Indian might bury the hatchet, carefully reburied the bottle. The tomahawk is war, the bottle was Baker Street; it would be ready to hand when the time came, but the time was not just yet.

The season, indeed, had never passed more peacefully. The sun shone, apples ripened, week after week slipped calmly away; then the sun withdrew itself, trees were bare, and the placid autumn slid into a tranquil winter of which the only outstanding event—apart, of course, from Christmas Day—was the nobbling of Arnold by Florrie Walpole.

It was not Lesley who put it like that, it was Mrs. Sprigg. Lesley and Mrs. Pomfret sent over notes of congratulation—Florrie loved getting notes—bought wedding presents at Walpoles in Aylesbury, and gave their promise to attend, all in a spirit of complete sincerity. But the village as a whole—though it too bought gifts, and though nothing on earth (save perhaps a machine-gun in the porch) could have kept it from the ceremony—the village as a whole agreed with Mrs. Sprigg. For Arnold Hasty was a catch: he earned money all the year round, he had pigs and a pension and a neat brick cottage. And he had Powers as well. He could have people up, anyone, even Mr. Povey; he could ask to see your wireless licence. ("Just about what 'e's fit for," Mrs. Sprigg used to say scornfully. "The last chap we 'ad used to lie out all night after poachers, Miss Frewen, but Arnold, it's all wireless with him. 'E likes to look at the sets.") This was no doubt true and Mr. Hasty himself would have been the last to deny it; but there are other qualities at least as dear to a prospective bride as the tendency to lie out, and these Arnold had in abundance. He was steady: an extreme shyness kept him off the women, as a squeamish stomach kept him off the drink. The village of High Westover was not notably abstemious—no village could be, with Mr. Povey in its midst; but whatever the celebration, whoever the host, alone in his virtue its policeman drank shandygaff.

In fact, anyone who married Arnold would have been said to have nobbled him; and a little becoming humility, therefore, would probably have done much to soften the tongue of public opinion;

but such was not Florrie's way. She had borne herself gallantly in a variety of circumstances, and it was hardly to be expected that with the banns safely past their third calling her exuberance should have failed her. Nor did it. If anything, it increased; and when the time came she marched up the aisle with veil a-flowing and on her beautiful face a look of happy surprise. Old Horace was there too, of course, and theoretically leading her; but for all the notice people took of him he might just as well have stayed at home. Florrie filled the bill. She had a white frock and veil, both with a great many yards of stuff in them, a white bouquet containing a great many chrysanthemums, and on her head a great deal of orange-blossom. When she made her responses it was in a loud, optimistic voice—far louder than Arnold's; but he was not to be outdone, he spoke up manfully, so that at the last the happy couple appeared to be hallooing cheerfully to each other, as Lesley had so often heard them on summer evenings.

"And if you ask me, he might have done a lot worse," said Mrs. Pomfret, as they emerged after the ceremony. "Florrie's got heaps of good qualities, with all her bounce. By the way, where was Gerald?"

Lesley laughed.

"Locked in the washhouse, to keep his face clean for the breakfast." It was quite true, and not nearly so brutal as it sounded, for the parlour, where he would have been locked normally, was full of wedding presents. These were handsome, useful, but above all numerous—so remarkably numerous, indeed, as almost to suggest that Florrie had artlessly mingled amongst them a good many trifles she had bought for herself. There were objects of art and objects of virtu, cut-glass vases and fireproof crockery; in the first of which categories, however, one expected masterpiece was conspicuous by its absence. (Many of the guests went and looked for it in the garden; and it was very generally whispered that old Povey was losing his grip.) There was a tea-set from Mrs. Povey (she disliked Florrie intensely, but Arnold was in the Force) and an inkstand from Sir Philip; while prominent amongst them all—indeed in the place of honour—blazed the outsize nightdress-case presented by Lesley herself. The word is chosen with care, as Lesley chose the case; covered all over with pink satin petals, plastered (at its rose's heart) with a plaque of gold sequins, the awful object loudly blazed. Even Arnold had noticed it, said Florrie, and it was the only one of the presents she was bothering to pack. For there was to be a honeymoon as well—there was everything one could think of—and at half-past three that afternoon the happy couple departed for Southend. They went flushed, triumphant (Arnold at least with no more than shandygaff) and taking Gerald with them; for, as the bride pointed out, he had never seen the sea.

"Won't it be rather cold?" asked Lesley, whom their exact destination had hitherto escaped. She had left the festivities early, a good two hours at least before Florrie started kissing people; but Mrs. Sprigg was there to the end.

"Cold?" repeated Mrs. Sprigg jovially. "*They* won't notice the cold. A good bracing up'll be just what they could do with. I 'ad *my* wedding in July, and the 'eat was something 'orrible." The bright shrew-mouse eye—brighter even than usual—turned suddenly on her employer. "Just you remember that, Miss Frewen, and don't be led away. They talk about 'June the month of roses,' but what I say is, let's 'ave a bit of mistletoe. If you ask *me*, Miss Frewen—"

"Speaking of mistletoe," observed Lesley swiftly, "isn't it time we made the puddings?"

II

It was indeed, it was the fourteenth of December; the reason Mrs. Sprigg had forgotten them being that she herself simply took a 'bus into Aylesbury and bought one at a shop. So did the other women; and probably in all High Westover that Christmas there were not more than three batches of puddings—at the Vicarage, at the Hall, and at the White Cottage—made ritually at home. Mrs. Pomfret and Sir Philip's cook, indeed, were almost equal experts, the one in the plain, the other in the rich; while Lesley the amateur obeyed all Mrs. Beeton's instructions, let Pat suck candied peel, and thoroughly enjoyed herself with the dark and odorous mess. The thought that it must be extremely fattening did just occur to her; but only fleetingly, and for the second year in succession, with a good appetite and a quiet mind, she ate three Christmas dinners.

There was one at the Pomfrets, on Christmas Day itself, one at the cottage the day after, and one at the Hall on New Year's Eve; the last of these functions being distinguished by a Haut Briton 1900 and the presence of Denis Cotton. He had flown over specially from somewhere in Switzerland, arriving (as Lesley was glad to observe) as innocently and justifiably pleased with himself as a cat with two tails. For he was to sleep at the Pomfrets' and fly back the next morning, so that all the danger—there was fog over the Channel—all that expense, had been incurred for no more than a brief three hours or so of his lady's company. It was a gesture indeed, and an eminently successful one: Mrs. Pomfret held up her hands, the Vicar shook his head, even the experienced Sir Philip—though his own more rococo taste would no doubt have added a snow-shower of camellias on the cottage roof—even the experienced Sir Philip was visibly impressed. As for Lesley, she displayed and felt almost as much pleasure as even Denis could have wished; for every circumstance of the visit seemed to her one more proof that his summer's passion would soon have crystallised into a romantic legend of early youth. Indeed, he was enjoying it already—his own devotion, the Christmas scene; she had a strong suspicion that he could really have stayed at least till to-morrow's luncheon, and was only refusing to do so because lunch would have spoiled the picture. To fly over for one evening— that was romance: to fly over for nearly a day, eat three square meals and hang about the house—that was merely a trip. The legend was in being, and with a clear conscience Lesley lent herself to its embellishment. From the first startled greeting to the last and solitary kiss, she was all an exquisite kindness that anointed his soul; and when at last they parted (as it might well be for ever) the legend had been rounded and enriched with a worthy epilogue.

'And—and I've got it too,' thought Lesley suddenly. She had opened her window, in spite of the cold, and was leaning still cloaked to admire a frosty sky: would that be in the legend too—New Year's morning and the smell of the fallow earth? She leaned farther, saw the puddles skinned with ice, and on the perfectly still air breath made visible. . . .

'I believe it's going to freeze!' thought Lesley, and mindful of Pat, pulled-to the window.

Chapter Seven

I

Her prophecy was fulfilled, though not for another month. At the beginning of February, there was ice not only on the puddles, but also skinning the canal; and three days later, just after breakfast, the under-gardener arrived with a message from the Hall.

"Sir Philip's compliments, there's skating on the lake, so will you and Master Patrick come up at once and not stay to potter?"

"Miss Frewen's compliments," replied Lesley promptly, "and she'll be up in ten minutes. Master Patrick has gone on the canal."

As soon as the man was gone she covered up the butter, lidded the marmalade, and ran upstairs to pull out her skating-dress. It was of privileged black, laced down the sides with a white cord: which lacing, she discovered, would now have to be loosened at least an inch. At any more leisured moment Lesley would have been seriously upset, but with the sun bright and the ice waiting she was already rubbing the vaseline from her skates before the original shock had time to stun her. 'Another inch—blast—thank goodness there's a slip!'—so ran her thoughts as she crammed on the velvet cap: snatching her scarf, they had changed to, 'Bulbs—didn't Sir Philip say I could have some tulips?' And as she ran out of the door she thought—'Oranges—one for Pat when he comes in, one for me after supper—must get some more this afternoon.'

The path across fields was hard as iron: no hunting, thought Lesley. They were by no means a hunting community, but Sir Philip, from sheer force of habit, always kept a wary eye on the weather, and liked to be sympathised with when his sport would have been spoiled. It was a weakness which Lesley, clean against her original humanitarian principles, shamelessly indulged; herself opening the conversation, as often as not, with the remark that this (frost, snow, flood or whatever it was) would put a stopper on the huntin'. It was the only phrase of which she felt at all confident: there was Jorrocks's 'ard 'igh road, of course—(was it Jorrocks?)—but Sir Philip always liked to get that in himself. And passing through the lower gate, Lesley determined that as soon as opportunity arose she would break new ground with a reference to scent. . . .

"There you are!" called Sir Philip, waving to her between the trees.

She held up her boots in reply and hurried forward. He was already on the ice, light and spidery in an antique skating-costume of tight black frieze, vaguely branden-burged and with collar of astrakhan. On his head was a round cap, also of astrakhan, on his hands a pair of white worsted gloves: and waving back his greeting Lesley suddenly wondered whether her own magpie colouring gave her the same ghostly look.

"This is splendid!" called Sir Philip, casually executing one more figure before returning to the bank. "I always knew you weren't a potterer. Now we shall get at least two hours."

"But the ice is going to last much longer than that!" exclaimed Lesley. "I can feel it freezing!"

Sir Philip shook his head.

"This afternoon," he exclaimed genially, "cowardice will compel me to throw it open to the mob. So if you can start a few good dangerous cracks, my dear, I shall take it as a favour."

"How deep is it?"

"Deep enough to drown the whole village. But don't be alarmed. If either you or Pat go through, the gardeners have instructions to fish you out."

"That's the most flattering thing we've ever had said to us," remarked Lesley, sitting down and beginning to put on her skates. Sir Philip watched with interest: his own were the long curly kind, such as are sometimes seen in engravings.

"You probably skate brilliantly," he said at last. "So did I, about fifty years ago. Those were the days, my dear, when ponds were frozen solid from November to February. That's what I call a winter."

Lesley looked judicious.

"It must have put a stopper on the huntin', though."

"You're right there. And that's an odd thing," said Sir Philip, "because I seem to remember huntin' too. Both of 'em right through the winter. . . ." He put out a hand and helped her down the bank: her skates bit on ice, and shooting forward alone she cut a whole series of eights in the centre of the ice. The first was tentative, the second neat; but the third and succeeding ones swept faster and faster till she broke away from the centre and finished on her impetus in a flourish of arabesques.

"Right as usual," called Sir Philip behind her. "You do skate beautifully. Let's waltz."

She spun to a halt.

"There's no music."

"Never mind, I'll hum." And to the sudden ghost of a waltz tune Lesley felt a thin old hand touch her waist, a thin old hand close on her wrist: and all at once they were flying away together over the dark and ringing ice.

At first she enjoyed it. Sir Philip waltzed not exactly well, but with a sort of ingrained precision. Each short, jerky movement was perfectly carried out; with no swing or elasticity, there was equally no wavering. Curbing her own speed, shortening her step, Lesley followed obediently, and even after a second time round had breath for compliments.

"You waltz like a professional," she said.

But Sir Philip did not answer: and sideways-glancing she saw that his lined old face was set in a mask of concentration. In the necessity of making certain movements with his feet, of continuing to make them long after he wanted to stop, all else had been forgotten. A partner he had, of course—one couldn't dance without a partner—but she had ceased to be Lesley Frewen. She was any young woman who could follow him, and who must be made to tire first. . . .

And beginning to tire, Lesley ceased to enjoy. An odd thought took her mind, and refused to be expelled: she remembered the water. It was there all the time, deep and dark beneath a brittle three inches of dance-floor; and at the edge, where the ducks were, the floor was broken away. Lesley shivered. The glow of swift movement had suddenly left her; she was numb all over, even to her feet, and through their two gloves, her own and his, Sir Philip's fingers felt cold as ice. As though there were nothing inside the worsted but thin cold bones with no flesh or blood to keep them warm. . . . The ice rang in her brain, on the veins at her wrist the bony fingers closed tighter and tighter: but still the neat, jerky movements never faltered. It was like dancing with a marionette, it was like dancing with Death. . . .

II

"My dear, I've made you dizzy!" said Sir Philip.

Lesley opened her eyes. The lake lay quiet beneath her feet, the trees stood moveless and in ordered rows. But at the nape of her neck there was still a numbness, as though an icy pressure had just been removed.

She tried to laugh.

"You have indeed. It must be years since I skated." They were moving towards the bank, Lesley leaning like any novice. She thought, 'I won't go into the house, I must go straight home'; and surreptitiously, while Sir Philip unlaced her boots, she pinched her cheeks to restore their colour. The ruse worked: his anxiety allayed, Sir Philip passed in one breath from remorse to reminiscence. For he had unlaced, in his time, more things than skating-boots, and in the plenitude of his relief was soon on the verge of a very wrong story indeed. But he stopped in time, and with the offer of the Rolls regained his equilibrium.

Lesley shook her head. She had got over her fright as quickly and completely as Pat got over a surfeit, but the impulse to be gone was still alive, and with the composite excuse of Mrs. Pomfret and a pudding, refusing even a glass of wine, she squeezed Sir Philip's hand, gathered up her belongings, and hurried back home by the way she had come.

III

The rest of the daylight she spent teaching Pat on the canal, which by two o'clock was almost as deserted as the lake that morning. The ice was just as good, the area far greater, but there was a sense of privilege about going up to the Hall which the Village as a whole found impossible to resist. The young Pomfrets stayed, however, watched Lesley do a drop-three, and thereafter followed at her heel like gulls after a ship. They were all four good natural skaters, and if only the frost held had every hope of being able to cut eights by the end of another day. There might be a special prayer for it, said Alec hopefully, like the ones for rain.

"No, there isn't," panted his sister, wobbling unsteadily round on an outside edge. "I looked all through this morning. But there's no reason why we shouldn't pray on our own. Is there, Miss Frewen?"

"None at all," said Lesley cheerfully; and indeed her agnosticism had always been of the mild, non-proselytising variety, a mere absence of taste, as it were, for anything to do with religion. What she was concerned with at the moment was the deplorable angle of Pat's left boot.

"Try and keep on the flat of the blade!" she called. "You'll never learn to skate like that!"

"But I can skate!" boasted Pat, precariously balancing on splayed-out ankles. "I can skate! Look at me!"

Without further waste of breath Lesley shot to his side and grasped him firmly by the back of the jacket.

"Now lift your feet *up*, Pat, as though you were walking through mud. Don't try to slide yet."

"But the others aren't walking!" protested Pat. "I want to slide!"

"The others began by walking, and you'll have to too," said Lesley patiently. And to herself, she thought, 'How much do they get at the Ice Club? Seven-and-six, isn't it, for half-an-hour? And dirt cheap at the price!'

The employment was not, indeed, one to which she was temperamentally inclined: requiring as it did more sympathy than skill and more patience than either. But she was desperately anxious that Pat should hold his own, and the sight of him so outshone lent her qualities she hardly recognised. With incredible persistence she forced him to plod up and down out of the way of the others, herself plodding likewise for his better encouragement. By the end of the afternoon an improvement was visible, and when at last she let him slide he slid evenly on both feet. Lesley watched him with triumph: he was nothing if not dogged, and if only the frost held, Alec would soon have a rival.

About four o'clock, just as they were tiring, Mrs. Pomfret appeared with a whole newly-baked cake, ready cut into slices for distribution among the hungry. They ate as they skated, for the sun was gone, and Lesley by special request gave a last exhibition. This time she waltzed alone, in a pattern as free as a gull's swooping: the ice rang under her skates, the good food crumbled in her mouth; never before—tingling with warmth, intoxicated with rhythm—had she felt so wholly alive.

Chapter Eight

I

Hurrying down Pig Lane with a suitcase in her hand, Lesley was accosted by Mr. Walpole.

"Went skatin' up at the Hall, Miss Frewen?"

"On the canal, mostly. I was up at the Hall in the morning."

"Ah," said Mr. Walpole, almost with animation, "you haven't heard, then. Sir Philip, he's been through the ice and got a proper wetting."

Lesley expressed her concern and hastened on. 'Dear me!' she thought, 'one thing after another!' The other thing, in this case, and the reason for her baggage—being the serious illness of Mrs. Pomfret's aunt. She was no ordinary aunt, but a second mother, having reared the childish Clara (as Mrs. Pomfret then was) from the age of three; and late the previous evening, as they all lay about exhausted after the day's exercise, a telegram had arrived referring briefly to pneumonia and requesting the niece's immediate presence. The ensuing flutter was considerable, for to even so placid a parent as Mrs. Pomfret the thought of leaving, at one night's notice, a home and four children, could not be other than highly disturbing; and she was at least approaching her wits' end when Lesley received a sudden inspiration and invited herself to stay.

"My dear! would you really?" exclaimed Mrs. Pomfret joyfully.

"Of course I will, and Pat can go in with the boys. He'll adore it. And I'll see they all change their stockings after rain and go to bed at the right times."

"—Seven, eight, and a quarter to nine," murmured Mrs. Pomfret. "My dear, you're a blessing in disguise—no, I don't mean that, do I?—and I'll go with an easy mind."

As swiftly and simply as that, all was arranged; and as swiftly and simply, Mrs. Pomfret having departed, did Lesley settle herself in. The ways of the Vicarage, indeed, were almost as well known to her as the ways of the cottage, though she had certainly not realised quite how enormous was the body of work its absent mistress had daily to get through. The darning alone was occupation for a nurserymaid, the making of puddings proceeded almost continuously, and it was not till the end of the third afternoon—for Mrs. Pomfret's absence was eventually prolonged for a fortnight—that Lesley found time to go up to the Hall, where Sir Philip received her in the library from a sort of cocoon of eiderdowns. He was taking his chill very seriously, with hot bottles, hot whisky, and a carriage foot-warmer.

II

"You *are* enjoying yourself," said Lesley.

Sir Philip grunted.

"The modern woman," he said. "Your grandmother, my dear, would at once have flown to my pillows. Take some sherry."

"But your pillows are beautiful," protested Lesley, doing as she was told. "Why should I come and disarrange them?"

"Because I should like you to. Because every man, when feeling a trifle uneasy, likes to believe that his women are feeling even more so. It panders to our sense of superiority."

Without a word Lesley set down her glass and went over to his chair. Causing as little discomfort as possible, she plumped up one

or two cushions, fiddled about with the bolster, and drew a travelling rug tighter about the whole.

"Thank you," said Sir Philip. "And now confess. Didn't you get
some slight satisfaction too?"

"Out of giving you pleasure I did," admitted Lesley honestly.
"Not out of the fussing itself. But then"—she paused, and looked at
him with humour—"I don't really come into the category of your
women."

"You don't feel it, then?" said Sir Philip placidly. "Now, I do. Perhaps because you're living in my cottage. I feel as though there were
possibly a relationship between us—nothing obligatory, you know,
but one of those curious, underground connections that make English history so fascinating." He reached out deliberately and lifted his
glass. "I feel, for instance, that if you were had up for exceeding the
speed limit, I should have to come and bail you out."

Lesley regarded him whimsically.

"You almost tempt me to buy a car," she said; and they fell into a
sudden deep silence, as though the conversation could now be carried on without the impediment of words. The fire crackled, a stable-
dog barked: far across the park Lesley could hear a faint hymn-tune
being tried over on five bells. Raising a long sallow hand, as though
to shield his eyes from the flame, Sir Philip said abruptly,

"My son was born in that cottage."

Involuntarily her eyes flew to the great Sargent, glowing and
sumptuous even in the dusk. Sir Philip shook his head.

"No. I have no heir. And *he* died at Gallipoli, of enteric."

On the other side of the hearth Lesley sat very still. Behind that
wrinkled hand, behind those wrinkled lids, a vision was moving:
she must not disturb it. And looking again at the Sargent, she suddenly thought, 'And *you*—what was *your* story?' But the portrait
kept its counsel.

"So you will understand," said Sir Philip, lowering his hand, "that
it seemed very natural for me to see a woman and child there again."

She said softly,

"Was that why you let it to me?"

"No. No." For a moment, half sadly, half humorously, he had tried to give himself the benefit of the doubt. "To tell the truth, I had almost forgotten. It's you, my dear, who have brought her back."

Simple as the first dairy-maid, Lesley raised incredulous eyes.

"She died, you see, more than thirty years ago," said Sir Philip. "You think it strange? Wrong in a man, perhaps, but I assure you, Lesley, not in the least strange. What is strange is that now, ever since you came here, I think of her almost constantly."

"You had never really forgotten at all," said Lesley.

The fire crackled, the dog barked: they would soon be sitting in darkness, with only a red fire to light the crystals, and Lady Kerr's portrait no more than a deeper shadow on the dim walls. The dog barked: the fire crackled: had bell-practice finished, or was the wind blowing another way?

"She had a laugh like a blackbird's," said Sir Philip.

III

Soon after, Lesley went away: she did not wish to mar, by their usual wit, an impression of such deep and tender intimacy. 'A laugh like a black-bird's!' What a phrase to end on! She said softly,

"I'll come again soon. To-morrow, perhaps, or at any rate the day after."

He looked at her with great kindness.

"When you can, my dear. But there are other things more important for you than I am."

The statement, from so confessed an egoist, made her open her eyes. The Pomfrets? The Pomfrets were certainly keeping her busy, but since when had Sir Philip thought of anyone but himself?

"You must be worse than I thought," said Lesley, and went away laughing.

She was not able to return on the morrow, however, nor for many days after, for Alec and Pat caught coughs, and she promptly sent them to bed. The measure was a drastic one, but other people's children are like other people's china; and with a fire in the boys' room already it seemed a waste not to put Pat in bed too. It all made more work, of course, but safety came first; as to the sufferers, they rather enjoyed themselves, for Lesley read aloud a good deal, out of an expurgated edition of the Arabian Nights, and they also invented the new occupation of trying to suck up the sugar off Turkish delight like lemonade through a straw. Neither made any progress, but Alec gave up first. With three other children in action the rest of the day's routine naturally proceeded as usual, while nine o'clock at night, when the last had gone to bed, opened a long and oddly domestic evening in the company of the Vicar. Sometimes they listened to the gramophone—Lesley with her darning, Mr. Pomfret with his pipe; but chiefly Mr. Pomfret talked. He did not, of course, actually prefer her company to his wife's, because he was a Vicar, but there was no doubt he enjoyed it. Lesley, on the other hand, after about the third session, became conscious of a slight disillusionment: his conversation was always good, but he had a preacher's wind, and she now first began to attribute to something other than pure unselfishness the unfailing good humour with which his wife saw him depart to spend an evening at the Hall. With the same good humour Lesley would have seen him off herself; but this resource was no longer available, for Sir Philip's chill seemed to have settled in his temper, and he had asked neither of them to dinner since Lesley's last visit. This sudden moroseness, explained the Vicar, was but the normal accompaniment of any slight indisposition, and his own parochial calls now took place in the morning and lasted about ten minutes. He went every day, however, returning occasionally with a message for Lesley, once with a hothouse bloom or two, but in general with no more to report than crabbedness and a tendency to swear.

"But how is the chill?" demanded Lesley, sniffing at her forced hyacinths.

"On the liver—or so he says. He also says that it's worse than gout."

"And I haven't been up for nearly a fortnight! Did you tell him I was coming to-morrow?"

To her extreme surprise, the Vicar looked suddenly distressed.

"Do you know, my dear," he said, "if I were you I don't think I should go. Being ill doesn't agree with him. He's got into one of his hermit-crab moods. . . ."

"You mean he said he didn't *want* me?" persisted Lesley.

The Vicar looked more distressed still.

"Well—not quite that exactly, but he'd evidently rather be left alone. At that age, I suppose, one feels entitled to a few crochets."

She listened with politeness; but in her heart she was both surprised and hurt. Sir Philip not want to see her! It was preposterous! It was inexplicable! Even out of mere courtesy, even if only for the sparing of a rebuff, he could surely have supported her company for a bare ten minutes! And concealing her chagrin, Lesley felt the hurt go deeper. For she who had believed herself—and surely after that last meeting had been right to believe herself—his dear friend, was now thus brusquely informed that he no longer wished to be amused. Or so she saw it, as she feigned indifference; and the hyacinths smelt less sweet.

At this juncture, however, and by a fortunate coincidence, her thoughts were effectually distracted by no less an event than the simultaneous arrival of two telegrams. One was from Mrs. Pomfret, announcing her return that afternoon: the other, for Lesley, contained a long and enthusiastic account of the 1933 Buick, ending with an invitation to lunch, the day following, at the Yellow Swan, at Thame. It was one of those communications, in fact, for which Elissa had been so long and deservedly famous.

'After all this time!' thought Lesley. 'Elissa!' By contrast with Sir Philip's capriciousness, her fidelity in friendship (though, as Lesley herself remarked, after all that time) was doubly welcome; and since her duties at the Vicarage would by then be over, Lesley wired back at once a grateful acceptance. Unlike the Locks, Elissa had forgotten to prepay an answer: but it was a shilling well spent on mental distraction.

By four o'clock that afternoon Mrs. Pomfret was back; and it speaks volumes for her character that she returned in genuinely good spirits. For the aunt, by whose will she would benefit to the extent of five hundred pounds, had against all expectation made a complete recovery. She was extremely grateful, however, for Mrs. Pomfret's attention, and was almost certainly going to send after her, as a token of esteem, the small garden roller she had so often admired.

With a sort of sorrowing affection, the Vicar took his wife's hand.

"That's splendid, my dear," he said, "and I expect we shall use it a lot. But the next time you're there, do you think you could admire that small oil-painting over the dining-room sofa? I have an idea it's a Raeburn."

Chapter Nine

I

In rather more of a hurry than she had intended, Lesley set out to meet Elissa. For she had meant to dress carefully, to spend a long time over her face; but after taking Pat up to the Vicarage, putting milk for the cats, and talking to Mrs. Sprigg, there was only just time to put on her hat and run for the 'bus. She went, in fact, just as she was, in a sweater of bright daffodil yellow, brown skirt and short leather jacket; a combination pleasing enough in its way, but definitely . . .

'Simple-minded,' thought Lesley, considering her image in the 'bus window. 'All I want is a buttonhole of wool flowers.' For a moment or two the reflection depressed her (especially when she remembered the cream-and-crimson chevrons of her latest knitting. They would have impressed anyone, even Elissa); but all other emotions were soon overshadowed by the pleasure of the approaching reunion.

Why this should have been so, Lesley did not stop to think. The gap in their acquaintance, now of nearly three years' duration, had been supported by her with no more than the most occasional and mildest pang; and no doubt the same with Elissa, who would have supported no pang at all, not even the mildest, without doing something about it. She now wanted to show her new car, and so remembered old acquaintance; but though Lesley knew this to be so, it in no way affected her present flow of affection. For Elissa—therein lay the spell!—came from the enchanted territory of Baker Street, wherein no one could do wrong; like a magic carpet she carried that territory with her, and Lesley joyfully looked forward to stepping upon it too. Her imagination, as will be seen, was still a little coloured by the Arabian Nights; and indeed there *was* something about Elissa that made her by no means out of place among—for example—those ambiguous widows who came to buy silk and vamped the merchants. . . . So ran Lesley's thoughts as the 'bus stopped, proceeded, and stopped again; and with every successive mile her impatience grew. This was unfortunate in a way, because as soon as she reached Thame it became gradually more and more apparent that Elissa, as usual, was going to be late.

And she was late; she was very late indeed. Lesley could have creamed her face and changed from top to toe, and now instead found no better distraction than the pile of illustrated papers in the lounge of the Yellow Swan. She did not dare go and look at the shops, in case Elissa came and missed her; and only a strong initial impetus enabled her spirits to rise superior to one hour and ten minutes of hunger and suspense. But rise they did, though only just: and at five past two, when a brand-new Buick slid gracefully into the square, she was able to go out and meet it with genuine pleasure.

"Elissa!"

With a swift wriggling movement, curiously reminiscent of getting out of bed, Elissa slipped from the low seat and looked inquiringly round. Then her eye was caught, she slammed-to the door, and an instant later had flung herself over the threshold and into the arms of her friend.

"Darling!" cried Elissa, quite in the old way.

"Darling!" responded Lesley, quite in the old way too.

"How lovely to see you! Come and look at my car!"

They went out on to the pavement and examined it minutely,

Elissa never ceasing to proclaim her unalloyed delight. It was the most marvellous car she'd ever had, it went like a bird, they had christened it with champagne, the upholstery of course was going to be altered, but the mascot—Lesley must look really carefully at the mascot—was really rather a gem, absolutely unique, made specially for her, Elissa, by a marvellous Latvian craftsman who was going to be deported. It represented a slim naked female embracing a policeman.

"And so you see, darling, I never get held up. They just take one look and wave me through. Now let's have a Martini, and then get at some lunch. I'm simply ravenous," said Elissa; and pulling out a chair she proceeded to order a small piece of fish and toast Melba.

Lesley heard her with mixed feelings. For the last hour and a half she had been frankly looking forward to her food, but if Elissa were really on a diet any marked display of appetite could scarcely look other than heartless. For a moment she wavered; then remembering with relief that Elissa never did eat anything, gratefully threw aside all scruples and ordered jugged hare. Or rather, to be exact, jugged hare, Brussels sprouts and sauté potatoes.

"My dear!" murmured Elissa. "Aren't you afraid of fat?"

"I know I ought to be," said Lesley guiltily. As unobtrusively as possible she took a roll and butter. "But being in the open air seems to give one such an appetite. Are you on diet again, darling?"

"No more than usual," replied Elissa rather severely. "I hate"— and she sketched a little gesture of disgust—"I do so hate being cluttered up with food."

Lesley frowned.

"But it *doesn't* clutter up, you know, really. I mean, most of it one actually needs, and the rest . . . well, at any rate it shouldn't clutter. Look at Pat, for instance. He eats enormously, but, roughly speaking, I know what happens to every mouthful."

"Pat! My dear, I never asked. How is he?"

"Very well indeed," said Lesley, still rather earnest in the defence of food. "I've left him at the Vicarage."

"Darling! How perfectly sweet! Do you mean to say you've got all matey with the Vicar?"

"I've just been staying there, to look after the children," said Lesley placidly. The jugged hare had arrived, looking extremely adequate: but fortunately Elissa, now furnished with her sole, was a very slow eater. She talked so much; she was talking so much now. . . .

And all through lunch, indeed, Elissa's high shrill voice chattered tirelessly on, marvelling at the Vicar, extolling her car, creating around them, as nothing else could have done, the sights and sounds of London at cocktail time: while all through lunch, obliquely in the Swan's silvery mirrors, Lesley scrutinised her friend.

Elissa—there was no doubt at all—had dressed very carefully indeed. Possibly it was the effect of her four years' exile, but Lesley felt she had never seen anything quite so smart as the trim little dark vermilion sports suit, the matching cap and gauntletted hogskin gloves. And as for her face—it would need a life-long experience of beauty-parlours to gauge exactly how many hours a week went to achieve its perfection. With a sudden sinking of the spirit, Lesley remembered that it was nearly three years since she had had her eyebrows plucked.

And meanwhile, from the other side of the table, a similar examination had been unobtrusively proceeding.

"But really, darling, I think you're looking very well. You've put on weight, of course"—Elissa's complacent glance flickered over her own mirrored slenderness—"but they say curves are going to be fashionable. Though they've said that for years, haven't they? Let's take our coffee in the other room."

But after they had crossed the hall—the same hall in which Lesley had once been taken for a Country Type—conversation flagged. Even Elissa's flow seemed suddenly to slacken, for she had already dealt with dress, drama, art and personalities; and to be the next person to speak after Elissa always made anyone else feel a little dull. Or was that too—Lesley asked herself—simply another notion born of a four-years' absence? Surely in Town she herself, for instance, had talked every bit as fast, made just as many epigrams, and would have thought no more of capping Elissa's stories than of criticising her clothes? Only here, she lacked material. There was Pat, of course; but he, like all her other preoccupations—of cats and gardens and Mrs. Pomfret's aunt—was obviously far too commonplace to amuse. . . .

"God, but this fire's hot!" said Elissa suddenly. "If I don't move my face will run." She pulled out a mirror, looked long and searchingly at the skin round her nostrils. "And now, darling"—the powder-box closed with a well-remembered snap—"tell me everything you've been doing for the last three years."

"Nothing much," said Lesley.

II

In the short silence a clock chimed in the hall. Elissa stirred.

"My dear, you really are rather marvellous," she said; and held up her bag to save her complexion from the fire.

Lesley looked up inquiringly.

"About Pat. Living in the country. Giving up everything you enjoyed. I mean, I've sometimes felt like giving up everything myself, but not in that way. (Only last year," threw out Elissa in parentheses, "I tried to go into a nunner; but they made difficulty after difficulty.) You know, my dear, we none of us ever expected you to stick it."

Wrinkling her forehead, Lesley tried to think back to the time when living in the country was something one deserved credit for. For four years, to be sure, the thought of returning to Town had been constantly at the back of her mind; but that was not to say that they had been four years of unmitigated pain. Far from it, thought Lesley honestly: her memory suddenly selecting, as a random nose-gay of favours, the herbaceous border, Pat shouting to Pincher, and Mrs. Pomfret's home-made cake. However, in Elissa's eyes she had apparently done something noble; and Elissa was not as a rule much given to praise.

"Oh, well," said Lesley, as nobly as she knew how, "it's nearly over now. Pat goes to school in September, and then I shall be free again."

With one of her long flickering glances Elissa again took in her friend's calm unpainted face, her unremarkable clothes, her general air of woman-no-longer-in-active-competition. . . .

"Darling! How nice it will be to have you back!" She spoke with sincerity: she felt she had never liked Lesley so much before. "I wonder if you could get your own flat again? Or there's a cottage to let in my mews—or lots of people are going to Chelsea—"

For half-an-hour more she babbled joyfully on, renting Lesley's new flat, hanging her new curtains, inviting her to Pont Street—as long as she liked, whenever she liked, and at a moment's notice—and in short forgetting all but the passage of time in a pure effusion of friendship. Then the clock struck, it was half-past three; and with a couple of fluttering kisses Elissa fled for her car.

A trifle more soberly, though with head still spinning from so much enthusiasm, Lesley followed across the square in the direction of the 'bus stop. Elissa would have loved to take her back, but there was a private view at four.

III

Returning a little wearied in the early dusk, Lesley saw Mr. Pomfret's black coat dark against her door. So he had stood all those years ago, just before disappearing from view by the simple expedient of slipping in at the front door and out the other side! But now he had evidently come to bring Pat, and she hastened forward to thank him.

"But you shouldn't have troubled," she cried. "He always runs back alone unless it's really dark. Has the roller come yet?"

"Not yet," said the Vicar.

And at once, at something in his voice, fear gripped her. Holding hard by the door-post, she said brusquely:

"Please don't try and prepare me. Has anything happened to Pat?"

With equal brusqueness the Vicar answered her.

"No, no. I'm sorry I frightened you. But it's bad news all the same. Sir Philip died this afternoon."

For a moment Lesley stared at him in silence; until, moistening her lips with her tongue, she was surprised by a sudden taste of salt. She said,

"But—but there was nothing wrong with him. Only that chill."

"He was seventy-five, and very frail. And—I'm afraid I've been deceiving you, my dear. He's been very ill all these weeks. Only he didn't want you, you see, to know that he was dying. *He* knew, I think, from the very beginning. And most of all, he didn't want you to see him die."

Lesley nodded. Not to spoil it, not to leave the wrong memory! She could understand that. A thought struck her.

"Who looked after him?"

"A nurse from Aylesbury. I fetched her myself, with the doctor. It was pleurisy, and he . . . hadn't the strength."

As though his words had released a flow of mechanical energy, Lesley rushed past him into the house, switched on the light, drew the blinds; until from close behind the Vicar's hand gripped her shoulder.

"Sit down," he said, "sit down and cry. You look as though you're going to faint."

"I don't think so," said Lesley. She steadied her voice, so that it made a queer dull noise in her own ears. She said,

"You ought to have told me."

Very gently, the Vicar forced her into a chair.

"My dear," he said, "it was his one pride and consolation, that you should be spared all useless pain. He didn't call it pain, he called it ugliness. How could I have told you?"

Lesley moistened her lips.

"Isn't there—isn't there any message for me?"

"Yes. He sent you his love," said the Vicar gently, "and said you were to cry a little, but not too much. And the other thing is—he's left you this cottage."

Chapter Ten

— ✿ —

I

Of all forms of property, freehold land (except of course in slum and other congested areas) demands most and gives least. Gives least, that is to say, in the matter of half-yearly dividends: for its profits are not of the kind that can be cleared through the bank for the benefit of an absentee landlord. They are for the most part, indeed, intangible, like those tenuous exports which should, but do not, redress the balance of trade: to describe them one must take refuge in comparisons, observing, for example, that though a share in British Celanese is a precious, an invaluable thing, one cannot watch it put forth grass; or that though Government Stock offers very good security, one has not to rise at six to see at its best. In diamonds, it is said, Jews find both commercial and æsthetic satisfaction; but even diamonds look the same at all four seasons. Land changes. It is brown in winter, green in spring: it supports—we speak of land, not House Property—three separate populations, the rooted, the ambulant, and the volatile. And to command these varied profits mere ownership is not enough: that is where the land demands. Unless the owner is there, on the spot, he loses all. For one cannot by proxy smell earth after rain, or hear a blackbird whistle; or set roots of cowslips in a wet green bank.

Lesley sat back on her heels (she had Pat's old prayermat, rein-forced with waterproof) and broke the last of the earthy clumps into two equal parts. They had been dug that morning out of Hor-ace Walpole's meadow, from a slope where the ground each April showed pale honey-gold; and the way to set them was to cut out a square of turf slightly smaller than the clump, then press apart the edges so that when the root had been inserted they would spring a little back and clip it in its place. Lesley had found this out for herself, and besides the delicious sensations at her finger-ends—the elasticity of the turf, the freshness of rain-wet—had thus the addi-tional pleasure of putting into practice a theory recently acquired.

But her mind was not wholly on her work. It strayed, in an idle and desultory manner, from the theory of cowslip-planting to the theory of freehold land; being chiefly occupied with the odd mental phenomenon contained in this fact: that though cottage, land and apple-trees all remained exactly what they were a week ago—though the fact of her ownership obviously made no objective difference to any one of them—the idea of returning permanently to Baker Street was now no longer either desirable or not desirable, possible or not possible: it was simply out of the question.

'I'll have to write to Elissa,' Lesley thought. Those daydreams at the Yellow Swan—how airy, how unreal! She fitted in the last root, felt the turf grip, and pressed down on either side till her palms were marked with a twig and a pebble. For the moment at any rate the problem was too much for her. And after all, why bother? The answer was there, however arrived at; and indeed from the moment brain and heart had recovered from their shock her first and still dominant emotion—stronger even than gratitude—was a feeling of immense simplification. Something had been settled for her; as though Sir Philip had reached out, with a last authoritative gesture, and put the young woman in her place.

II

That afternoon, under a lowering March sky, Lesley went up to the Hall for the first time since its master's death. Pat and Pincher accompanied her, but she left them on the terrace and went alone into the quiet house.

It was already dead. The clocks ticked, a fire burned on the library hearth: but in room after speckless room she instinctively hushed her step. The breath had left them: the light was out: and what a slender and flickering candle it had been that lit those lofty and succeeding rooms! Behind the green baize door of the butler's pantry a fat tallow dip was doubtless still burning; but where Lesley walked not a foot might have fallen for fifty years. In Sir Philip's big chair—how long since she had last seen him? Only a month?—the cushions lay freshly plumped; one looked for the red official cords, and a notice 'Not to be sat in.' Lesley put out her hand as she had done only a month ago to smooth the immaculate pillows, and was suddenly aware that she could not see. Tears blurred her eyes and ran easily down her cheeks: a wholesome and simple grief that relieved and washed the heart. She thought,

'I wish I had been here. Whatever he said, he may have wanted me really. Because we did love each other.' And with her hand on his chair Lesley tried to think that last thought again, very clearly and strongly, so that if Sir Philip were still within reach, he might hear and perhaps take pleasure. But though she stood receptive, no answering thought came back: the dead were gone, and left no echo.

On the lawn outside she found Pat and Pincher chasing birds in the dusk. They stopped when they saw her, and came back to the terrace; and from Pat's suddenly concentrated face she knew that he was going to ask questions.

"What did Sir Philip die of, Frewen?"

"He caught a chill, Pat, and he was very old."

"How old?"

"Seventy-five."

"That's *very* old, isn't it?" asked Pat anxiously.

Lesley nodded. A sudden memory made her voice uncertain. For that girl, Pat's mother, had been no more than twenty-four, both her own youth and her child's still almost untouched. And forgetful for a moment even of Sir Philip, Lesley turned away her head and wept again.

III

On their way back by road (for the field-paths were like glue after a two-days' rain) Patrick, who had been walking for some time in thoughtful silence, suddenly observed that the Pomfrets were having a potato roast.

"I should have thought it was too wet for bonfires," said Lesley. "Won't they put it off?"

Pat shook his head.

"Alec's having it," he explained, "to celebrate the battle of Hyderabad, and he's been keeping the wood and things dry under his bed. Can I take some potatoes?"

"How many?" asked Lesley automatically; for she had never forgotten the time when they took some burnt almonds till there were none left.

"Five. Or if you come too, six. Why don't you, Frewen? It's going to be lovely, and we're just there."

"I thought you wanted to go home for the potatoes?"

In Pat's face candour struggled with diplomacy; and as usual, candour won.

"As a matter of *fact*, Frewen, they're there already. We took them up yesterday, when we went back to tea and you'd gone to the Post Office. But they weren't going to be roasted without asking, and if you'd said no I was going to bring them all back." He looked at her anxiously, well aware that his case, though sound, was a trifle subtle;

and Pincher looked at her too. They both looked at her, and with such an odd similarity of regard that in spite of her melancholy Lesley laughed aloud. Immediately Pincher leapt up, Pat relaxed into a smile, and they turned up the lane to the Vicarage gate.

Only a few yards' progress sufficed to inform them that the genius of General Napier was already being celebrated. A great billow of smoke came drifting over the hedge, making Pat break into a run and Pincher leap more than ever. Their haste was infectious; and with no great eagerness for either burnt potatoes or burnt fingers, Lesley was hurried along into such an impetus that when they finally burst on the group round the bonfire, it was with every appearance of equal enthusiasm.

"It's all right!" shouted Pat at once. "We can have them!" He made a bee-line for a small paper-basket, in which was evidently cached his personal hoard, while the four young Pomfrets, making bee-lines in the opposite direction, swarmed about Lesley with a potato apiece. They were not quite baked enough, and exceedingly hot to the touch; but in the vigorous firelit scene, at once so wild and so familiar, the eye at any rate found compensation. For the bonfire was going strong, sending up long tongues of flame that lit now an overhanging branch, now Pat's eager face, now a whole frieze of agitated figures: it was not perhaps the best kind of bonfire for potatoes, but as Pat had promised, it was very lovely.

"Here's one all ready buttered," said Alec out of the smoke. It was indeed, both inside and out: the jacket dropped fatness as it passed from hand to hand. 'Where's Pincher?' thought Lesley; and moving a pace or two back from the firelight, saw the figure of Mrs. Pomfret advancing up the path. She made a solid dark figure even in the twilight, for unlike Lesley, she had gone into mourning.

"My dear! How nice to see you!" she cried; for with something of Sir Philip's own temper Lesley had for the week past been avoiding all company. This Mrs. Pomfret, though loyally following Henry's advice to leave her alone, found hard to understand. Her own impulses in affliction were firstly to give, and secondly to receive, articulate sympathy, and it was therefore with very real pleasure that she now interpreted Lesley's presence as a tacit signal for the opening of hearts.

"I *have* so wanted to see you," she began candidly, "but Henry told me not to come, and that's why I didn't."

"It was very understanding of you," said Lesley. She gripped the potato so hard that it broke between her fingers in a buttery mess. 'Pincher!' she thought again, and calling him from the fire gave it him to eat.

"Because, my dear—in spite of everything else—I can't tell you how glad I am. I mean about the cottage. You have so deserved it," said Mrs. Pomfret sincerely.

Against Lesley's palm came the rasp of Pincher's tongue; she moved her hand and caught him by the collar. No one could be kinder than Mrs. Pomfret, no one more genuine in unselfish affection. Sir Philip had left the Vicarage nothing, and she wore her mourning in all sincerity; but somehow she—she had it all wrong. . . .

"Why deserved?" asked Lesley, almost with coldness. "I used to go up to the Hall because I enjoyed it. If it amused him, it amused me just as much. I used to dine there about four times a week, and the sherry alone would have rewarded any amount of virtue."

"I suppose it would," agreed Mrs. Pomfret, but a little uncertainly. "I know the dinners were always lovely. But I wasn't thinking of Sir Philip, I was thinking of Pat. You do deserve something there."

"Rubbish!" said Lesley rudely. A phrase from the past sounded in her ear: 'That good woman Mrs. Pomfret. . . .' Well, she was good, a lot better than Sir Philip, who was practically a wicked baronet; but how much harder to make understand! And then remembering the Vicar, Lesley felt her irritation abate. Those long domestic evenings! When had Mrs. Pomfret practice in understanding? She wasn't required to understand, only to listen. Half the time she didn't even do that, but sat, as now, gazing at the nearest point of interest—bonfire, sock, or dinner-plate—and thinking about her children. . . . A good deal more moderately, Lesley went on,

"That was rude of me, but it's just how I feel. When I remember, for instance, how you took Pat completely off my hands all that first winter—when I never even said thank you—I feel I ought to rake out the ashes and put them on my head."

"No, don't do that," said Mrs. Pomfret absently, "there are still some potatoes in them. . . . What were you saying, dear?"

Lesley laughed.

"I'm trying to eat humble pie, and you won't take any notice. My one consolation is that Sir Philip would agree with me. *He* knew there was no damned merit about it. He just gave me the cottage because he enjoyed giving it." She broke off, aware that her voice was not to be trusted; and moving a little back from the fire, said presently,

"About the Hall itself—does the Vicar know yet what will happen to it?"

"My dear, I don't know. It all goes to those people called Brooke, but whether they'll live there is another matter. Henry says they'll turn it into an old English road-house, but I think that's just the weather." She glanced anxiously at the sky, but it was too dark to forecast.

"The servants are there still," said Lesley. "I went up this afternoon."

Her companion nodded.

"Yes, they're to have their wages until the Brookes come and make up their minds. Henry says Sir Philip left a special message for Mr. Brooke advising him, if he *did* stay, to keep on the cook. There's money, too, you know."

And in spite of all her goodness, she could not quite suppress a sigh. For it did seem just a little . . . tantalising, that after two serious alarms and one actual death, all they had come in for was a small garden-roller.

Chapter Eleven

I

The news that the Brookes proposed to take up their residence at the Hall was heard with satisfaction as far as Aylesbury, where many a tradesman had visualised with dismay a closed house and no weekly order. The Brookes were to come—the Brookes indeed had been: for in a one-hour's visit, witnessed only by the Vicar, they had inspected the house, reinstated the servants, and announced their intention of settling in at once.

"And a good thing too," said Florrie, who as Mrs. Hasty was now one of the leaders of public opinion. "My cousin George, he's under-gardener there. I s'pose you'll go up and call right away, Miss Frewen?"

She spoke a trifle wistfully; she would dearly have liked to call herself; but there were still one or two limits at which even wedded aplomb stopped short. Her husband's public position, indeed, would sooner or later almost certainly effect an introduction, but Florrie's impetuous and social nature chafed at the delay. So she added simply,

"And if they should be wanting a kitten, Miss Frewen, would you say we've got five?"

She drew back a pace (they had been standing in converse at the police-station door), and let Lesley see past to where, in a patch of sunlight on the red bricks, lay an empty saucer and the five kittens, all fast asleep and plumped out with milk like five little leather bottles.

"We shan't drown 'em for a week or two," said Florrie cheerfully.

II

Though feeling very little gratitude for her privilege, Lesley went up to the Hill on the actual morning of the day the Brookes moved in. Her own inclinations would have kept her away, for having known the place alive she had no wish to revisit its empty and fossilised shell; but she had also the curiously definite feeling that the Brookes were Sir Philip's guests, who arriving in the absence of their host ought at least to find someone to welcome them. They would have with them, moreover, their two boys, who might very well be carried off to the cottage out of the way of moving in; so impelled by both these reasons, together with the faintest, the not-altogether-to-be-denied touch of curiosity, Lesley took formal hat and gloves and walked up to the Hall.

A certain delicacy, a wish not to appear too much at home, sent her past the lower gate and up to the front-door. It stood wide open, as though the small pile of trunks within had only just arrived, but there was no sign of either butler or maid-servants. Not having rung the bell for three years, the idea of now doing so never entered her head; and delicacy notwithstanding Lesley walked straight into the house and through to the library.

The Brookes were there. Through the open door, in the moment before they heard her, she saw them both. They were standing perfectly still in the centre of the floor, looking not at the room nor the garden, but at each other. The man was about forty-five, tall, fair, very thin, and with a face just saved from haggardness by a one-day tan: his wife, probably a year or two younger, carried a head of short black curls very erect on square thin shoulders: and in spite of every difference in height and colouring, they somehow managed to present an odd resemblance.

At the sound of Lesley's step on the parquet, they both turned, the man to show, in full-face, a high narrow forehead. Lesley said,

"I'm Miss Frewen, from the White Cottage. Is there anything I can do?"

The woman took a quick step forward.

"Miss Frewen? We know your name, of course, from Mr. Pomfret. How nice of you to come!"

They all shook hands, Charles Brooke with a short quick grip, very soon over, that gave Lesley the queer impression that he disliked doing it. But there was no lack of cordiality in his greeting; they were both obviously glad to see her, in spite of the fact that she could do them no service. For the Hall was in apple-pie order, and the trunks in the entrance held their only effects.

"Then I won't stay and keep you," said Lesley, "but if your children would like to be shown the village, I've a small boy of my own who would make an admirable guide."

Mrs. Brooke looked puzzled.

"Children?" she repeated. "You don't mean Jack and David? They're outside, on the lawn." She motioned towards the window, and following her glance Lesley saw a couple of tall youths, aged about sixteen and seventeen, examining the astrolabe. Like their father, they both wore grey flannels and tweed coats, but without his knack of making them seem merely threadbare instead of cheap; they looked somehow used to cheap clothes, at home in them; just as they did not look at home on that shaven lawn. Charles Brooke in the library was already the master of the house: his sons might have been the first arrivals for a hospital féte;

'At that age, their father was still at school,' Lesley thought. 'They have been junior clerks somewhere. . . .' Aloud, she said,

"How absurd of me! Do you know, I really expected to see two small boys? It's Sir Philip's fault really: he never could remember that children grew up."

Mrs. Brooke turned eagerly.

"Mr. Pomfret said you knew Sir Philip better than anybody. I wish, some day, you'd talk to us about him. You see—it seems so strange—we know nothing at all."

Lesley nodded. She would talk to them of course, but not just yet; and not in that room, where to speak of Sir Philip was like discussing him before his face. For the first time during the visit, her distress was as great as she had anticipated; and as soon as politeness allowed she spoke of Pat's dinner-time and got up to go.

Her hosts seemed to part from her with genuine reluctance; they all went out together, pausing on the lawn for Mrs. Brooke to introduce her sons, who in voice and manner, as well as in dress, followed at some little distance behind their father. Then Charles Brooke excused himself to speak to a gardener, while the two women went on alone in the direction of the lower gate. For perhaps twenty yards they walked in silence, all superficial conversation having been exhausted in the house; then without any warning, Mrs. Brooke stood still.

"Miss Frewen," she said, "I've got to tell someone. You don't know what it *means*. For the last four years my husband's been trying to sell cars." She laughed uncertainly, fluttering out a pair of small hard hands that were somehow much older than the rest of her. "In the Marylebone Road, you know, where they have to stand in the doorway, and be friendly with people. . . .

('That handshake!' thought Lesley.)

". . . And ask them to have drinks. And once a month we used to put on evening clothes and go and have dinner at that half-crown place opposite the Palladium. We didn't dare miss, you know, though sometimes I've grudged the money. And once we met a man who'd been in his ship, and Charles gave him ten shillings. . . ." Mrs. Brooke broke off abruptly and turned away her head. Far down by the lake Lesley could see a long thin figure standing motionless between the trees. She said,

"I wish—I do wish Sir Philip had known you."

Mrs. Brooke nodded.

"You were very great friends, weren't you?"

"Yes. You see—" Lesley hesitated, suddenly uncertain, like one who has forgotten the wording of a message; and again her companion turned with that flutter of the hands.

"Miss Frewen, please say anything you like to me. I can understand exactly how you feel, belonging here and knowing him so well. You must tell us everything he liked done, and how it was all kept. We won't change anything."

"*No!*" said Lesley, with sudden vehemence. "You mustn't think of it like that. As though it were dead. Like a museum." The words, so totally opposed to all she had been thinking for the past weeks, seemed to have been put into her mouth. She looked back at the house and lawn: all the windows were open, the two boys, now joined by a very old retriever, lay flat on the grass with the dog between them. They had less of a tripperish look, seemed almost at home. The butler came out from the library, asked a question, and then glancing towards the lake moved stately down to meet his master. With much the same gait, the dog followed him and was called back. The boys laughed, the dog barked; and the house was alive.

Chapter Twelve

I

As soon as the Brookes were fairly settled in, there began to appear at the Hall a constant succession of visitors. They were all very much alike—the men, in pre-war tweeds, so far past the point of mere shabbiness that they might have been taken for dukes, the wives with harassed complexions and home-made clothes who sat and watched their husbands exactly as Mrs. Brooke watched Charles. There were also several small children, considerably better dressed than their parents, and with the beginning of the summer holidays, said Mrs. Brooke, there were going to be more.

"You don't know, I suppose," said Lesley thoughtfully, "anyone with a boy at the Bluecoat School? Pat's going to the Prep. there in September, and I would like him to get used to the clothes first. Just seeing them on another boy, I mean, and realising that they're not anything to feel awkward about. I couldn't explain half so well."

Mrs. Brooke looked at her with admiration.

"I do think you're splendid," she said simply. "So does Charles. He says it's one of the most courageous things he's ever heard of. I hope one day Pat will be properly grateful."

"I hope he'll be nothing of the sort," said Lesley. "I think of all the mill-stones round a child's neck gratitude is the worst. What parents do for them they do purely by instinct: they'd be unhappy if they didn't." She broke off, smiling at her own heat and at Mrs. Brooke's startled face. "A child's instinct is to take without thanking: it's a sort of natural insurance against the time when it in turn will have to give without being thanked."

"My dear, you're so—so detached," said Mrs. Brooke, half-way between admiration and mistrust. "And of course it's what every mother knows in a way, though she won't let herself believe it. It's her duty to sacrifice; as you say, she'd be unhappy if she didn't. But you hadn't that duty: you took it up of your own free will. Oughtn't Pat to be grateful for that?"

Lesley smiled.

"I remember quite well the reasons why I adopted him. I had been very bored in London, and had also failed to look my best at an important dinner-party. At least, I thought it was important. . . . The next day I went down to my aunt's, and found her at her wits' end to know what to do with Pat. I thought that if I adopted him it would provide me with a new and amusing topic of conversation. If I'd known what I was taking on I shouldn't have done it. And when I *did* know. . . . I felt like wrapping him in a shawl and leaving him on a doorstep."

"But you didn't, did you?" said Mrs. Brooke.

For a minute or two they sat silent, so that in the garden all about them could be heard a multitude of soft warm-weather sounds. But Lesley listened only subconsciously, her mind being busied with three separate and absorbing thoughts: of Pat, of the new rose-bed, and of two important letters received a day earlier. One was from Graham Whittal, explaining, a trifle curtly, that Patrick had got his presentation: the other, from Christ's Hospital, contained a solid body of information and some forms to be filled in. These she had completed without difficulty: the boy had not had Roseola ('Rose-rash'), nor any of the other ailments with which, as she discovered in surprise, the average parent presumedly had to cope. In fact, the only thing he had had, apart from a few colds, was chicken-pox; and

that he had at the Vicarage, where he and two of the Pomfrets all
sickened together on the same day. So Pat simply stayed where he
was, while Lesley took Alec and the eldest girl back to the cottage
and kept them there in quarantine till the danger was past. They
did not catch it, and Mrs. Pomfret in her gratitude made nothing of
nursing Pat.

'I *have* been lucky,' Lesley had thought, filling in the last of the
blanks with a prideful 'No'; and reading further, saw that Pat would
also have to run the gauntlet of medical examination in Town, to
take place within the last few days before the Michaelmas term, and
an entrance examination, also in Town, some weeks earlier. To both
of these, however, she looked forward with complete confidence; for
Pat was exactly as healthy as a child could be, and unless obviously
a half-wit (wrote Graham Whittal) no presentation-boy ever failed
in his entrance. Pat might not be brilliant; but he definitely wasn't
a half-wit; his sums went very, very slowly, but they nearly always
came out right. . . .

A movement on the terrace distracted Lesley's thoughts. It was
the old retriever—his name was Daniel—stretching slowly in the
sun as though about to take exercise; but he looked about him, evidently thought better of it, and slowly lay down again. Children
laughed, a thrush sang; and the may smelled stronger than the lilac.

"It all seems so ungrateful," said Mrs. Brooke suddenly. "No,
I don't mean that. I *know* we're not ungrateful, but I do wish we
could have shown it. If only he had sent for us! Was he ill very long,
Lesley?"

"A few weeks. No one except the Vicar even knew it was serious."

"We wondered, you see, because everything was left in such perfect order. There's only been one bill to settle ever since we came
here, and that was for the bird-bath."

"*Bird-bath?*" said Lesley, startled.

"The big, rather ornate one down by the stables, that Mr. Povey
got for him. It was only set up a few hours before he died, you know,
and Mr. Povey very honestly came and offered to take it away again;

but of course we couldn't let him, and Charles paid for it on the spot. Though I must say," added Mrs. Brooke temperately, "it's not the kind of thing we either of us really care for."

II

As soon as the summer holidays were well in swing, Mrs. Brooke, with her indefatigable good nature, succeeded in producing a small boy in a blue stuff gown and yellow stockings. His name was Jackson, he arrived unaccompanied, and spent the first afternoon in organising an all-fight-all-boxing tournament among himself, his fellow-guests, Pat and the young Pomfrets. The first four bouts took place next morning, after which secrecy became impossible, and Pat, the smallest Pomfret, and the smallest guest were immediately scratched by Lesley, Mrs. Pomfret and the smallest guest's mother. The seniors, however, were allowed to proceed, and according to Mrs. Pomfret, received private coaching from their fathers in the Hall barn.

"You'd better let Pat come too," said the Vicar to Lesley, "I promise he shan't get killed;" and a day or two later, when boxing-lessons had become a regular feature of the house-party, the master of ceremonies himself voluntarily observed that young Craigie showed promise.

"*Craigie?*" repeated Lesley, in genuine bewilderment.

"He means Patrick," interpreted the Vicar, "and he's quite right. Pat's always going to be slow, but he hangs on like a bulldog. You don't want to turn him into a prize-fighter, I suppose?"

"At the moment," said Lesley, "he wants to be a policeman. And really, you know, if he sticks to it, and with all these new regulations, there might be a lot of things worse."

It was her serious opinion, for she had privately little doubt that Patrick, with a good education and his already outstanding character, would rapidly rise to a room in Scotland Yard and the privilege of putting down riots. He would be good, she thought, with riots: firm yet kind, and very thorough. . . .

In the meantime, however, her chief anxiety was that he should make a friend of young Jackson, who on better acquaintance proved to have more sides to his character than she had previously imagined. For beside his passion for boxing there flourished a passion for music, and he spent whole afternoons listening to Bach, Beethoven and Mozart on the Vicar's gramophone. He never discussed, he simply listened, but in response to Lesley's inquiry admitted that some of the chaps at Housey were quite keen on music.

('Housey!' thought Lesley, 'I must remember that!')

He was also something of a naturalist, and infected Pat with a desire to watch birds; for on learning that young Craigie was destined for Housey too, he at once extended his patronage in the most liberal way imaginable. All day long Pat ran at his heels and imbibed information; and on the day before the entrance exam., which took place in Town, Jackson saw him off at the station with a whole four ounces of peppermint.

Lesley was there too, of course, but a trifle in the background; she sat in her corner, and looked at Pat, and tried hard to think of him as Craigie.

III

Not many weeks later, walking up to the Hall from the lower gate, Lesley observed on the edge of the lawn, in the tentative attitude of the explorer, a small brown boy in a minute green bathing-dress. Advancing up the path, she at once identified him as either the two-year Wootten or the three-year Pratt, for her intercourse with the Brooke house-parties was giving her the memory of a reception-clerk. Before she could address him, however, Pincher, with habitual impetuosity, had bounded amicably forward and bowled him over. The fall was soft—into a bed of marguerites: but there were mothers,

Lesley knew, to whom a sound skin spelt internal injuries. Rebuking Pincher as she ran, she hurried forward and dropped on her knees on the flowering grass.

There was no need for alarm. The two-year Wootten (for such he turned out to be) lay like Moses in the bulrushes, snugly cradled among the green stems. The situation delighted him. He waved his legs, he roared with laughter: he reached up to the white flower-heads, he hugged them to his breast. And Lesley, leaning above like Pharaoh's daughter, thought suddenly:

'But I don't remember Pat like that!'

The next instant she was laughing at her folly. Of course she didn't remember Pat at two: she hadn't had him till he was four-and-a-half. And quite casually, there slipped into her mind the odd, the unprecedented thought of a child of her own. It seemed so unre-markable, however, that she at once forgot it again; and picking up her Moses, with Pincher at heel, continued towards the house to tell the Brookes Pat had passed.

Chapter Thirteen

I

At the beginning of that September when Lesley was to have returned permanently to Town, she went up with Patrick and stayed precisely six days. Of these, moreover, only three were spent with Elissa; for there was a two-day gap between Pat's medical examination and his departure from Victoria, and in those two days Lesley had early decided that he ought to see life. The backbone of most youthful conversation is boasting pure and simple, and she did not wish him to reach school totally ignorant of both the Zoo and Madame Tussaud's. There was also the Natural History Museum, and Maskelyne's Temple of Magic; and with such a programme as that it was obviously impossible that they should stay in Pont Street. When Lesley wrote finally to Elissa, therefore, it was to put off her own unencumbered visit till the afternoon of the ninth; and in the meantime, on Mrs. Brooke's recommendation, they would provide themselves with a room in a small Bayswater hotel.

But why, it may be asked, with so carte blanche an invitation—whenever she liked, for how long she liked, and at a moment's notice—did Lesley not choose to stay longer in Pont Street? And the answer was broadly speaking this, that in the course of an hour's reflection she had progressed from a vague idea of a few new frocks to the figure-supported conclusion that a week with Elissa was going to cost at least forty pounds. She would have to get some sort of walking-suit, together with shoes and stockings, hat, bag and gloves; she would have to get an afternoon or cocktail outfit (together with shoes and stockings, hat, bag and gloves). She would have to get at least two evening dresses (necessitating shoes and stockings, bags and gloves). If evening cloaks had changed much, she would have to get an evening cloak. And if she stepped an inch outside Oxford Street, the sum would be doubled.

For the first time in her life the idea of buying clothes afforded Lesley practically no pleasure. She was a woman with whom the need to be well dressed ranked very soon indeed after the need to eat and the need to sleep; and for four years, in her Chanel jumpers and tweed skirts, in her cool gingham and stiff piqué, she had been exactly as well dressed as it was possible to be. And to signalise her return to Town (however temporary) by abandoning that standard was something so contrary to her nature that she never even considered it. If she went to Town for a week, forty pounds she must spend; and forty pounds was more than a twelfth of her income.

There was another point. When the forty pounds for clothes was translated into forty pounds for the cottage—into rose-bushes, that is to say, and into bricking the hearth, and into a gate-leg table—the disproportion was very striking. It was so remarkably striking, in fact, that she couldn't consider that either.

The two points, it will be seen, had thus rapidly developed into the twin horns of a dilemma; but it was at this critical juncture that Lesley suddenly saw a way out. A week in Town was a stay, and as such demanded complete equipment; but to dash up for three days, say—the time to do a couple of theatres and a party—that was different. For that one could wear country clothes till dinner-time, and cover the rest with a single new gown; and after thinking a little longer of her rose-trees, Lesley felt that six days altogether was quite as much as she wanted.

II

The life seen by Patrick was an unqualified success. They spent a morning (fine) at the Zoo, a morning (wet) at the Natural History Museum: an afternoon at Maskelyne's, and an evening at the cinema. The other afternoon Pat had his medical exam., and the other evening he went to bed early; and every nook and cranny in between was filled with either tea-shops or Boys' Departments. For there was still the matter of his underwear list, which Lesley, having never been brought up in the Public School tradition, had no hesitation in augmenting as she thought fit. She put in nothing that could embarrass him, but she doubled the number of vests; and everything that didn't come from Jaeger's came from the Army and Navy Stores.

No forty-eight hours could have been spent more agreeably: the only fly in the ointment—and that in Lesley's alone—was the absence of Graham Whittal. To her suggestion for a meeting, dispatched in excellent time, he had replied with a curt six lines (softened, to be sure, by a ten-shilling note for Pat) to the effect that he would be away in Scotland till the end of the month; and without (she told herself) any adequate reason, Lesley felt snubbed. She was also extremely disappointed, for she wanted to show Pat off, to display him to old Whittal as the worthy recipient of any man's bounty; and now (for he would certainly not interest Elissa, and Aunt Alice was away as well) there was no one to display him to at all.

But for Pat none of these heartburnings existed, and he enjoyed himself with concentrated energy not only in recognised places of amusement, but also on 'buses, in lifts, and crossing the street. There was something about him, indeed, that made Lesley think of the Locks: what old Horace had been to them, a mounted policeman was to Pat. Policemen, indeed, now fascinated him more than ever, and he and Lesley spent the last hour before the train hanging about Scotland Yard (in any case quite handy for Victoria) and eating ices at a near-by Lyons. It was the cheapest form of amusement Lesley had ever encountered, nor, since the luggage was already at the station, did they need a taxi afterwards; but in a spirit of recklessness Lesley hailed one all the same, and they drove up in style with a porter to open the door.

"I want the train for Christ's Hospital," said Lesley, experimentally.

"Bluecoats?" said the porter. "Over there on seventeen, Madam"; and following his direction they came upon a part of the station covered with small boys. The majority, like Pat, had a parent or guardian; and the majority of guardians seemed to be members of the clergy. These did not stay long, Lesley noted, but deposited their young and went away; while those charges whose guardians lingered wore expressions of slight moroseness. Lesley noted that too, and stationing Pat by a bookstall, near a group of the unattended, went off to find some person in authority. She marked him at once, a tall young master, looking cheerful though harassed, and towards whom more than one other woman was even then making her way. But Lesley happened to be nearest, and got in first.

"I've got a boy for Christ's Hospital," she said. "Shall I just leave him here?"

"Yes, do. That's right. He'll be all right," replied the master rapidly. He did not see her, he did not see Pat: they were merely an Importunate Female and Another Kid. Fully aware that she was being a nuisance, Lesley placed herself squarely in the young man's path, caught and held his reluctant eye, and directed it towards Patrick's flaming head.

"That's the one," she said clearly, "with the bright red hair. His name is Patrick Craigie."

"That's right. He'll be all right," repeated the young man.

Slightly reassured—for Pat's hair, once seen, could never be quite forgotten—Lesley moved out of the way. Her next move was obviously to say good-bye and go home; but she felt a curious reluctance to do so. For though she had no real fear for Pat's welfare—since he possessed, in such an eminent degree, the capacity to lie low and take his bearings—she could not help feeling that however much they might call him Craigie, he was still, after all, a very small boy.

However, there was no sense in lingering. Returning to the bookstall, where Pat was already in conversation with some of the unattached, she said cheerfully,

"Well, Pat, it's nearly time. Shall you be all right, if I leave you?"

"Oh, *yes,*" said Pat simply.

('If I don't go now,' thought Lesley, 'I'll be an Importunate Female to him too.')

"Good-bye, then, Pat. Write as soon as you can."

They shook hands, and with a considerable effort she turned on her heel and walked straight down the platform.

Under cover of a luggage-lift, however, she halted and looked back: they were still all over the place, seething round the tall master like a new entry of hounds. Just where she had left him stood young Craigie, still in converse with one or two others; and seeing him thus surrounded by his peers, Lesley stood still a minute and surveyed the fruit of her four years' labour. A boy here and there looked quicker, more lively, perhaps, but for sheer sturdy health, and above all for sheer composure, not one could compare. Pat stood squarely on both feet, did not fidget, and was not to be jostled out of his chosen position. When someone knocked somebody else's cap off, he took no part in the scuffle, but merely seemed to stand a little more squarely than before, in case anyone should be going to knock *his*. No one did. He listened more than he talked, watched more than he listened, and all with a mingled expression of wariness and excitement.

The fruit was good.

Lesley looked, sighed, and gave him her blessing; then she left the station and took a 'bus to Elissa's.

PART V

Chapter One

I

In the matter of the party for Lesley Frewen, Elissa really did her best. She found a four-year-old engagement-book, and went through every man mentioned in it, trying hard to remember which, if any of them, had been Lesley's lovers. In this way she revived a good many sentimental memories of her own, but achieved no other result; and was just about to discard the book altogether when her eye was caught by a sprawling entry at the beginning of August. It covered three days, and it said: 'Lesley week-end: Toby's car.'

Toby's car! And in it, in the back, Bryan Collingwood! Well, Toby at least—dear Toby! had transferred his allegiance; but hadn't Bryan been very badly hit indeed? In any case, those two would do to start with: and moving to the telephone Elissa began alphabetically with Toby Ashton.

It was so long since she had last 'phoned him that she had to look up the number: Mayfair 001. It seemed vaguely unexpected: surely he used to be 110? With deliberately cultivated trustfulness, however—she was trying to rely more and more on the Unseen—Elissa repeated it to Exchange and hoped for the best.

Her faith was justified.

"Hello?"

Nice deep voice—dear Toby!

"Hello, Toby darling!"

"This is Mr. Ashton's valet speaking. . . ."

"Oh! Well, can I speak to Mr. Ashton, please?"

"I'm afraid Mr. Ashton is not—"

He broke off, and in the short pause that followed she could hear him speak to someone else: then the 'phone evidently changed hands, for a new voice took up the thread.

"Hello!"

"Hello, Toby darling. This is Elissa."

"*Elis*—? Oh! *Elissa!*" exclaimed the 'phone resourcefully. "How are you, darling?"

"Oh, still alive. Toby, you remember Lesley Frewen?"

"No," said Toby.

"My dear, of course you do. We went down and stayed with her. At a cottage in the country, about three or four years ago. It was rather a flop."

"Then I'm sure I don't remember. I always put flops straight out of my mind."

"Well, anyway, Toby, she's coming back to Town for a few days, and I've got to give a party. To-day week. Could you come early, say about nine o'clock, and have a preliminary cocktail?"

But Toby had not heard. He was just remembering something.

"Lesley Frewen—hadn't she a small boy? I mean, wasn't that why she went into the country in the first place?"

"Darling, how clever of you! That's the woman. But it wasn't her own infant. At least, I don't *think* it was," said Elissa doubtfully. "Anyway—nine o'clock?"

"If I possibly can, darling. But there is just a chance," said Toby Ashton, "that I may have to fly over to Paris. . . ."

So that was no good. Without nurturing any false hopes, Elissa went back to the telephone book and turned up the C's. Collingwood, Bryan L., Flat K.16, Beverley Court: she gave the number, trusted as before, and was presently aware of a voice at her ear.

"That you, Bryan, darling?"

"No, it isn't," said the voice. "This is Mrs. Collingwood."

'Of course, how stupid of me!' exclaimed Elissa, with considerable sang-froid. "I couldn't remember the surname. . . . Listen, can you come to a party here, to-day week, and bring Bryan with you? I shall have Lesley Frewen staying here, and I'm sure they'd enjoy seeing each other. Oh, by the way, this is Elissa speaking."

"Thank you," said the voice tartly, "I haven't the least idea—"

"Wait!" cried Elissa, suddenly inspired. "Natasha!"

"— What you're talking about," concluded the voice.

"Well, Bryan will tell you," said Elissa sweetly; and with extreme deliberation hung up the receiver.

So that was no good either, and the party would have to remain just as she had originally designed it—art, stage, and literature (all three, naturally, of recognised and amusing brands) with for high light Andrew Bentall. And remembering that name, Elissa smiled. He had been difficult to pin down, for architects, as soon as they became famous, always had a secretary; and secretaries (or so Elissa was convinced) lie without scruple or remorse. But she had prevailed at last, and that distinguished presence was now a certainty. For the rest, to fill up all gaps, there would be one or two thirsty young men, because the older women liked them, and just a sprinkling of the rich, because they were so comforting to have about. And if in all that Lesley couldn't find someone to mate with—well, it would just be a pity.

'Anyway—I've done my best,' thought Elissa complacently; and that being so, felt completely justified in accepting, for the day her guest was to appear, a rather fascinating invitation to spend the afternoon on a houseboat and the evening at a riverside club. She left Pont Street, therefore, exactly ten minutes after Lesley arrived, and returned about three a.m.: which meant (since the latter retired at eleven) no further interview until the early following morning, when Lesley, awaking as usual, at a quarter past seven, out of sheer heedless bonhomie, slipped down the passage and knocked on Elissa's door.

"I thought you were the orange-juice," said Elissa, sitting up and reaching for a bed-jacket. Her expression, though still a good deal blurred by the remains of some skin-food, was almost certainly not one of happy surprise. "Couldn't you sleep, darling, or have the maids been making a racket?"

"Oh, no, I slept beautifully," said Lesley. "I—I just wanted to know where the bathroom was."

"Darling! Didn't that fool Parker tell you? You're having the little green one at the end of the passage." She picked up a hand-mirror and stared thoughtfully at her chin: jerked it first to the left, then to the right. "And if you see anyone along the way, darling, just send them straight along to me."

The congé was unmistakable, but for a moment longer an uneasy sense of guilt made Lesley stand her ground.

"It wasn't really Parker's fault, darling. She showed me everything last night, only I couldn't remember the doors. They—they all look so alike."

"Well, next time you come, darling," said Elissa irritably, "I'll get some W.C. labels."

Unhappily conscious that she had made a fool of herself, Lesley opened the door and retired to her own room. An obscure melancholy was burdening her heart, so sudden and unexpected that she instinctively looked up to see if the day were clouding over. But no, the sun still climbed in a cloudless sky, the flowers at the window were still transparent with light. If a note had jarred, one must try to forget it: and standing barefoot on a patch of sun Lesley did her best to eliminate from memory Elissa's morning face.

|

It was soon eliminated at any rate from view, for when they met again, at about eleven o'clock, Elissa advanced with her usual radiant countenance. She was dressed for driving, and at once made it clear that Lesley was not going too.

"My dear—dinner at seven," she announced briskly, "an ungodly hour, because of the mob afterwards. And there'll be lunch here at one, though I probably shan't be back. What are *your* plans, darling?"

'She feels she ought to send me to Saint Paul's!' thought Lesley; and indeed almost before she had time to answer Elissa added hastily,

"If ever you feel like going to the Zoo, darling, do tell me in time, and I'll ring up Cyril Poullett. I met him at the Ballet Circle—a perfectly fascinating little man who looks after the snakes. He takes them out and waves them about. . . ." She sketched a vaguely sinuous gesture, as though of a waved snake, and picked up her bag. "Or what about the Park? It's a perfect day."

Lesley made haste to relieve her friend's mind. She had lots to do—shopping and hair to begin with: would doubtless be out to lunch herself; and was in fact away from the house while the Buick still waited. Elissa caught her up at the corner, waved and flashed on; and Lesley, after taking a leisurely look at the Park, caught a 'bus to Hyde Park Corner. Her destination was Kensington High Street, where for reasons of economy (and of course keeping its *provenance* from Elissa) she hoped to purchase a new evening-dress; but the sight of Piccadilly drew her off her course, and turning left instead of right she started to walk slowly towards the Circus.

And now, as never in her life before, she savoured the multiple and exquisite sensations that together made up a stroll down Piccadilly. Pleasure of eye and of ear: the smooth clean pavement underfoot: the full river of traffic so evenly flowing: the infinite variety of face, figure, clothing and scent that on every side caught and fed her attention. A brilliant and settled sky had brought out all the women in their lightest clothes: they walked with light, buoyant steps, happily conscious of giving pleasure, and sideways-glancing into the windows of the motor-shops, where the ample space between Rolls and Rolls could mirror, Lesley noted, at least three slim silhouettes at one and the same time. From a hundred vermilion 'buses, many of them in full career, prehensile conductors leaned out to look at the ladies: or with one hand curved about the mouth (the other as it were their sole link with life) shouted flavour-some pleasantries to men working on the road. For the road was up, as usual, opposite the Ritz, where a homely little encampment struck a contrasting note of simple comfort. Along the adjacent barrier a dozen or more *flaneurs* formed an oasis of quiet and contemplation; the men with the pneumatic drills, though they answered readily enough to the 'bus conductors, took no more notice than a row of sparrows.

'I'd quite forgotten!' thought Lesley, looking about her, as in a foreign land, with interest and enjoyment; and as in a foreign land she tried to store up every detail and incident—a chance grouping of roadmenders, a repartee from a 'bus—to take back to the Pomfrets. For she had indeed the advantage of most travellers in being certain of her audience; the Pomfrets would want to know *everything*, and so would the Brookes. So Lesley walked slowly, taking it all in, and being struck more than once by the particularly good-humoured expressions on the faces of the people she passed. Everyone she looked at seemed on the point of smiling, especially the pukka or pre-war sahibs then arriving at their clubs; and one at least of them almost stood still in her path. Lesley looked again; it was Graham Whittal.

"Uncle Graham!" she cried accusingly.

"My dear Lesley!"

"You told me you were going to be in Scotland! If this had been yesterday you could have seen Pat!" She half turned, and made a despairing motion towards Victoria. "When did you come back?"

"Last night," said Mr. Whittal unhesitatingly. "If you're going shopping, may I come and carry for you?"

She accepted with pleasure, and directing his steps towards Piccadilly Circus began at once to describe with what flying colours Pat had passed the Doctor. As far as could be judged, he had absolutely nothing wrong with him; and though at lessons he might be a trifle slower than some children, good health, at that age, was obviously far more important. Didn't Uncle Graham think so?

'Devonshire cream!' thought old Whittal.

It was the phrase that had come into his mind on first seeing her, before he realised who she was: an involuntary tribute to something charming and unusual on the Piccadilly pavements. There was a freshness about her, and an air of enjoyment—nothing like it, for setting off a pretty woman. 'Devonshire cream!' had thought old Whittal. 'Very refreshing!'

And even after the shock of recognition, the impression remained. The creamy-sunburned complexion, that look about the eyes that comes only from eight hours' sleep: the soft lower lip, and slight fullness under the chin; she had developed a kind, easy beauty that was extraordinarily grateful to the jaded eye. . . .

"But you'll see him at Christmas," Lesley was saying. "I do hope it'll freeze! Let's cross over, Uncle Graham, and look in Fortnums?"

He took her arm and piloted her through the traffic, Lesley entrusting herself to his guidance in a manner which he at once felt to be charming, womanly, and entirely new. In the old days, as far as he could remember, it had always been she who showed a tendency to guide *him:* yes, she used to grip him by the elbow and nearly land him under a bus. . . .

"*Ah!*" said Lesley, as they achieved the opposite pavement. And she glanced at him admiringly: he knew she did.

"When you've looked your fill," he said, "we'll go in and have some coffee." Her face under the curve of hat-brim—it was delightful! And his glance moving downwards, he noted with pleasure that in spite of nearly five years in the country she hadn't at all let herself go. On the contrary! She had lost her slouch, carried her head up and her shoulders back; as though no longer ashamed, thought old Whittal, of having a chest.

Lesley drew a deep breath.

"Do you know," she said, "that when first I had the cottage I used to *shop* here?" She turned to watch the effect, so obviously expecting him to look shocked that he at once did so.

"Good God!" cried Mr. Whittal.

Lesley nodded.

"I did. I used to have things down all ready in dishes: I ate the things out and sent the dishes back again. It nearly ruined me."

"But you stopped in time?" pleaded Mr. Whittal.

"Only just. And I know all the dishes *didn't* get back, because Florrie told me afterwards that Mrs. Sprigg used to lend them out all over the village." She took a last look, and accompanied him inside. But the recollection of Mrs. Sprigg's perfidy appeared to have sobered her; and after ordering chocolate and a brioche, and drinking the best part of the former in silence, she asked suddenly,

"Why did you say you were going to be in Scotland, Uncle Graham? Didn't you want to see me?"

"No," said old Whittal, with equal frankness; and to his extreme surprise saw her look neither annoyed nor astonished but merely a trifle more earnest.

"I should have thought you'd have wanted to see Pat," she said simply.

"Pat? I never thought of him. All I knew was that I didn't want to see you."

"But why?"

"Because the last time we met you had struck me as an extremely unpleasant young woman. My dear Lesley, you can't think how I disliked you. You no doubt disliked me too: you thought me an Early Victorian relic. But I can tell you one thing, my dear: if I hadn't been Early Victorian I wouldn't have lifted a finger to help you. What I did I did simply and solely because we were blood relations: which is a tie I believe your detached young modern doesn't recognise. Afterwards, on the other hand, I became quite advanced: I never wanted to set eyes on you again, and I determined that I wouldn't."

There was a short pause.

"And yet here you are," murmured Lesley at length, "giving me chocolate at Fortnums."

He nodded.

"That's because I have the strength of mind to acknowledge my errors. Not that it was an error, at the time. But now that I've confessed and repented—would it amuse you to come to the theatre to-night?"

"I'd love to," said Lesley, "but not to-night, because Elissa's giving a party. And that reminds me—I've got to get a frock."

Old Whittal looked at her.

"Get one like Devonshire cream," he said.

Chapter Two

I

In the end it was a shade nearer ivory; but it had the right smooth creaminess and the right golden tinge where a fold curved under: and old Graham Whittal not only chose it, unaided, out of a shop in Bruton Street, but paid for it as well. (The other thing he paid for that afternoon was a Nelson's Column in Goss to take back to Mrs. Sprigg.) Lesley accepted his bounty with unfeigned pleasure, and did her best to make him come and see it at Elissa's party; but he said he would wait until the night after, having encountered Elissa once previously, and feeling no desire to renew the acquaintance.

Dressing that evening after early dinner, Lesley was aware of a strange yet familiar sensation that was making the blood beat in her cheek. It was the feeling   how exactly she recognised it!—of the last half-hour before a party, and it always improved her looks. Well, that was fortunate, with Elissa and all Elissa's beauties set out in their array; but as Lesley looked in the glass, she did not feel dissatisfied. Her skin was sunburnt, but smoothly and agreeably so, just a shade or two deeper (save where the pearls at her ear made cheek and throat golden) than her Devonshire cream gown. The dark smooth waves, though still looser than five years ago, lay close and glossy after the visit to the hairdresser; and though her new scarlet lipstick was so good a match as to be almost imperceptible, it could not really mar (decided Lesley) the whole effect.

And that the whole effect was good, she knew by the way Elissa looked at her.

"Darling, you *have* put on weight," said Elissa sympathetically. She herself was wearing blue, a deep, deep blue like the sky on a summer night; and when given time to arrange her thighs, looked as thin as a toothpick.

Without attempting any defence (for really there was none possible) Lesley took herself and her finery down to the drawing-room. It now had a bar in it permanently, and a bar-tender on occasion, and since this was an occasion *par excellence*, he was just reporting for duty as Lesley came down.

They entered together, and he at once offered to mix her something; but Lesley, no longer sure of her head, declined politely. He seemed a nice little man, very anxious to oblige, and in case her refusal had hurt him, she now said the first thing that came into her head. She said,

"I've just been seeing my small boy off to school."

The bar-tender at once looked interested.

"Indeed, Madam? May I ask which?"

"Bluecoat."

"Ah, that's a *good* school, that is," said the bar-tender with enthusiasm. "A neighbour of mine, Madam, who works in an insurance office in the City, had the good fortune to get his boy there—very brilliant boy, I believe—and they tell me he's doing wonders."

"How old is he?" asked Lesley quickly.

"Fourteen-and-a-half, Madam."

"Oh, dear! Mine's not quite nine. Would they ever come across each other, do you think?"

"Well, as to that, Madam, of course I can't say; but if you'd like me to give you his name—"

Lesley would have liked it very much indeed, for a brilliant and really bigger boy—Jackson was only twelve—was just the person she wanted to keep an eye on Pat's career; but at that precise moment their conversation was interrupted by Elissa herself with a bunch of first arrivals. The barman was at once busy, Lesley swept away; and before she had time even to look at herself, the party had begun.

And never, thought Lesley, was such a party before.

Never in her life had she seen so many attractive women: never in her life met so many brilliant men. And not only brilliant, but charming as well; they came and talked to her one after another while she listened fascinated. Mr. Poullett in particular, could hardly tear himself away; he begged, he urged, he implored her with passion to come and look at his snakes.

"I'd love to," said Lesley sincerely; and indeed the thought of Pat's missed opportunity went straight to her heart.

"When?" asked Mr. Poullett.

"The Christmas holidays, perhaps," said Lesley.

And after Mr. Poullett came a man called Ribera (but he was obviously American), who spoke for a full fifteen minutes on modern Italian art; another man lectured on *Nacktkultur;* a third, with a small beard, on the history of the gold standard. Lesley drank one cocktail after another, and felt herself getting more and more intellectual: whenever she asked a question, they at once called it intelligent. At the end of an hour or two, however, she began to need air, and by a good deal of tact and a little swift movement managed to escape alone to the tiny balcony. But she had not even been there more than a few minutes, thinking restfully of the cottage and wondering how Pat slept, when a very tall man was suddenly standing beside her. She had noted him earlier as looking distinguished but cross, and was now relieved to observe the distinction predominate.

He said,

"Tell me what you're thinking about."

"Rose-bushes," answered Lesley truthfully.

Subtly his face changed.

"In that frock, of course," he said; and there was a difference in his voice too, a sudden infusion of boredom.—'Like picking up a book and finding you've read it,' thought Lesley vaguely. Then realising for the first time the implications of his remark, she woke up and defended herself.

"But I mean real rose-trees," she explained, "not—not the conversational sort. Three Barbara Richards, one Etoile de Hollande, three Madam Butterfly, three Mrs. Barraclough, and a Rev. Page Roberts. Is that eleven or twelve?"

"Eleven," said the man.

"Then I can have one more. Do you know anything about Julien Potin?"

"He's a sort of hybrid-tea. But why have another one? Wouldn't it be more original to have eleven?"

"At the place where I'm going," explained Lesley, "they have them at so much a dozen—assorted, you know. I believe they practically throw one in. And it's silly to waste a rose bush just to be original."

"You don't know how I agree with you," said the man, quite fervently. "By the way—my name's Bentall."

"The architect," supplied Lesley. She had heard about him from Elissa. "Do you like cottages?"

"If they're old enough, I do."

At once she told him all about hers, stepping back inside the room to make a comparison of floor-space, indicating with gestures of the hands the girth of its outside walls. Mr. Bentall said they sounded marvellous, and expressed so hot a desire to see them for himself that it was only common kindness to invite him, if ever he should be in Bucks, to pay them a visit.

"May I, really?" said Mr. Bentall eagerly. "What sort of a day? Sunday?"

A Sunday, agreed Lesley, would do very well.

"Next Sunday?" said Mr. Bentall.

There was no reason against it.

"Now tell me something else," said Mr. Bentall. "I've twice offered to get you a drink, and both times you've refused. But if you *really* don't want one, why do you keep looking so anxiously at the bar?"

"I'm not," said Lesley, stung. "I'm looking at the barman."

"Then why him?"

"Because one of his neighbours has a brilliant boy at the Blue-coat School, and so have I. I mean—mine's not brilliant, he's only just got there; and I thought this other boy, who's fourteen, might be a good person to keep an eye on him. And the barman was just giving me his name when everyone came in."

Just as the barman himself had done earlier in the evening, Mr. Bentall at once looked extremely interested.

"But Elissa tells me you're staying here," he said. "Can't you catch him at the end?"

"I shall if I can, but he may slip away. They do, you know, when the drink begins to run out. And with all these people here I don't like to ask him now. He might feel it was unprofessional, and I'm sure Elissa would."

"Well, I'll help to keep an eye on him," promised Mr. Bentall. "Now tell me about your boy."

"Oh, he isn't mine really," said Lesley, conscious that she should perhaps have said that before, "I only adopted him. But I've had him nearly five years, and he went to school yesterday. *That* was really why I took the cottage, of course, and now it's mine I somehow don't want to leave it. When you see it on Sunday—"

"*Darlings,*" cried Elissa gaily, "I'm going to tear you apart and cast you to the lions. Everyone wants to make love to you, Lesley, and a good few would like Andrew to make love to them. *Avanti!*"

Resistance was useless. A moment later, and they were seated on opposite sides of the room, the architect with Elissa, Lesley in the power of a small and dapper Italian. His admiration was ardent, but his English poor, and she was extremely glad to be borne down on by a small plump-breasted Frenchwoman with enormous pearls.

"Lesley Frewen!" cried Mrs. Carnegie. "Let me look at you!"

She did so at length, and announced herself satisfied.

"You 'ave kept young," she said approvingly. "So 'ave I. 'Ave you seen Sasha?"

"Not yet," said Lesley.

"'E is of very-ry, very-ry good family," explained Mrs. Carnegie. "I found 'im in Paris, and when I 'ave to do something for him—'e 'as no shirt even, poor boy—'e wept like a baby. You shall see 'im."

She turned round and raised her voice.

At once, from the group round the bar, there emerged a tall and strikingly handsome young man. He advanced toward his patroness, kissed Lesley's hand, and immediately suggested that they should all go and dance.

"No," said Mrs. Carnegie, "Miss Frewen, she is staying 'ere, so she must remain. But you and I, if you like, Sasha."

Sasha considered.

"We will go, then," he said at last, "and it would also be nice to have supper. Good-bye, Miss Frewen." He kissed her hand again, while Mrs. Carnegie kissed her cheeks: they were a very affectionate couple.

'But she *has* kept young all the same,' thought Lesley, 'younger than Elissa. . . .'

As the reflection indicates, she was no longer enjoying herself: and a moment later the party, which had been steadily losing its brightness, at last snuffed out. The moment of snuffing, for Lesley at least, was a quite definite one: it was the moment in which she glanced round the thinning room and saw that Andrew Bentall was gone. For the last hour and more she had, like everyone else, been drinking, chattering, and moving from one chair to another; but whichever way her moves took her, they had brought her no nearer to Mr. Bentall: he was being courted, cajoled, swarmed over by beautiful ladies, and whenever he broke free Elissa was on him like a flash. The pride of her party, it was his business to circulate; or if not in circulation, to devote himself to his hostess.

A ridiculous disappointment filled Lesley's heart. She felt defrauded of something—simply of saying good-night to him, per-haps; she remembered that they had made no real arrangements for Sunday. And glancing round the room again she saw that in her second and fruitless preoccupation she had also missed the barman. It was three o'clock, the barman was gone; and as soon as the last few guests had gone too, Lesley left Elissa talking to the man called Ribera, and went slowly upstairs.

II

And at that moment her name was called from below. She turned, and looking down saw a tall dark figure standing in the hall.

"Miss Frewen!" called Andrew Bentall.

Lesley ran down to him.

"Name of brilliant boy—James Turner. Home address: 6, Green Lane, Sheen."

"How did you find out?"

"Waylaid the barman on the way out. Look here, can't I see you again before Sunday? To-morrow night, for instance?"

She thought of old Whittal, and shook her head.

"Lunch or tea, then? Lunch? I'll call for you at one," said Mr. Bentall.

Then she gave him her hand, and they said good-night to each other.

Chapter Three

———— ✻ ————

I

Having enjoyed almost every minute of her visit, Lesley returned to High Westover at the prearranged time. Elissa did indeed, over the very last cocktail, invite her to stay longer, but in so fleeting a parentheses that it slipped by almost unheard, and in no way impeded the flow of their last conversation.

"And if at any time *you* feel like the country, darling," finished Lesley, "just wire and come down. There's a bathroom now." She hesitated: it was the opportunity she had for three days been seeking, the opportunity to tell Elissa about the cottage; but it had come too late. And if she did tell Elissa, what would Elissa say? '*Don't you get a pension as well, darling?*'—something like that; amusing, of course, but not what one really wanted to hear said about Sir Philip. Old Whittal had been different. . . . So Lesley held her tongue, kissed Elissa for the last time, and about an hour and a half later was walking up Pig Lane in the company of Mrs. Hasty. They had met at the station, and Florrie with her usual good humour volunteered to carry a bag.

"I'm going that way meself, to see the old 'uns," she said. "Did he get off all right, Miss Frewen?"

"Rather. There were lots of other boys, and a master to look after them. He didn't seem a bit worried."

"Ah! Pat was always like that, wasn't he? Never turns a hair. But how you brought yourself to part with 'im, Miss Frewen, I just can't think. I know I couldn't part with my Gerald," said Florrie earnestly.

A slight difference between the two cases did present itself to Lesley, but she forbore to mention it. Florrie's sympathy was obviously genuine, and to a certain extent deserved; she *would* miss Pat very much indeed, and if at the moment she didn't quite realise it, that was because her mind was as though preoccupied with something more important. What it was, she could not yet quite tell: but to be more important than Pat it would have to be very important indeed. . . .

"'N did you have a good time yourself?" asked Florrie.

"Very, thank you," said Lesley. "I went to two theatres and a conjuring show with Pat, and Madame Tussaud's and a cinema."

Florrie was visibly impressed.

"My cousin George, he went to Tussaud's once. He said it was ever so handy, just near the station. (Did I tell you the Pomfrets' roller had come?) But you missed the Conservative Concert, Miss Frewen, it was last Wen'sday night."

"Oh, dear!" said Lesley. "Was it good?"

"Ever so good, except for Mrs. Povey singing three times. They couldn't stop her, you see, because old man Povey was doing the refreshments cheap."

Thinking of the bird-bath, Lesley laughed aloud; and then for some minutes they walked in silence. The air, after the air of London, was like brown bread after white: from the hedges on either hand came the sweet warm scent of ripening blackberries. Lesley lifted her head, and saw bright between the trees the roof of the White Cottage.

"My! There's a yellow leaf already," said Florrie. "Whist-drives'll be starting soon."

II

A little later that same evening, but before she went up to see the Brookes, Lesley walked in her orchard. Mrs. Sprigg was just gone, happy in the possession of Nelson's Column; she had had high tea on the table, and water for a bath. . . .

It was pleasant in the orchard. Leaves touched by autumn, and grass warm in the sun. Setting sun, and so with a peculiar softness in the last of its light. Lesley walked slowly between the trees, till she came to the Walpole fence. On the other side of the yard someone was making a bonfire, and with every puff of wind came the good smell of woodsmoke. So leaning, so looking, her thoughts came slowly; thoughts of Patrick when he should be older, thoughts of the garden next year: all thoughts with a future to them. And there was a thought amongst them that was quite new, yet like the woodsmoke pervasive; and as when woodsmoke blows through an orchard, the orchard becomes more lovely, so were Pat and the garden suddenly dearer for it.

'To-morrow, when Andrew comes,' thought Lesley.

About the Author

Margery Sharp (1905–1991) is renowned for her sparkling wit and insight into human nature, which are liberally displayed in her critically acclaimed social comedies of class and manners. Born in Yorkshire, England, she wrote pieces for *Punch* magazine after attending college and art school. In 1930, she published her first novel, *Rhododendron Pie*, and in 1938, she married Maj. Geoffrey Castle. Sharp wrote twenty-six novels, three of which, *Britannia Mews*, *Cluny Brown*, and *The Nutmeg Tree*, were made into feature films, and fourteen children's books, including *The Rescuers*, which was adapted into two Disney animated films.

MARGERY SHARP

FROM OPEN ROAD MEDIA

OPEN ROAD
INTEGRATED MEDIA

INTEGRATED MEDIA

Find a full list of our authors and
titles at www.openroadmedia.com

FOLLOW US
@OpenRoadMedia